soaked

STACY KESTWICK

soaked

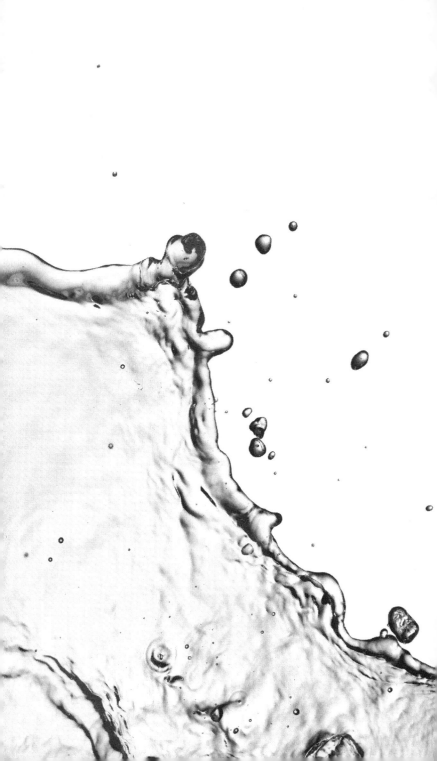

prologue

West

HELL WAS NOTHING LIKE I envisioned.

Brilliant blue sky. Sun beating down. Steady breeze. Calm seas. Fish biting. Classic rock on the satellite radio. No other boats around as far as the eye could see. Cold beer and soda in the Yeti. Beautiful, bikini-clad Italian woman posing against the bow.

Most men would've killed to be in my deck shoes. Considered this paradise.

I, on the other hand, would have sold my soul to be anywhere but here.

I prayed to a merciful God for help. A pop-up rainstorm. A hurricane. Parting of the seas.

Anything.

Anything but another three hours of watching Aubrey try

to sell her melons like a vendor at a farmer's market. I'd already sampled them years ago. They were as fake as the rest of her, and I wouldn't be going back for more.

Luckily, my clients, the Young brothers, seemed oblivious for the most part. They were here purely for the fishing tournament. We were after marlin today and already had a great contender on ice.

They'd brought along Mr. Perotti, Aubrey's dad, as a thank you to him for being their lawyer through the process of starting up their new rental supply company.

That was Aubrey's angle. The same company was generously donating their services to the gala she was chairwoman of at the end of the summer, and she'd *just wanted to thank them in person.* She'd practically cooed as she said it, and when they'd politely invited her to join them today, she'd been fucking *delighted.* My idea of a thank you tended to be a head nod and a fist bump. Aubrey's was a little different.

She might as well have given them a striptease, based on the amount of fabric she had left on her body after she took off her blue cover-up. Calling it a bikini was generous. But maybe unnecessary displays of skin were a familial defect. Mr. Perotti's shorts were half as long as mine and twice as tight. Although Aubrey was a lot less hairy than her dad. Got to give credit where credit is due.

And not helping matters any, Mr. Perotti's efforts to pimp out his daughter to me were about as subtle as a used car salesman up against a deadline. He'd all but bent her over so I could check out what was underneath her hood. It was disturbing as fuck what that man said about his spawn with a few beers in him. Like when he praised the sturdiness of her hips, saying her mama was the same way. I swear my fucking balls shrank to the size of marbles at that visual.

Honestly, I felt bad for Aubrey. Pity was the strongest emotion she evoked in me these days. I got why she did it—threw herself at me the way she did. Her dad had made it clear since we were kids that a good marriage was what he expected of her. The way to make him proud. And he'd decided I was the ideal son-in-law, the son of his best friend. I think he assumed this whole charter fishing *experiment*—his word, not mine—would blow over soon and I'd take my rightful place as the next president of Montgomery Golf, the way my parents had always hoped I would, too. And Aubrey would be right there next to me, the perfect trophy wife.

Too bad no one ever asked me what I wanted.

I'd tried to play their game for years. Went to Wharton, escorted Aubrey to every charity ball and event I was forced to attend. Hell, I even sampled the wares she kept shoving at me. My willpower in my early twenties had only been so strong.

But none of it had felt real. None of it fired my blood or sparked my ambition.

Not the way running my own company did. Even if it was small, it was mine. I did it. It was *my* blood, sweat, and tears that made it work.

And Sadie.

Fuck, that girl had me feeling things I didn't even understand.

Had me doing things I would've called my brother a pussy for. Leaving love notes. Smelling her hair. Sneaking into her room at night just to wrap her in my arms, feel her snuggle back into me. Craving her touch like an addict. All I knew when it came to her was I wanted more.

I wanted it all.

Her soft smiles. Her sweet laughter. Her green eyes finding mine. Her small hands on my skin. Her long legs wrapping around my waist. Her sexy moans in my ear.

Her nights. Her mornings. Her *tomorrows*.

I loved her, I just hadn't found the right way to tell her yet.

That word was scary as shit, you know?

It felt fragile, like if I didn't handle it right, it would crumble and disintegrate right in front of me. Like a sand dollar. You ever tried picking one of those up? My rough fingers crushed them every time.

Aubrey stretched at the prow, arms straight, back arched, head tipped to the sun. Breasts and ass jutting out. I rolled my eyes. You'd think by now she'd realize we weren't happening. But I got it. I was her chance to escape.

Her overprotective Italian father wasn't going to let her move out of the house until he was passing her off to a husband. One he approved of. So I was the only option she could see. I knew that. And I felt bad for her. But not enough to be manipulated into being with her. When her parents weren't around, and she forget she had ulterior motives, she really wasn't that bad. Her sense of humor was wicked sarcastic, and she was smarter than her parents

realized. But they were bound and determined to marry her off .
. . and soon. It had slowly become their all-consuming mission.

Personally, I thought Aubrey was willing to do anything just
to make the nonsense stop. Even if it meant throwing herself at
me every chance she got.

What a fucking waste of time and energy.

I had to give the Young brothers credit; they barely glanced at
her. They were going to do well in the business world. Adapting
on the fly to a situation was a necessary part of strong leadership,
and the brothers had moved quickly—plying an accommodating
Mr. Perotti with beer until he passed out. His hairy stomach rose
and fell with each breath as he snored in one of the beanbags. I
cranked the music louder to cover the sounds.

Situation handled.

Except by that point, the beer was almost gone.

I looked in the cooler with longing, grabbing a bottle of water
instead of the lone can of Bud Light. What I wouldn't give to be
able to drink myself into oblivion right now. Black out and not
remember any of this.

But I was businessman too. So I'd play the part of the helpful
but unobtrusive guide, at least for another few hours. I'd made it
this far, I was practically home free.

I underestimated hell though.

It had multiple levels.

I'd forgotten.

As Aubrey pushed away from the railing and sashayed my
way, she stumbled in those strappy wedge heels she was wearing,

falling to the deck with a shout and then clutching her ankle and whimpering.

The brothers looked at her, then over at me.

Mr. Perotti snored from the beanbag.

I guessed that made her my problem.

Clenching my jaw as I made my way around the center console, I squatted next to where she lay crumbled on the deck.

"You okay?"

Her dark eyes met mine, wet with tears.

Ah fuck, had she actually injured herself?

I sighed. "Where does it hurt?"

A tear slid down her cheek. Her mascara must've been waterproof, because it stayed perfect. She sniffled. "My an-ankle."

Removing her ridiculous shoe—who the fuck wore heels on a boat?—I moved her ankle through its range of motion. She flinched and cried out and, shit, it was already starting to swell.

Fucking lovely.

The three hours left in the trip were an exercise in perseverance.

Aubrey was not a good patient.

By the end, I'd considered dumping her overboard to the sharks no less than four times. I figured her boobs would work as suitable floatation devices. I wouldn't even have to sacrifice a life jacket.

Her dad was worthless. When we stopped at the tournament marina, where the marlin we'd caught took second place, he left with the Young brothers to go to a bar to celebrate. Still wearing his short swim trunks.

"You're headed back to the city marina, right? Near the MUSC emergency room?" He clapped me hard on the shoulder, squeezing. "You don't mind taking Aubrey, do you? She'd rather hang out with you than me, I'm sure." He'd wiggled his caterpillar eyebrows and winked.

I closed my eyes in defeat, taking a slow breath to calm myself. *My God, why hast thou forsaken me?*

"No problem." The words barely made it past my gritted teeth.

"Thanks, son." He slapped my back before heading down the dock after the Youngs.

I cranked the radio to angry rock as I motored to the other marina, drowning out Aubrey's pointless attempts at conversation from the beanbag.

Looking at my watch and cursing, knowing there was nothing quick about a trip to the ER, not after fighting traffic through the city and back again, I sent Sadie a text, letting her know I'd be headed her way after I finished up with things here.

Of all days, why did this have to happen on our last night together for the next three weeks?

When we docked, I hauled a lame Aubrey into my arms, forced to carry her. The swelling had subsided some, but she swore she couldn't handle putting any weight on it. Whatever. I just needed to get her dropped off at the ER. Then I could come back and pack up things on the boat while she got seen. Her dad could pick her up as far as I was concerned.

She rubbed against me, talking some shit about me being her hero. I laughed to keep from strangling her.

I needed to get back to Reynolds Island.

I needed to get back to Sadie.

chapter
one

Sadie

I TEETERED PRECARIOUSLY ON THE edge of rage, trying not to let the shock push me off the cliff into the pain of his betrayal. I needed to hold on to the anger right now. It was the glue keeping me intact.

My mind whirred, manufacturing scenes of West romancing Aubrey, of West laughing at my naivety, of their wedding, their future kids, their picture-fucking-perfect life. The episodes played on the IMAX of my mind—the images too big, the volume too loud to fully process. I was immobile, held captive by the *what ifs*. The *never woulds*.

I inhaled carefully, my motions delicate. Abrupt movement might shatter the fragile grip I had on my control. And if I lost that, I wasn't sure which way I would tumble—fury or agony. I just knew it would be violent. And I couldn't allow that. It meant she—Aubrey—would have won. That he was never mine.

Squeezing my eyes shut, I exhaled. It was all I could manage.

As my world shattered around me, everything blurred, as if trying to soften the blow. My breath caught, my chest fighting the most natural of instincts beneath the pain crushing it.

Flexing my hands against the wrought iron table, I searched blindly for stability, a way to anchor myself in this awful new reality. My palms slid until my fingers curled around the edge, squeezing until my knuckles turned white.

I was a lit fuse. I wasn't sure if the detonation would be an implosion or an explosion.

But destruction was inevitable.

I licked my dry lips.

Inhaled.

Exhaled.

I concentrated on the expansion of my ribs. The deflation of my chest.

Rise.

Fall.

In.

Out.

I focused on my lungs. Because I couldn't bear to think about my heart.

ON MY DRIVE HOME, I got a text. From Aubrey.

Save your pride and walk away now. He's gonna dump you tonight. He's already tired of you and your trip is the perfect time for him to make a clean break. Hell, he didn't even wait for you to leave. He's been with me all day. Woman to woman, I thought I owed you a head's up.

She'd attached a picture of West kneeling in front of her long, bare legs. He looked like he was about to take off her shoes for her. How fucking thoughtful of him.

"YOU WANT TO GO TO Anchor now? I thought the plan was to meet the guys at the Wreck?" Rue leaned against my doorway, effortlessly sexy in a short skirt and loose tank.

I twisted my hips, checking my backside in the mirror. Panty lines weren't going to be a problem because I wasn't wearing any.

"Plans change. All the time. Without warning."

Her eyes narrowed. "What's that mean?"

I faced forward again and smoothed my hands down my snug black dress, coasting them over the curve of my hips. With my tan and my wild blond curls, I looked sexy.

More important, I *felt* sexy. Too bad for West it was no longer for him. I didn't know who the lucky man was yet, but somebody was going to be unwrapping me later.

After all, wasn't that the quickest way to get over a guy?

I flicked my eyes to my best friend, willing her to understand without having to explain it all.

"We're going to Anchor. And we're gonna drink. And we're gonna dance. And we're gonna see where that leads." It probably would've sounded more fun if my eyes weren't dead and my voice wasn't leaden.

Rue wrinkled her brow as she studied me. She was quiet for a long moment. "He fucked up?"

I jutted my chin out and clenched my jaw, dropping my head in a jerky nod. *I'm not gonna cry. He's not worth it.*

"I hear there's a good DJ tonight. Should be a big crowd."

My lips curved, more sneer than smile. "Fucking perfect. You ready?"

She didn't budge from the doorway. "*I am. Are you?*" Her voice was soft, the concern peeking through in her tone.

"No." I barked out a harsh laugh. "No. And I know this is a shitty way to deal with it. But it's all I've got right now. Okay?"

Rue smiled sadly, her expression soft. "I hear you, babe. Let me tell you though, from experience, it's probably not gonna work. It's gonna be a distraction at best, a regret at the worst."

I met her eyes, my gaze steady. "I'm okay with that."

She sighed. "Let's go break some hearts then."

Too fucking late.

Too fucking late.

******

My hip throbbed where I'd fallen harder than I meant to against the table. I slid the empty bottle farther away from me.

Beer was my drink of choice tonight because I planned to keep them coming nice and steady all night. That was number five. I think.

My phone chirped. Again. It'd been making noise for the last two hours. I peered down at it, tipsy enough to finally be curious what *he'd* have to say. The messages filled my screen and then some.

I'm back.

I can't wait to see you.

Are you almost ready?

I'm here. Where are you?

Sadie, are you okay?

Why aren't you answering?

There were more. His *concern* was evident.

Too bad.

He'd fucking sunk his own ship.

A giggle slipped out. *His own ship!* I covered my mouth with my hand, my eyes watering with tears. It wasn't that funny. It really wasn't.

Aubrey's fake tits could be his flotation device. I was sure he had lots of practice hanging on to them.

My laughter died abruptly.

I studied my own breasts where they peeked out of the black jersey of my dress. They looked great tonight, but there was at least a cup size of extra padding in my bra propping the girls up. Aubrey's boudoir photoshoot came to mind. Hers were fake, but they were well done. She'd dropped some serious cash on those babies.

I cupped my chest, wondering if quantity was better than quality when it came to tit size.

My fingers squeezed experimentally. They were good breasts. Sensitive. Perky. Clad in my most expensive bra. *Somebody* tonight was going to appreciate them.

But not *him*.

Resolved, I woke my phone up. Typed out a response and hit send before I could second guess myself.

I've got some things to take care of. You understand.

My screen immediately lit up with an incoming message, but I powered it off and left the text unread.

Tonight wasn't about him.

It was about anybody *but* him.

I picked up my fresh bottle of beer and took a long pull. I'd been ordering them two at a time; I was efficient like that.

Rue put an arm around me, her lips wrapped around her own dark brown glass bottle. Releasing it with a pop, she leaned her head against me. With those heels, she would've been the same height as me if I was in flats, but I was rocking some serious shoes tonight too, so she only came to my chin.

I hugged her to my side. The soft press of her generous curves against me was all natural. Her girls were going free tonight and, depending how she moved and lifted her arms, she was showing off some major side boob.

Reaching over, I hefted one of her tits through her top. Heavy. Warm. Kind of smooshy. I bet guys liked that.

Or maybe guys—maybe *West*—preferred Aubrey's artificial wonders?

"What's that about?" Rue swatted my hand away.

I poked at my chest. "Do you think this is why?"

Sighing, she took her two hands and gave my tits a quick squeeze. "They're boobs. They jiggle. They have nipples. Guys like nipples. It's really not more complicated than that. The only thing they might like better is seeing two girls play with each other's tits."

She glanced around, and when I realized what she was doing, I followed suit.

We were attracting a bit of an audience. An all-male audience.

She turned to whisper in my ear, plastering herself fully against my side. "Come on, let's dance and give these boys a show."

Knowing how much she loved being the center of attention, and ready to stir up a little trouble myself, I held her hand as she led me onto the dance floor.

Don't get me wrong, Rue was gorgeous, my bestie, and we lived together. I'd dance dirty with her all night long for the fun of it.

But it'd never go past that. I liked cock. So did she. Plain and simple.

We found a spot and faced each other, her hands on my waist and mine in the air. The bass was pulsing, the beat throbbing, and we found our groove, sliding sinuously against each other. In less than the space of two verses, we were surrounded by men presented with a dilemma—to stand back and watch or to approach and try to get a piece of the action.

The timid ones watched. Those weren't the ones we were after anyway.

The bolder ones moved closer. Hands slipped over my hips. One confident man wedged himself between us, so we sandwiched him.

And I didn't give a fuck about anything except dancing, getting lost in the moment, and the sensation of being *wanted*.

Even if it was by strangers whose hands didn't know how I liked to be stroked, or that the back of my knees were ticklish, or that—if he did it right—just massaging my feet could be erotic enough to make me wet. No, tonight I wasn't picky.

Tonight, I was fine with quantity over quality.

Maybe I could learn something from West after all.

The guy behind me moved closer, effectively trapping me between him and the man almost flush with my chest. Palms traced from my hips down the front of my thighs while the lanky guy before me cupped my neck and stared into my eyes. An erection pressed into my ass and another into my stomach. I ran my hands down the impressive set of abs in front of me. And I shamelessly compared size. The guy I was facing had a bigger cock and better moves.

Winner, winner, chicken dinner.

Licking my lips, I dropped low then rose up slowly, sliding against his hard body. His dark eyes flared with heat, and he pushed a thigh between my legs, dislodging the guy behind me.

No big loss.

Wrapping a hand around my hip, he pulled me closer, my dress riding up my legs until his thigh was pressed against my bare core. The dance floor was packed, and I was just shy of sharing my secrets with anyone who cared to look. As we moved, the friction of the rough denim against me drew a moan from my lips. He grinned wickedly and gripped my ass, pulling me higher. If he didn't know I was pantiless before, he knew now.

I bit my lip and slipped my hands under the edge of his shirt. His warm muscles contracted as I drew my nails along the waistband of his low-slung jeans.

Moving against him, feeling his reactions to me, filled me with a sense of power. It was dirty and heady and wrong and everything I needed this night to be.

I didn't want pretty words and soft emotions.

I needed a guy to take the initiative and sweep me away with raw chemistry and bad decisions made after too much alcohol.

I needed to spread my legs and forget how *he* felt moving between them, and instead lose myself in the unknown, dangerous appeal of a stranger.

For a second, I froze, and I tugged his head closer to me. "Your name's not Jared, is it?"

He looked confused. "No, I'm—"

"Doesn't matter. As long it's not Jared. I don't have a good history with Jareds." Or . . . Wests. But I couldn't imagine there was more than one of *those* in the area.

He smirked down at me as he ran his hands up my sides, his thumbs stroking the undersides of my breasts. "Honey, you can call me whatever the hell you want tonight."

I pressed against him, crushing my chest to his. "I don't want to call you anything. Words aren't real high on my priority list."

He chuckled, eyes half-closing as his hands retreated back to my hips. He withdrew his leg and spun me until he was pressed against me from behind, bending his knees slightly so he could nestle his hard length between my ass cheeks.

His hips thrust against me and I lifted my hands over my head and back until they looped behind his neck. The scruff on his face tickled where it pressed against my jawline, scraping my soft skin.

"God, I love the South."

I hummed my agreement. "We're big on . . . *hospitality* around here."

He groaned as I scraped my nails along the base of his scalp. "And I was told everything moved slower down South."

"Not tonight."

His hips mimicked what I hoped we'd be doing horizontally soon while his hands wandered the rest of me. I didn't look to see if anyone noticed. I just watched his hands—part of me vibrating with arousal, another part detached—as they traced over my stomach, ribs, neck, upper arms. The sides of my boobs. Followed my hip toward my core before veering away at the last second.

Another hand pushed his away roughly, yanked me from his embrace.

A hand wearing a royal blue hair tie.

Familiar eyes blazed into mine.

"Sadie—*what the fuck?*"

Huh. He'd found me.

I tried to turn back to my dance partner, but West had a firm grip on my wrist. I hadn't noticed that. I tugged, but his fingers tightened in response.

What the fuck? He wanted to know what. The. Fuck?

I laughed.

Looked in his beautiful, blue-gray eyes and laughed.

"I'm dancing."

West tucked me close to his tense body, turning us so that he physically separated me from my new friend.

"What's going on? Did this asshole slip you something?"

I met his gaze. Smirked in contempt. "Nope. We were just starting to get to know each other."

Mouth tight and nostrils flaring, his fingers squeezed my wrist, his grip almost painful. "We're leaving."

I dug in my heels as he started to pull me off the dance floor. Or, at least, I tried. Digging in your stilettos when you were being manhandled by a guy who was still inches taller than you in your highest heels wasn't super effective. I stumbled, forced to clutch his arm to avoid face-planting.

My pride had me matching his long-legged stride. When we reached the dim overhang outside the bar, my ears ringing from the sudden quietness, I'd hit my limit.

"Stop!"

The venom in my voice got his attention, and he froze, turning back to face me. His fingers still circled my wrist.

His eyes raced over my face, brows knit with confusion. Scrubbing his hand across his short hair in agitation, he stared at me. "Are you mad at me? Is this some kind of fucked up revenge for missing our date Wednesday?"

I licked my lips, forcing my somewhat sluggish brain to think before reacting. I was tipsy, but not wasted. "Nope. Just making a new friend."

He cocked his head to the side, the muscle in his jaw ticking. "What's going on here?"

"Why don't you tell me?!"

He took a ragged breath, caging me against the stucco building with his arm. He loomed over me, and I hated the way he was using his size to his advantage. "You leave tomorrow, and I get back from Charleston, and you won't even see me? And then I find you here looking for a hook up?" Gray thunderclouds raged in his eyes and his arm muscles flexed spasmodically.

Meeting his glare with one of my own, I straightened, glad for the extra height my shoes gave me, even if I did feel a little unsteady. "I know."

"You know what?"

"*I know*, and you don't have to pretend anymore."

chapter
two

HE LEANED DOWN UNTIL ONLY A whisper separated us. I exhaled, my entire world shrinking to just his face. The rough stubble where he hadn't shaved. The harsh slash of his eyebrows. His narrowed blue-gray eyes piercing me, shaking my resolve. I bit my lip, and his gaze flickered down at the small action. He took a step closer, crowding me. His skin was hotter than the humid air surrounding us.

When I inhaled, I expected to smell her. Some combo of musk and suntan lotion and sweat and money.

But he smelled like him—citrus and salt. He'd been considerate then. Washed her off before he came looking for me.

"I can stop pretending? Stop pretending I don't want to turn you over my knee and make your perfect little ass red for letting another guy put his hands on you? That I would've taken him down if it wouldn't have taken away time I want to be spending with you—time I'd much rather pass in a bed together instead of arguing outside a bar?"

He released my wrist, his hand sliding up my arm until his fingers circled my throat. His thumb covered my pulse and his lips thinned.

"Is that from me? Or from that stand-in back there?"

My mouth parted and I sagged against the wall. What the fuck was happening? I pressed my legs together, ashamed of the moisture pooling there, furious that he still heated my blood and weakened my knees despite everything.

"I saw you. I saw her. I saw the pictures. I. Know." My voice betrayed my strong words, though, breaking with each painful statement.

His fingers shifted behind my neck, forcing my head up to meet his gaze.

"Stop talking in fucking riddles."

I wasn't. Riddles were funny. This—this wasn't funny at all.

"You're leaving me. You're going back to her. Hell, I don't know if you ever left her."

He dropped his arm and took a step back, rubbing his eyes with the heels of his hands. He cursed under his breath. "I will never fucking understand women. What the hell are you talking about? You're the one leaving. To Grand Cayman. Tomorrow. The only *her* I'm going back to while you're gone is my boat. And the only *her* I thought I was with was you."

I pushed off the wall until I stood on my own. Part of me

knew having this conversation now, with alcohol loosening my tongue, was a terrible idea. But that part of me was outvoted by pride and anger and the sheer fucking desire to hurt him back.

"Then why was Aubrey in your arms this afternoon?" Sheer venom dripped from every word.

He stiffened, eyes widening in either guilt or surprise. I couldn't tell which.

"What are you talking about?"

"Are you seriously gonna deny it?"

"I—" He opened and closed his mouth, and then looked down at his feet like maybe the answer was lost somewhere down there with the cigarette butts and empty beer bottles before raising his eyes back to mine. He shook his head. "How do you even *know* about that?"

"Wow. *That's* your response? That's what you have to say?"

I blinked, stupefied.

Turning, I stumbled away from him, off the concrete patio and into the oyster shell parking lot. I teetered, unsteady on my heels as the world fell apart beneath me.

Hot tears pricked my eyes. I gritted my teeth together, hating the female propensity toward crying in both sadness and anger. It felt weak, and although I could barely see through my traitorous eyes to walk straight, my muscles were tense with fury.

They weren't tears of self-pity. Not one single drop.

"Sadie." My name was a warning. An order to stop.

Fuck him and what he wanted.

I picked my way deeper into the dark parking lot.

"Sadie!"

I lifted my hand then delicately raised my middle finger.

Before I could lower my arm, he was there—lifting me up and tossing me over his shoulder.

The warm breeze caressed the bottom of my ass where my dress no longer covered me.

I struggled against his hold even though I knew it was pointless. Instead, he gripped me tighter, one arm anchored across the back of my thighs, the other discovering what was missing from my outfit.

He paused the second his fingers touched bare skin instead of lace or silk.

"Seriously?" His harsh laugh echoed in the empty night. "I don't know whether to strangle you for dancing with that guy like this or fuck you right here in the parking lot."

"You won't be touching me anymore!" My nails raked across his back.

"The hell I won't. You're mine."

He palmed the curve where ass met thigh, rubbing my sensitive skin, squeezing me. My body was a rebellious slut, betraying me with its urge to push into his hand.

When we reached his truck—the big, shiny white one, not the junker—he pitched me into the back seat, following me in and hovering over me. My dress was twisted around my hips, and one strap was falling off my arm, the top curve of my breast bare to his view. I scrambled to the other side, but he was faster, hitting the child lock button so I couldn't open it from my position.

His finger traced my cleavage, pulling my strap down further, dipping low between my pushed up breasts. Leaning down, he nipped the side of my neck before trailing kisses down to my collarbone.

"Is this what I can't touch? All this soft skin that's just begging for me?"

His stubble scraped my throat and a moan escaped before I could stop it.

"Get off me!" I hissed, pushing up with my hips to dislodge him. The door behind him was still open, our feet sticking out.

He ground himself over my exposed mound, his erection hard and straining behind his zipper. "Don't worry, babe. We're both gonna get off."

Oh, yes. Please.

Yanking my arms above my head, he captured my mouth in a savage kiss—taking more than he gave. My tongue fought his, but my hips answered his thrusts, rolling in a heady response.

Holding my wrists with one hand, his other drifted down my arm and up to the base of my neck, fisting a handful of hair and angling my head the way he wanted it. His hard lips slanted over mine again and again. I strained in his hold but my mouth met his, welcomed him, sought each slide, lick, and nibble he dropped on me. When he twisted away for a breath, I followed, nipping his lip until he rejoined the action, his biceps bunching and flexing.

"Fuck, yes." He growled in my ear, tugging on the lobe before shifting lower down my body.

My heels dug into his lower back, thighs I didn't remember

moving wrapped tight around him. My hips ground without shame against him even as my hands twisted to free themselves.

"We're *over*."

He pushed my bra cup aside with his nose and latched onto my nipple, sucking hard. My back bowed, offering him more of my freed breast. His other hand released my hair and yanked the other dress strap off, the fragile fabric tearing. Cupping and squeezing my swollen flesh, he hummed low in his throat. I couldn't think past his hands, his mouth.

Lifting his head and pulling on the pebbled bud until it popped free, his stormy eyes seared mine with dark promises.

"We're just getting started."

I glared, bit my lip, and bucked again—whether my hips were begging for more or trying to push him away, I couldn't tell.

"Let me go." *Dear God, don't stop.*

He shook his head, his eyes daring me, but he released my wrists. My body gave him the answer he wanted though when I rocked my hips restlessly, and he closed his eyes and dropped back down to my breasts, sucking and squeezing. I panted with each delicious flick of his tongue and pull of his lips, the sting of his teeth twisting me tighter, making me forget everything but where we connected.

My hands fisted his shirt, yanking, and he raised up, tearing it off with one hand and throwing it to the floor. I dragged my nails across his back, pulling his head closer to my chest.

"Stay." The pain in that one word sliced deep into my jagged emotions.

I shook my head, but pressed closer.

"Don't go tomorrow."

"It doesn't matter. We're done. I won't do this again." I clung to my convictions and his hard body with equal desperation.

He moved, ripping my dress farther to bare more skin for his mouth to explore.

"You're wrong. We're gonna do this all night."

I was torn, knowing this was wrong, but wanting one last time with him. One last time to burn the feel of his skin against mine, his mouth, his hands, his cock—all of it—into memory.

"No!"

He groaned, rising up on his elbows to look at me through hooded eyes.

"Are you really gonna deny this? I don't know what the fuck you're talking about with Aubrey—about going back to her—but the only woman I give a fuck about is underneath me, and I promise you, she is gonna be thoroughly satisfied before I'm done with her."

He started to lick a trail down to my navel, my dress destroyed, split at the top and bunched at the bottom, when I caught his chin and made him look at me.

"I was there today. I fucking *saw* you carrying her."

He paused—the moment frozen, dark and intense between us. We were both breathing hard from arousal and anger and uncertainty, and the tears I'd been holding back threatened to spill over.

"You were there *today*? In Charleston? At the marina?"

I nodded, my heart stuttering in its sprint under my ribs.

"Why the fuck didn't you say something?"

I swallowed hard past the lump in my throat. "You'd made your choice. It was obvious."

"I made my choice weeks ago. Apparently it hasn't been obvious enough." With a harsh noise, he pulled himself higher up my body, my breasts crushed beneath his chest, his heat scorching me.

Framing my face with his hands and forcing me to meet his stare, he gazed down at me, his eyes harsh and fierce. His thumb stroked over my tender lower lip and he chuckled once, the rough sound vibrating in my own chest.

"This isn't how I wanted to do this. I had a plan—but leave it to you and your hard-headed stubbornness—" he cut himself off and pressed a kiss, soft and tender, to my forehead.

The unexpected change in pace gave me whiplash.

"I love you, Sadie."

I tried to shake my head, sure I hadn't heard him right.

"Yes. I. Love. You. I thought—I thought you knew. I thought my actions showed it. The paper airplanes, crawling in your window to cuddle for a few hours, your hair tie that I can't bring myself to take off my wrist—how could you not know? Do you think I take moonlit walks with all my female friends? That I get so crazy going up my back stairs that I can't even wait the few steps it would take to get to my bed with just any woman? I can't hardly pass a fucking Krispy Kreme anymore without getting a hard-on. Gives a whole new meaning to the HOT NOW sign in the window."

I stilled beneath him. That was everything I'd wanted to hear—but now couldn't bear. My heart felt like it was in a blender, my emotions chopped to bits and flying everywhere. He was lying—I'd seen him with her with my own two eyes. The pictures in his nightstand. The lunch meetings he conveniently didn't mention.

But I wanted desperately to believe him too. His eyes shone with sincerity, and the memories of all the times we were together, just *together*, came roaring back. Not the sex. The other times. His stubbornness trying to coax me into the ocean. Lying on the hammock, legs intertwined. The way our bodies automatically curled together in sleep.

The look on his face dropped, twisted, grew more determined. "I know you feel this connection we have, Sadie. It's undeniable." Reaching one hand between us, he plunged a finger into me. I was wet, more than ready for him and my hips surged up. He added a second and it was all I could do to focus on his words. "You think you respond this way because we click physically? You think this is just biological compatibility? You think this is just hormones at work?"

He worked me, pumping me with his hand, the heel of his palm circling my clit. I couldn't answer, my body on sensory overload. I gasped his name. It was the only thought in my mind.

"You think you could feel this way with just anybody?"

When he withdrew from me abruptly, a cry of need wrenched from my throat. I was so close now. He unzipped his pants, pushing them down just far enough to free himself. He settled between my thighs, his cock a welcome warmth against my sensitive skin.

I squirmed, searching for pressure, friction, anything to ease this feeling inside me, despite knowing this was wrong, knowing this was goodbye.

"You don't think it's gotten better between us for a reason? I know you love me—you don't even have to say it. I thought you knew it too. I thought the way our bodies spoke to each other made it clear—you don't reach these heights, feel this passion, experience this utter perfection without love."

"You don't love me," I gasped, tilting my hips until he was poised at my entrance.

"The hell I don't!" he roared, impaling me with one hard thrust.

We both paused, the fullness of him stretching me, completing me, overwhelmed everything else. His neck muscles bulged, and his ass flexed under my hands. Even yelling at each other, nothing had ever felt more right than being joined with him.

And even if I never got to experience it again after tonight, I knew I'd never forget how he felt inside me. His long, hot length, greedy and impatient, moving now at a savage pace.

He dropped his mouth to my neck, sucking hard. Marking me.

I clutched him tighter, squeezed harder, slid against him, met each thrust. I wanted everything he could give me one last time.

He changed his angle, rolling his hips on the downward stroke, making sure my clit wasn't ignored. We moved together, scaling the precipice until it was too much and I was right there at the peak. Tears fell from my eyes as my orgasm burst through me, scary in its intensity, its finality.

Another pump, one more, and he joined me, my name a harsh cry on his lips.

He buried his face in my shoulder, his chest heaving, as he pulsed deep within me. We stayed like that for a long minute, aftershocks rocking both of us as we caught our breath.

With a satisfied groan, he twisted, our sweaty bodies sticking to the leather seats as he rolled until I lay spent across his chest, my cheek pressed to the thundering pulse of his heart.

He ran his hand down my hair.

"Stay," he whispered. "You're mine. Fuck, if I'm doing something wrong, talk to me, teach me. But you can't go. Not like this."

I brushed my lips over his damp skin.

"I can't, West. I can't do this again. I shouldn't ever have to wonder if I can trust you. Have to wonder if you're with her, thinking of her, touching her."

He started to protest, but I covered his mouth with my hand.

"You want to talk about actions? You were carrying her! She was draped all over you! You were laughing!"

My hand was ripped off his mouth.

"She's an idiot who twisted her fucking ankle and I was taking her to the ER—"

"You know what?" I interrupted. "I don't fucking care. I'm sure you have an excuse. You always do. I'm sure you have a perfectly good reason for having half-naked pictures of her in your nightstand too."

He wrinkled his brow. "I have no idea what you're talking about."

I bit the inside of my cheek to keep from screaming. Scooping his shirt off the floorboard, I slid it over my head, grateful it would be long enough to cover my dripping sex. Glaring at him, I scrambled out of the truck. I didn't even register the sharp edges of the crushed oyster shells digging into my bare feet.

"Why don't you check when you get home? Then you can tell me what completely legitimate excuse you have for that. Because, I'm *sure* you have one."

Tucking himself back inside his pants and zipping up, he followed me.

"Sadie, don't do this. Don't go. Catch a later flight. Turn down the job. Let's work this out."

I turned flat eyes on him, ignoring the hand he stretched in my direction. "There's nothing to work out. We're done."

"We're *not* done! Quit saying that!"

Stepping close, I kissed him one last time, softly, lips closed. A final goodbye.

"You really love me, West? Let me go. Just let me go."

chapter
three

I WAITED LIKE A FOOL. LAID IN bed, wide awake, dry-eyed, trembling at times with arousal and other times with anger. I wanted to scream and yell and beat my fists on his chest. Kiss him senseless and fuck him until we were too tired to talk anymore. My lips wanted to whisper in his ear that I loved him too, that we'd make this work. I plotted Aubrey's demise with increasing detail. The ways I'd prove her wrong. Prove West did love me— that we were perfect for each other.

But I didn't get to do any of that.

Because he never came.

Not when I got up to get a glass of warm milk. Not when the stars mocked me when I looked out the window for his truck— again. Not when the gray fingers of dawn stretched awake. Not while I showered off the last remnants I had of *us*, the last of him on me, our musky smell replaced with my usual cheap watermelon products. Not while I finished packing, my body on autopilot as I plucked toiletries from my bathroom counter. Not as I hauled two oversized suitcases to the curb and waited for Grady to pick me up on the way to the Savannah airport.

He didn't show last minute, running to the gate, desperate for a last attempt to convince me to stay.

He didn't text. Didn't call. Didn't appear.

He never came.

He let me go.

He let me go.

He let me go.

You know what was great about airplanes? They served alcohol. Even in the morning. Today was only a travel day, according to Grady. I wasn't officially on the clock, so why not start the day with a screwdriver? I didn't remember much else from the first flight—Savannah to Miami. Just that one screwdriver I nursed the entire way. I was stuck next to some foreign businessman in coach who thankfully ignored me, leaving me to brood in my drink and stare unseeing out the window.

As I looked at the miniature landscape spread out thousands of feet below me, I remembered exactly how small I really was in this great big world. That my pain was nothing compared to all the problems that existed and plagued the world. Poverty, hunger, illiteracy, crime, discrimination. My heartbreak was so far down that list of problems.

And yet, I felt crushed by it.

Shattered. Cracked. Betrayed.

But not destroyed. I was too fucking stubborn to let a guy utterly destroy me again.

No. If nothing else, I had my pride.

And my pride demanded that by the time I arrive in the Caribbean, my wallowing would end. I had one more flight to pout and then I had to pull on my big girl panties.

If West was too dumb to realize what he fucked up, that was on him—not me.

I was a *damn* fine catch.

Any man should be *lucky* to have me by his side. Fucking honored.

I downed the last gulp of my screwdriver and allowed myself a tight, bitter smile. Anger was so much easier than denial. I was making nice progress through the stages of grief.

Miami was a blur. Grady and I had to race to make our connection—which actually turned out to be a decent-sized plane. Like the first leg of the trip, he sat in first class and I sat mid-plane in a seat over the wing. This time, my seatmate was a man traveling solo who looked only a few years older than me. And, unlike last time, this guy didn't seem content to ignore me.

After stuffing a carryon in the overhead bin, he turned to face me, reaching out to shake my hand. "Hey. I'm Nick."

Begrudgingly giving him my hand, I lifted my face to his. "Sadie."

His warm fingers held mine a moment too long, and I tugged it back, tucking it under my thigh. He had dark eyes, like the color West preferred his coffee. The memory made me scowl.

Nick's eyes widened and he looked over his shoulder. "Is something wrong? Do you get airsick or something?"

I blushed, embarrassed at taking out my frustration on this innocent guy. "No. I—I'm fine."

He paused, his gaze drifting over my features. I wondered what he saw as he studied my face before his focus dropped to take in the rest of me. I glanced down, self-consciously. The scooped neck of my top had twisted a little from my seatbelt, and the barest edge of my lavender bra peeked out on one side. I fumbled with the cotton fabric, adjusting it back in place.

A smile lingered on his lips when I looked back up at him. "Yes, you are," he said softly.

I fidgeted. Was he flirting? I took a minute to absorb the rest of him. He skin was bronzed, and his brown hair was streaked from the sun. Faint laugh lines cracked the sharp planes of his face, his full lips still tipped in a grin.

Why the hell was I noticing his lips?

I didn't allow my survey to drop below his smooth-shaven chin and the strong angle of his jaw, but his shoulders were brushing mine, so he was clearly broad.

Alcohol. I needed more alcohol.

The flight attendant went through the safety talk and Nick

paid attention, which was noticeable only because most passengers were ignoring it. He glanced over his shoulder to locate the emergency exit, two rows behind us.

When the plane began its taxi to the runway, he gripped the armrests tightly, dislodging my elbow in the process.

"Sorry," he gritted out.

"Nervous?"

"Nope."

I raised my eyebrows.

He grimaced. "Scared shitless is a better description."

I bit my lip so I wouldn't smile, but he saw the small motion.

"Most plane crashes occur within two minutes of takeoff. Once we're in the air, I'll be fine. It's just those first two minutes."

He braced himself with his feet, his thighs flexing under his gray pants.

"Talk to me. Distract me." His eyes pleaded with me, belaying the gruff tone to his voice.

"Ummm. Okay." I paused, my mind blank. "Are you single?"

What the fuck? Where had that question come from?

"Yes. You?"

I clenched my jaw, turned away for a second. "Yup. Very."

His eyes narrowed as he observed me. "What'd he do?"

"What?"

"What'd the idiot do?"

"He was an idiot." I shrugged.

"Clearly."

Shaking my head, I turned the question back on him. "What

about you? Why are you single?"

"I travel a lot for work. It makes it hard."

That word. I couldn't help my eyes from flicking down to his crotch.

The muscles in his arm relaxed as he laughed at me. "Yeah, it can be a problem sometimes. But I handle it."

I coughed. Did he mean what I thought?

The laugh lines around his eyes deepened as he struggled to keep a straight face.

"Is it a problem that comes up a lot?" What the fuck was wrong with me this morning? I blamed my lack of filter on my way-too-early-in-the-morning drink.

He kept his voice serious. "Just morning and night."

I snickered and he relaxed the rest of the way, his knuckles no longer white against the armrest.

"I've mastered some coping techniques. I could teach you. You may need them in the future, if you run into any more idiots."

I blinked. Damn, he was bold. I looked down where his hand rested between us, unconsciously checking out his fingers. Long and lean. Surprisingly lean for such a broad guy.

"I've had a lot of experience—"

"I'm sure you have," I interrupted.

" . . . and it'd be a shame for all that knowledge to just go to waste," he finished.

"We do live in a wasteful society these days."

"It's sad, really."

This was the moment we should've busted out laughing. But,

instead, we stared at each other, the tension rising between us. And I was grateful. This—this is what I needed. To spend a few hours flirting harmlessly with a good-looking guy I'd never see again. To take my mind off West. To remember there were other fish in the sea, other men who would find me attractive.

"I think we're past the two minute mark now." I broke the thick silence.

"Does that mean you're done talking to me?"

"Are you still scared?"

"Terrified. I think you should hold my hand." His eyes twinkled with mischief.

"I'm sure."

"It would help." His face was the very picture of sincerity.

"How do you know?" I couldn't help but smile at his audacity.

"I don't. But I won't know until I try." He scooped my hand into his, his grip loose and easy. He seemed at ease touching me, someone he'd known less than half an hour.

And oddly, I was okay with it. His vibe was so relaxed, I didn't feel that weirdness that normally happens when a stranger enters my personal space. He left our hands dangling between us, his tan a slightly more olive tone than my own.

"Do you often hold hands with strangers?" I'd never met someone like him. I was intrigued.

"The pretty ones—as often as I can. But I'm shallow. I pass on the ugly ones."

"Worried it's contagious?"

He winked. "Are you implying I'm good looking?"

I opened my mouth then snapped it shut. Tried again. "I mean, I'd say you're about a six right now. A solid six." I nodded to reinforce my words.

He shook his head. "I'm at least an eight."

"Eh, that might be pushing it." Teasing him felt natural. And he *was* an eight. Maybe a nine.

"You should see me when I'm trying."

"You're not trying right now?"

"Nah. This is my laidback, casual look. When I go for devastatingly handsome, *that's* when you should look out. You can't start looking your best. You have to build up to it, give them something to look forward to. Otherwise, they're disappointed every time after that first encounter."

I paused. That actually wasn't terrible advice.

He nudged me with his broad shoulder. "I told you. Lots of experience."

The flight attendant stopped next to our row, took our drink orders. I picked another screwdriver, accepting the tiny liquor bottle and plastic cup of orange juice. He ordered the same.

He let go of my hand so we could assemble our drinks and my fingers felt cool without his shared warmth.

"So, is Grand Cayman your final stop?" I was curious now.

He nodded. "I got a last minute assignment. I'm a photographer."

"Me too!"

We spent the rest of the flight talking shop, debating techniques, and sharing tips. He was a lot more technical than

I was, and I paid attention, even jotted down some notes on my phone.

When he spoke about his work, his face lit up and he used his hands. His passion for the field was clear. And contagious. We traded customer horror stories and compared equipment. He was a big fan of having multiple lenses and using additional lighting equipment. I was more of an in-the-moment, use-what's-available kind of girl. Less is more and all that. He spent at least thirty minutes trying to convince me of the merits of his camera of choice—one that cost three times my current favorite.

We got so lost in our conversation, the landing took me by surprise, the slight bounce as we touched down startling me and making me automatically latch onto his arm.

He muscle flexed under my palm, his other hand coming up to cover mine. "You okay there?"

I nodded, embarrassed. "Sorry about that."

I started to withdraw my fingers, but he held tight for a moment, until I met his eyes.

"You grabbing my arm? Absolutely nothing to be sorry about." He released his grip slowly and I pulled away. The simple action of my fingers sliding across his bicep felt loaded with the way he was watching me.

I licked my lips and turned away to hide my edginess, peering out the window at the island airport, palm trees swaying beyond the runway and not a cloud in the sky.

"I guess we're here."

"It's too bad."

"I forgot to ask you," I said, facing him again, ignoring his remark. "Do you have a card or something? I'd love to see some of your work."

He leaned to the side and pulled his wallet out of his back pocket, extracting a business card and handing it to me. Bold letters splashed across the top: NICK BENTLEY, photographer.

Nick *Bentley? The* Nick Bentley? The huge, big shot, famous photographer Nick Bentley?

I dropped the card, my hand coming up to cover my mouth. I wasn't even remotely in his league, and I'd been arguing methodology with him? Mortified wasn't a strong enough word to begin to describe how I felt.

"Have you heard of me?" His head was cocked to the side and his voice held only curiosity, not arrogance.

I nodded, unable to meet his gaze now. "Yeah," I laughed, self-depreciatingly. "I've heard of you."

"And that's a bad thing?"

"No," I backtracked. "No! I've seen your work. You're amazing."

"Thank you," he said. He tilted my chin up, his touch feather-light, and waited until I made eye contact with him. "You seem pretty amazing yourself."

I snorted. *Oh my fucking God, I snorted!?* "I wouldn't exactly say I've got the same experience as you."

"I offered to share my expertise." His smile deepened. "The offer still stands."

I wasn't sure if he was talking about his photography skills or his skills with the other, *harder* issues that we'd been talking about earlier. His smirk didn't clarify the matter either.

"I'm sure you'll be busy."

"I'd make time for you," he countered smoothly.

"Where did you say your assignment was again?"

"Oh. I'll be shooting at a new resort here on the island for a few weeks. Water's Edge. How 'bout you? Where will you be?"

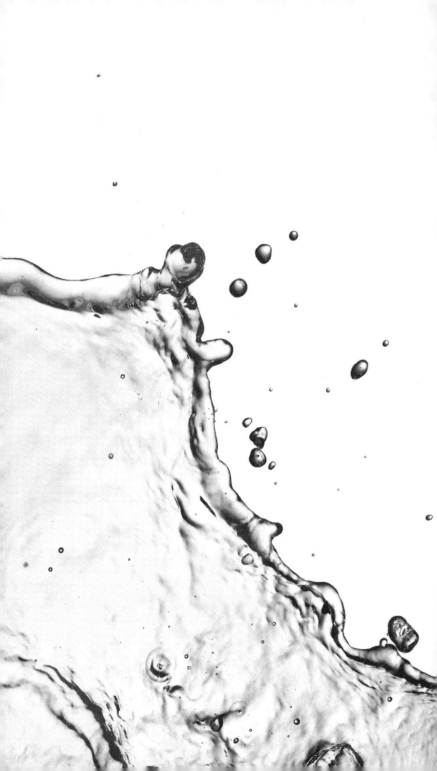

chapter
four

I WAS GOING TO KILL GRADY.

The Grand Cayman resort opening was his big break within the organization. It was his to organize, manage, advertise, handle, oversee—all that stuff. He'd told me it was basically a make it or break it situation. If he rocked it, he moved up to a VP position within the company. If he dropped the ball, he'd remain a mid-level manager overseeing the Reynolds Island property—not exactly their hottest location, even if he had personal ties to the area.

And he'd told me that he was impressed by my skills—trusted me to come up with a killer campaign.

How could he not have told me they'd hired Nick fucking Bentley too?

I guess that faith in me only went so far. I fumed silently as we went through customs and gathered our luggage.

Once we were situated in the shiny new minivan that would shuttle us to the resort, I couldn't hold it in any longer. I tapped Grady's shoulder in front of me. He twisted to face me and raised his eyebrows in question. Struggling to keep my voice level and professional, I asked, "Did you hire Nick—"

I was cut off when a hand shot out—stopping the door from closing all the way. Nick ducked inside and squeezed onto the bench seat next to me, his splayed thigh pressing against the length of mine. The heat of him burned right through my casual, linen-blend pants. I moved my leg over an inch and his followed me, maintaining the contact.

Leaning forward to the seat in front of us where Grady was, Nick punched his shoulder. "Grady! Man, it's good to see you again. It's been what—two years? I was sorry to hear about—"

"I've been *great!*" Grady interrupted, shooting Nick a look before glancing meaningfully at me. "I caught your show at the Galleria when I was in Chicago last year. I even bought a piece myself."

Nick settled back next to me, stretching his arm out along the seat behind my head. What was he doing?

Grady glanced at me, head cocked in question, clearly wondering if I was going to finish my earlier remark, but I shook my head slightly.

"So this is the hot new talent you were telling me about?" Nick tipped his head in my direction. "I have to say, I agree about the hot part. I can't wait to see what she can do."

My jaw dropped at his boldness, and I flushed from my face down to my chest. Was the air conditioner in this vehicle broken or something?

Grady rolled his eyes. "Easy, boy. Remember what I hired you to do and lay off the extracurricular activities for a change."

The resort opening was Grady's responsibility, his chance to shine. I guess he didn't have as much confidence in my abilities as I thought if he'd hired Nick Bentley too. And considering Nick was a fucking *legend* in the photography world, it was clear who was playing second string here.

They had a silent exchange, their pointed stares doing all the talking.

"So it's like that, is it?" Nick's voice was light, teasing.

"It's complicated. And I don't need you making it worse."

Nick glanced down at me, studying me more closely. I glared daggers into the back of Grady's head, pretending not to notice Nick's obvious interest.

"Complicated, huh? Complications are what make life so interesting."

"Nick." Grady's voice held a warning.

"So what's the schedule for today, boss?" Highly uncomfortable, I tried to change the subject.

Grady smiled and waved his hand dismissively. "No work today. Settle in, explore the resort some, see what you'll be working with. Tomorrow is soon enough to start blocking out your shots." He paused. "I thought you might like to join me for dinner later though? Around seven?"

"Yes, that'd be great!" I'd wondered if I'd be eating alone.

"Yeah, Grady, dinner at seven sounds perfect," Nick echoed, smirking at him. "I can't wait."

Grady narrowed his eyes in warning before facing front again and pulling out his phone.

I bit my lip.

What the hell had I gotten myself into?

AFTER I UNPACKED, I sent Rue a text to let her know I'd arrived safe and sound. Then I scrolled up to West's number. Rubbing my thumb over the edge of my phone, I hesitated. I knew what I needed to do for my own sanity. For my heart. The temptation was too great otherwise. Even though I was hundreds of miles away, he was still *right there* in my iPhone.

Biting my lip, I reluctantly blocked his number.

The phone mocked me. Practically screamed at me that it wasn't going to work. His name hovered on the screen, memories of him threatening to overwhelm me. Groaning, I pressed a few more buttons, deleting his contact info all together. It was the only way. I had to have a clean break.

I threw the phone angrily away from me onto the pillow-top mattress where it bounced harmlessly before settling on the edge of the pillow.

The giant king-sized bed with its fluffy white duvet and extra pillows.

Where I'd be sleeping solo.

By choice, I reminded myself sternly.

The phone wasn't the only place West still lingered, though. Pulling out my laptop, I logged on to the complimentary Wi-Fi and ruthlessly blocked West on my Facebook account, not allowing myself to check for any new updates. While I was at it, I blocked Aubrey too.

Good riddance to her.

Closing my eyes, I breathed deep. I should've felt relief from my attempt to cut him out, but my chest constricted tightly, mocking me for thinking it would be that simple.

As if my skin would forget that quickly what he felt like, trailing his fingers down my spine. My lips, what he tasted like. My hands, the way he felt hard and hot and pulsing in my palm as I stroked him. My thighs, the weight of him pressing down on top of me, opening me up.

My nipples tightened, and a familiar achiness in my core made my hips restless.

No. West might be gone, but my body hadn't forgotten. Not by a long shot.

Frustrated, I forced myself off the bed, hoping to halt my painful wayward memories.

As I stepped onto my third floor balcony, the salty air played with the ends of my hair while I studied the resort. There were a dozen stucco buildings topped with red clay tiles, two freeform pools, and more palm trees than I could ever count. Peacocks freely wandered the property, and the ocean was a beautiful, clear pale aqua that slowly bled into sapphire in the distance. The bright white sand of Seven Mile Beach was dotted with crisp white chairs and yellow cabanas. Inland, tennis courts cut harsh geometrics into the natural landscape and a scaled-down kids' waterpark was tucked into a shady corner. One side of the resort was family centered, while the other side catered to couples looking for romance.

My room was decidedly on the half meant for couples.

Sighing, I settled onto a padded chaise, cracking open a can of Coke made with real sugar, and urged myself to appreciate all the beauty surrounding me.

The resort was doing a soft opening for a few weeks before the highly publicized grand opening next month. It was time for the staff to work out the kinks and find their sea legs.

And time for me to make my mark.

Trading my Coke for my camera, I raised it to my eye, using the zoom lens to study different angles from my vantage point and mentally marking spots I wanted to explore more thoroughly later. The poolside bar. The activity center where brightly colored catamarans and wind-surfing sails fluttered in the steady ocean breeze. A peacock meandered down a sidewalk and I watched him, hoping he might spread his feathers and put on a show for me, but no such luck.

Panning back to my own building, a man waving his arm caught my attention.

Nick.

Three balconies over.

Shirtless.

Whoa.

I lowered my camera. He was bulkier than I expected—more of a gym body physique than an actual I-use-these-muscles-to-perform-work build like West had. But holy six-pack, Batman. The guy was ripped. And . . . tanned. Did he work shirtless frequently? Would it be a sight I'd be seeing often?

Maybe he used a gym tanning bed. I smirked.

My mind followed that train of thought briefly, wondering about the presence or absence of tan lines.

Not that I'd be finding out.

Damn, it was hot out here. I took another sip of my soda, fanning myself with my hand and wishing the ocean breeze reached this high.

A faint clicking sound drew my eyes back up.

Nick again.

Taking *my* picture. I must have been so stuck on his abs I'd missed the camera in his hands. Ducking automatically, I threw my arms across my face, shielding myself and laughing.

"I'm not fair game," I called out.

"Says who?" he shot back. "Grady? I didn't think he was serious about that on the ride over."

That hadn't been what I'd meant at all.

"We're . . ." I struggled with how to finish the sentence.

"I like the start of that. *We're* what?"

I waved my hand between us. "We're colleagues or something.

I don't really understand how we're splitting the work here, but the only *we* involves us working together."

He tipped his head and lowered the camera from his face.

"We're not working together so much as parallel. Didn't Grady explain this to you already?"

I growled softly under my breath.

Was every man in my life keeping things from me?

"Not exactly," I clipped out.

"I'm shooting the couples campaign. Dark, romantic, sultry. You're doing the family one. Bright, inviting, and open. Innocent. Cheerful. That type of thing." He shrugged one shoulder like it was obvious.

"I can do romantic," I muttered, slightly offended.

"Not like me."

Shit, he'd heard me. And what the fuck was that supposed to mean?

"I'm more than happy to tutor you while I'm here." He smiled and cocked an eyebrow. "Teach you some new tricks. Show you what I know."

"There's nothing wrong with my style." I gritted my teeth.

"I'm sure there's not. I bet it's perfectly commercial and happy. I just meant, if you wanted to explore some other options."

I paused, unsure if we were only talking about photography or not.

He smirked. "Just think about it. I'll see you at dinner, Sadie."

With that, he disappeared into his room, leaving me pondering his intent.

And his offer.

A<small>FTER AN AWKWARD MEAL</small> where Nick flirted outrageously with me, Grady caught my arm before I could escape back to my room. Nick started to linger as well, but when Grady pointedly said he's see him tomorrow, Nick took the hint and exited ahead of us. Although not until after he gave me a lingering hug where his hand strayed low on my back, making Grady cough in annoyance.

Leading me out onto the oyster-shell encrusted sidewalk that edged the beach and reminded me of Reynolds Island, Grady steered us toward the pavilion that housed both the evening entertainment and a ballroom for events.

"I was wondering if you could do me a favor while we're here." Clearing his throat, Grady shoved his hands in the pockets of his slacks.

Expecting a warning to stay away from Nick, I nodded briskly. "Of course, whatever you want."

"I, uh . . ." he hesitated, his eyebrows furrowing. "I was hoping you'd be my partner for some dance lessons. They have salsa classes at night and some other ones." He stopped walking and faced me. "Obviously this is completely platonic, and I'd actually prefer you not mention this to our friends."

Thrown completely off guard, I studied him. He wouldn't quite meet my gaze, and his hand came up to awkwardly rub the back of his neck.

"Look," he started. "I understand if you're not interested. I just saw that they offered lessons, and I know the basics, but I've never had a chance to learn some of the fancier, complicated ones that the girls back home know."

"The girls back home? Or one girl in particular you're trying to impress?" One with dark brown hair with hot pink tips who loved to go out to clubs and shake what her mother gave her. I sensed there was something more between him and Rue, despite her claims to the contrary.

He started to stammer out a response, but I cut him off, giving him an easy out so I didn't overstep my bounds.

"Marissa, right? Isn't that her name?" That was the anime pixie looking girl who'd been by his side when we met.

He blinked at me and shifted his weight from one foot to the other, confusion written all of his face before he caught himself. "R-right. Marissa—"

"Grady." I interrupted him again, my heart softening a little at his obvious discomfort. "I'd be honored. But only because I want to help the girl you were thinking about." I paused and waited for him to make eye contact. "Not Marissa. The *other* girl."

"There is no other girl." He watched me warily. "Just Marissa."

"Okay." I humored him and laughed softly. "Sure. We'll do this for *her*. She likes dancing?"

"Uh, yeah. Loves it." He sounded uncertain, and I knew he was still thinking about Rue and not our conversation. "Besides, I thought you could benefit too. There's a certain guy who knows all these dances already from his fancy upbringing. How much would it shock him for you to show up at the Gala with some new moves of your own?" His voice lowered and his eyes took on a gleeful sparkle. "Plus, can you imagine how pissed Aubrey would be if we learned some sexy moves and stole the attention from her at her own event?"

I could indeed picture her face. And, as childish as it sounded, I'd love more than anything to be able to beat Aubrey at something. Maybe West would take a good look at what he was missing out on too. The stupid asshole.

"Am I dressed okay?" I motioned to my flats and sundress combo.

"You look fine. I don't think they care what we wear for lessons. But you might want to practice in heels next time. I would think it feels different? I don't know how that works actually." He hesitated. "You know he isn't giving up on you, right? He told me you ended it, but I don't think he plans on listening."

"*He* ended it. Not me. And anything he said otherwise is just another one of his fucking lies." The flat tone of my voice was meant to discourage the line of conversation.

"What? West said you took something the wrong way, but he was going to explain it and he thought y'all would be fine."

"Oh, really? He'd just *explain* it and things would be *fine*?" I laughed. The idea of that happening was ludicrous. "Considering I've blocked him from contacting me, I wish him luck with that."

Grady frowned. "You know nothing is going on between him and Aubrey, right?"

I huffed out another laugh and raised my eyebrows. West had fooled Grady too.

"Sadie." His voice was serious. "I've never seen West look at another woman the way he looks at you. You and her, there's no competition. You're it for him. Don't let her fuck you two up. Don't let her win."

"She can have him. If it's a competition, I don't want the prize anymore."

He shook his head, but I raised my hand to stop any further arguments.

"Truce for tonight? You don't mention him, and I won't mention who you're really taking these classes for."

Relief filtered across his face. "Deal." His lips quirked and he stuck his arm out for me.

Tucking my hand in the crook of his elbow, I tugged him forward along the sidewalk again. "I think we have some dance lessons to get to."

Aubrey may have snagged West, but Grady was right. Stealing the limelight from her during the Gala? I definitely wanted to see her face when that happened.

I'd just discovered a newfound passion for dancing.

chapter
five

THE KNOCK ON THE DOOR came sooner than I'd anticipated. Tightening the belt of the thick white terrycloth robe around my waist, I hurried to let room service in. After last night, I wasn't up for another meal with Nick quite yet. As attractive as he was, and as much as I appreciated some male attention, he was a little too much of a good thing. More than I could handle pre-coffee anyway.

An older island man set my tray on the table and made a quick escape, refusing the tip I tried to give him twice. Shaking my head in exasperation, I shoved the cash in my pocket. Crossing the room to the tray, I doctored up my cup of coffee to make it sweeter and carried it into the bathroom with me. I removed the fluffy towel I'd had turbaned around my head and brushed out the tangles in my hair so it could air dry while I ate.

Picking up my Kindle on the way back to the table, I propped it open and removed the stainless steel cover over my plate. French toast, strawberries, and bacon. The powdered-sugar-covered, maple-syrup-drenched fried bread was the closest thing on the menu I could find to doughnuts. I was reaching for the napkin rolled around my silverware when I faltered.

Tucked neatly onto the corner of the tray was a paper airplane with my name on it.

In West's handwriting.

Hand shaking, I plucked it from the tray, my brow wrinkling as I stared at it. How in the fuck had he managed to get this delivered?

But before I could give in to temptation and actually read the note folded inside, I deposited it in the bottom drawer of my dresser and slammed it closed in satisfaction.

Out of sight.

Except, when I finally cut off a bite of my doughnut-substitute, I was thinking about the time West brought doughnuts for dessert on his boat, *Vitamin Sea*. I eyed my orange juice accusingly. The traitor.

Had I even ordered orange juice? Had he arranged for that little reminder as well?

And now my French toast was soggy after sitting in the syrup for too long.

And it was absolutely all his damn fault.

Waking up my Kindle and picking a romance to read at random, I tried to lose myself in the cowboy who dominated the opening. I dipped my bacon in the excess syrup and crunched my way through two chapters.

By the time I finished my French toast—hey, it was soggy, not ruined—and my strawberries, I was a good forty pages into it.

Then it hit me.

I was reading a fucking *Western*.

Powering the Kindle off in disgust, I apologized mentally to Foster, the book boyfriend I was going to have to abandon prematurely. He didn't deserve a DNF.

He was better than that.

He was strong and loyal and sweet and so achingly in love with the rancher's daughter my teeth hurt just thinking about it. The stupid, spoiled whore daughter didn't realize what she was missing out on. Clare. What kind of name was that anyway? Especially since it was the newly hired veterinarian who was going to rock his world by the end. I liked her. Meghan. She had spunk. Foster had just helped rescue her after the stallion knocked her into the mud on her ass.

And offered to let her use his shower.

But forgot to give her a towel.

Yeah, I was gonna have to leave her hanging.

No happy ending for either of us.

I swallowed the last of my coffee, but I refused to touch the orange juice. On principle alone.

Take that, asshole.

By the time the caffeine had fully hit my system, I was dressed and down on the beach, camera in hand, ready to attack this project head on. My hair was whipping wildly in the strong breeze, the damp strands drying in the humidity. Wavy, tousled beach hair was totally a look. The jury was still out on whether it was a look I could pull off.

I surveyed the long, pristine shoreline, unsure where to start.

The resort wasn't very crowded yet, even though it was mid-morning. A handful of surfers caught some wind-enhanced waves. A couple who'd planted themselves on matching striped towels in the sand were a shade of brown that indicated they'd be roasting themselves again all day. Some employees dressed in royal-blue and white uniforms stood laughing in a small bunch near the catamaran shack. My eyes lingered on the color of their shirts, my fingers automatically circling my wrist.

It was the same color blue as my hair tie that West had claimed. I hated that I couldn't even see that color without thinking of him. Remembering us. Missing *us*.

I wondered if he was still wearing it.

Or if Aubrey had stolen that too.

Blowing a strand of hair from between my lips, I twisted my mouth to one side, not seeing anything that inspired me right off. I aimed the camera at the palm trees edging the property, but it was such a generic shot it wasn't even worth bothering with.

"Good morning."

The greeting whispered only inches from my ear scared the shit out of me, making me gasp and almost jump out of skin.

Thank God the camera was on a strap around my neck.

"You look great this morning. Those beds are amazing, aren't they?" Nick invaded my personal space, wrapping me in a one-armed hug I didn't return.

My loose tunic billowed around me, but the black bikini top protected my girly bits from his blatant perusal. My shorts on the other hand, did little to conceal my legs from his dark gaze.

I side-stepped out of his embrace. "Morning to you too."

He lifted his own camera slightly, and dipped his chin toward mine. "What are we shooting this morning?"

"We?" I repeated, raising my eyebrows.

"Sure," he said, his stance relaxed even as he maintained an almost uncomfortable level of eye contact with me. "We. I thought it'd be fun to shoot the same subject for a bit. Maybe compare results. Make sure our styles are gonna be complimentary for this campaign."

Well. When he put it that way, it sounded downright reasonable.

I waved a hand at the empty lounge chairs that stood waiting to be filled with future skin cancer victims. "Not much really going on yet this morning."

"I disagree." He winked. "I think there's plenty going on here."

He reached out and snagged a wayward curl from my face and tucked it behind my ear, letting his fingers graze the length of my neck.

Biting my lip, I twisted away and fashioned a loose, messy bun at the nape of my neck, securing it with the hair tie from my wrist. Pink this time. He was oblivious of my attempt at creating distance between us and stayed firmly planted by my side.

He pointed past me to the water, his arm grazing me. "That surfer there? See him? The one with the tattoo of birds on his back? That's our subject."

I studied the man he indicated. The guy was hot. Both his sculpted body *and* the way he handled his board—slicing smoothly through the water with an intuitiveness that spoke of years of experience and a fluidity the other surfers couldn't match.

Nice choice.

"Check in with each other in twenty minutes?"

He shrugged. "If you need that long to get some good images, sure. Twenty minutes works."

I narrowed my eyes.

Game on.

Adjusting the setting on my camera, I edged closer to the shoreline. Nick followed, but then continued walking right into the ocean until he was waist deep. I hadn't realized until just then his yellow trimmed navy shorts were board shorts. He seemed unconcerned about his shirt, not bothering to remove it.

"What are you doing?" I yelled to be heard over the wind.

"Taking pictures." He winked. "What are you doing?"

Shaking my head at him, I lifted my camera to my face, moving farther across the sand so Nick didn't ruin my shot. I kept my angle wide. The way I framed the shot, the surfer acted as the exclamation point at the end of the sentence the wave was writing, its foamy curl chasing him.

I zoomed out more, letting the focus on the bare-chested man grow blurry, featuring instead his smallness contrasted to the vast expanse of turquoise water behind him, his red board a bright slash of color near the bottom edge of the frame.

The wave dissipated and the surfer paddled back out to catch another one. A wall of water hid him from view, playing hide and seek with me. I took pictures through three more sets that he expertly rode, oblivious to the two photographers capturing the action.

When time was up, Nick wordlessly handed me his camera and accepted mine.

We flipped through each other's work.

Mine was good. I knew it.

His was stunning. Absolutely breathtaking.

He'd gone for more detailed photos. The surfer's hand as it caressed the top of a swell. His victorious grin and upraised arm at the end of a good ride. The slope of his shoulder as he sat on the board, watching for the perfect wave to ride in. The beads of water running down his back.

I sucked in a breath. It was fucking hot.

"Today's lesson." Nick's voice was serious this time, no hint of playfulness. "Sometimes the parts are better than the whole. There's beauty in everybody, and choosing to focus on those details can be much more intriguing than looking at the entire subject. It's more intimate. It lets the viewer fill in the blanks with their own imagination, substitute the missing pieces with their own fantasies. And that's where the magic happens."

Handing my camera back, he tipped his chin at it. "Your technique is good. Nothing to be ashamed of. But step outside the box some and try it my way this time."

Nodding, I studied the surfer again, with new eyes. Not him versus the water. Or even him and the board. But the fragments.

The bunching of his back muscles, obscuring the script of his tattoo. The way the waistband of his shorts was higher on the left hip than the right. The angle of his throat as he raised his head up to the sun.

As I headed closer to the water, I realized Nick was walking the opposite direction, back toward the resort. "Where are you going?" I called after him.

"I got *my* shots for the morning. I'll catch up with you at lunch." He didn't wait for a response.

My nose wrinkled at his arrogance, even though he made a valid point. His work was impressive, and I wasn't too proud to accept I could learn a thing or two from him.

Refocusing on the surfer, I concentrated on Nick's words. Catching slivers of time that evoked a feeling but left the final interpretation up to the viewer.

The surfer's feet in the air, the surfboard a good foot beneath him, as he jumped off at the end of a wave. His profile, his jawline sharp and classic. His legs as he pushed up into the proper stance. A gratuitous shot of his ass as he bent over the board. It wasn't until the end of my session that I moved my focus away from body shots and tried to get a few of his face. His eyes. The smirk on his mouth. The sun reflecting off the angle of his cheekbones as he flew by me.

Finishing, I hurried to my room, eager to upload and edit my session.

When I got to the shot of his eyes, I froze.

I knew those eyes.

The surfer with the beautiful body, who's rippling muscles I'd captured in high-density megapixels, was Grady.

LUNCH WAS STRAINED. I couldn't look at Grady without blushing, even though I hadn't really done anything wrong. It wasn't that I was attracted to Grady—but taking a bunch of half-naked photos probably crossed the line of appropriate behavior toward your boss. Even if he was also a friend. Grady sent a few assessing gazes my way, cocking his head as if he was trying to figure me out, but whatever he was thinking, he kept quiet in front of Nick.

And Nick, oh, he was enjoying himself.

The twinkle in his eye and the way he laughed at my discomfort made it clear he'd known all along who the surfer was. The bastard.

I was mortified. And felt oddly guilty, like I'd somehow betrayed Rue by noticing just how gorgeous Grady was. I mean, he wasn't West, but *damn*, she had pretty good taste when it came to him. She could deny it all she wanted to, but she couldn't stop staring at him whenever he was around.

Dancing lessons later that night were even worse. Although, at least Nick wasn't there for those.

I was stiff and stepped on Grady's toes repeatedly, half a beat behind the music. I miscounted the steps, turning left instead of right, crashing into him and knocking us into another couple. He'd finally given up and taken me aside, waving at the instructor to continue without us.

"Are you okay? You've seemed off since lunch with Nick. Has he done something? I can have a word with him if I need to." Grady shook his head in exasperation. "He's always been a relentless flirt around pretty girls."

I shook my head in denial, my cheeks warming. "No. He's fine. I . . . I was just embarrassed by how much better than me he was when we worked together this morning." I improvised on the fly, hoping he bought it.

Looking unconvinced, he studied my face. "He told me he was going to try to work with you some while you're here. I thought you might be excited to work with someone of his caliber, but if he's a problem, I need you to let me know. I told West I'd look out for you while we're here."

The mention of West threw me. And pissed me off. I didn't need *looking after.*

I counted to five and forced myself to take a deep breath. It didn't help. "West lost that right when he chose Aubrey over me." I enunciated each word, trying to keep my anger in check.

Grady bit back a grin. "Easy, tiger. Don't kill the messenger."

"I'll give you a message for him," I muttered. "I don't even need words. Just one finger."

"I'll be sure to pass that along." He tried to smother his laugh.

"But seriously, about Nick—everything okay there?"

I hesitated, but nodded. I was a big girl. He wasn't anything I couldn't handle myself.

But speaking of messengers . . .

A flash of inspiration struck. I'd email the pictures of Grady to Rue, as a present. And I'd leave the face shots until last. Although I doubted it would take her nearly as long as it did me to realize who the surfer was. I had a feeling she was more familiar with his body than she led me to believe.

Finally able to relax, at ease with my conscience knowing I wouldn't be hiding anything from my best friend, Grady and I struggled through a few new salsa moves, building on the basics we'd learned last night. He returned the favor from earlier, crushing my toes under his feet as we worked through the different elements.

As I looked down, concentrating on the steps, I had another epiphany. Something I hadn't noticed during my photo session that morning.

And I couldn't stop my smile.

No wonder Rue couldn't seem to move on from whatever history there was between them.

Grady had some big ass feet.

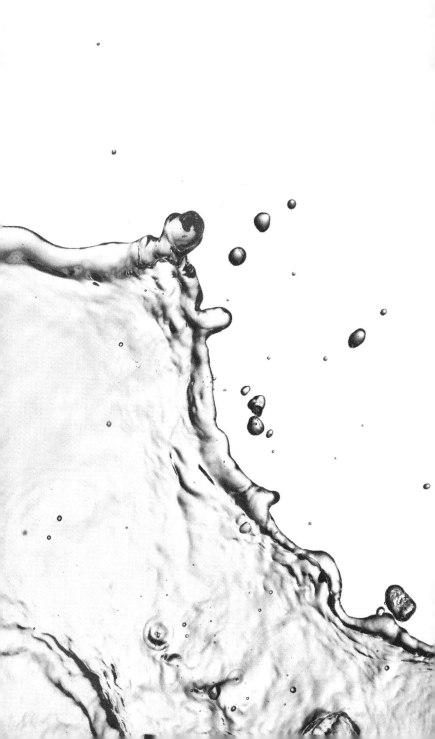

chapter
six

WHEN I OPENED MY LAPTOP the next morning to send the pictures to Rue, I already had an email waiting for me. A workout routine—complete with playlist—courtesy of Theo who warned *pics or it doesn't count* and gloated that I'd thank him when I didn't come back from vacation with a lard ass from lazing away in paradise. Theo was probably my closest friend after Rue and also my personal trainer. It was because of him working my ass off on a regular basis that I could indulge in my Krispy Kreme habit. He also mentioned I should expect another workout email tomorrow.

Well, yay.

But . . . he had a point. There might not be doughnuts here, but I wasn't exactly watching my calories. I pinched my stomach and wrinkled my nose.

After sending the shots of Grady to Rue with the simple subject line "You're welcome," I grudgingly put on workout clothes and headed to the resort gym. Better to just get it over with for the day.

Turned out, someone else had the same idea. Nick was there—in all his sweaty glory—on the treadmill just inside the door, three-and-half miles into a workout, according to the red digital numbers. Damn overachiever.

Except, wait. Theo's words came to mind and, without a word of explanation to Nick, who was watching me quizzically, I snapped a quick photo of the treadmill's workout summary display.

Photographic proof of a workout. Maybe it wasn't *my* workout, but now I had back-up if this session hurt as bad as I expected it to.

Tugging his earbuds out, Nick slowed to a fast walk. He pointed to my phone. "What was that about?"

"My trainer." I stepped on an elliptical in the corner and began warming up. "He said I owed him three miles of cardio today. With photographic proof. Plus, it's arm day."

He smirked. "Do you have to send him proof of that too?"

"Weights are on the honor system." I tried to look offended, but knew I failed when he laughed at me.

"You're clearly very trustworthy."

"Yup." I popped my earbuds in and scrolled to the playlist I'd downloaded that morning. I had to smile—Theo remembered my penchant for organizing my music by letter. This one was chock full of J's. Jason Derulo, Justin Timberlake, and Justin Beiber.

"Need me to spot you for anything?"

I shook my head. "I'll be fine, but thanks. I don't want to hold you up."

He shrugged and nudged the speed back up on the treadmill. I could see him out of the corner of my eye, but after the first few songs, as I got into the zone, I forgot about him.

My mind wandered inevitably to West. Wondering what he was doing today, if he missed me, if his bed had felt just as empty as mine had last night. I daydreamed my way through an encounter where, instead of freezing like a deer in the headlights when I saw West carrying Aubrey in his arms in Charleston, I confronted them, and he obligingly dumped her overboard and whisked me away to the Caribbean aboard the *Vitamin Sea*. The newspaper ran the appalling story of Aubrey Perotti showing her face in public without looking pageant-ready, and she had an allergic reaction to her sunscreen which resulted in a permanent skin disfigurement, a red oblong phallic inflammation that started on her nose and extended to her forehead. People began calling her Dickhead behind her back, not that I ever saw her again.

Hell, no. I was busy. Days upon days of makeup sex followed, where my flexibility and loud enthusiasm became legendary at the marina we docked at. A winning lottery ticket extended the spur-of-the-moment trip indefinitely, and we eloped a month later under a tropical, starlit sky, complete with a towering Krispy Kreme doughnut wedding cake, after which we had more days upon days of history-making honeymoon sex. I gave Gumby a run for his money, had enviable thigh gap, and became multi-orgasmic.

I sighed.

Three miles later—yes, on my own, stupid conscience—I captured the requisite proof on my phone and collapsed on the mats, breathing hard.

Nick's concerned face appeared above me, sweat dripping off his chin and on to me. I blinked in surprise, and, wrinkling my nose, scooted farther back. "You're getting me all wet!" Okay, yes, I was already damp from my own workout, but him dripping on me like that was just plain gross.

"Finally. You admit it." He ran his gaze over my panting body, lingering on my heaving chest. "Looks like I've stolen your breath too."

I rolled my eyes, but accepted his outstretched hand and let him pull me to my feet.

Holding on to a nearby weight machine for balance, I tucked my foot up to my butt and stretched my quads. "You're still here." Two points for stating the obvious.

He smirked. "I've been enjoying the scenery."

I ignored him and switched legs. If watching me jiggle was the best view he could find in this resort, he needed an eye exam. And a new line.

Opening up Theo's email again, I scanned the list of exercises he'd sent me. This gym didn't have a wall of mirrors like I was used to, but I didn't need them to check my form. Instead, floor-to-ceiling windows faced the ocean, giving the whole workout area more of a Zen-like vibe.

I hefted a light set of weights and commenced punishing my triceps for my indiscretions at the dessert table yesterday. Arm day sucked.

Thirty minutes later, stretching my exhausted muscles one last time, I glanced around. Two other people were powering through their workouts, matching looks of sheer joy on their faces. Ugh. They were *those* kind of workout people. And Nick was still there, his expensive camera pointed right at me.

I yanked my earbuds out and reflexively put my hand over my face, blocking his shot. "What are you doing?"

He lowered the camera, switched it to display mode, and handed it over to me. "I would've thought it was obvious." His grin was positively roguish.

Scowling, I flipped through a couple dozen shots of *me*. He'd captured tight close-ups, much like I'd taken of Grady the day before. The sleek flex of my arm. The strong line of my spine as I bent over for triceps rows. The curve of my throat as I'd tipped my face up to catch my breath.

And I looked . . . hot. More than hot, I looked strong, toned . . . *sexy*.

I was stunned. This was not what I saw when I looked in the mirror.

"I'm good, aren't I?" He loomed over my shoulder, looking at the images with me. His ego ruined it.

Turning, I shoved the camera at him, catching him in the stomach. "I didn't give you permission to take those."

"I didn't ask." He raised his eyebrows and looked amused.

I rubbed my arm across my forehead, sweat dripping down my body. I felt gross and sticky. I knew I smelled. It was like his pictures had captured an alternative reality, where I glistened and followed a Paleo diet and got an appropriate amount of sleep every night. It was pretty, but it wasn't real.

"Not cool, Nick. Do we need to set some basic ground rules here?"

He looked at his camera, then me, through eyes that downright shone with mischief. "I'll tell you what. Next time I take sexy photos of you, it'll be because you asked me to. Is that good enough?"

I laughed. "And what makes you think I'd ever do that?" I drained the rest of my water bottle and wiped my neck with a towel.

He leaned closer and lowered his voice. "Because I think you like the way I see you. And you like the way it makes you feel knowing I see you like that. Hot, damp—"

I smacked him with my *hot, damp* towel and narrowed my eyes.

He chuckled. "Meet me for breakfast in thirty minutes. Today's lesson involves food."

****

Breakfast was served buffet style, and after Theo's workout, I piled my plate high—although I avoided the pancakes because they made me think of West and the time he'd made them for me.

I settled into the chair next to Nick, who was already digging into a veggie omelet, and a waitress set a glass of orange juice and coffee down in front of me. I turned to refuse the juice but she was already walking away. When I faced the table again, Nick was looking at me oddly.

"What?" I asked.

He pointed to my beverages with his fork.

A small, folded paper plane was tucked between my orange juice and coffee mug.

He started to reach for it, but I snatched it up, glancing at it long enough to confirm that West's handwriting was scrawled across the paper, and shoved it into the pocket of my khaki shorts.

"Did the waitress bring this?" I glanced at him, the hair on the back of my neck standing up.

He shrugged around a mouthful of eggs. "I guess? It wasn't here when I sat down."

How did they know how to find me? How did he arrange this? I bit my lip and looked around. Nothing seemed out of the ordinary.

"He's good." Nick's words drew my attention back to him.

"Who's good?"

"Him. Paper airplane guy. That's a slick move there."

"How do you know it's from a guy?"

He leveled an exasperated look at me. "Who am I supposed to think it's from? Your fairy godmother?" He snickered.

I ran my hand over my pocket, feeling the paper crinkle.

"Is it from the idiot? The one we talked about on the plane? The one who was stupid enough to let you go?"

I nodded once then shoved a bite of French toast in my

mouth, not even tasting it.

Nick raised his eyebrows. "Maybe he's not as big an idiot as you thought."

"Can we not talk about him? I'd like to at least attempt to enjoy my breakfast."

"Ooooh, touchy."

"Didn't you want to talk about food?"

"Yes. I did." He regarded me silently for a moment, as if trying to decide whether or not to press the issue of the plane. Whatever he saw in my face must have convinced him to drop it. "The assignment today revolves around the sensuality of food and eating and capturing the moment, but not making it look like a cow chewing on cud. There's a fine line."

"Assignment?" I put my fork down, smoothed my napkin across my lap while I took a deep breath. "Am I some sort of charity case here? What's up with the lessons and assignments? I thought we'd both already been hired to do a job?" My voice rose toward the end along with my temper.

Nick took a long swallow of his coffee. "We have. And you're right, normally I wouldn't work with a colleague this way. But I see hidden potential in you—raw talent that needs some refinement. What you do is good, very good in fact. You have a great eye, but your emotional range is a little stunted. Everything you do is bright, cheery, soft. There's so much more to explore. Shadowed, dark, moody, seduc—"

"What's that got to do with food?"

"Seriously? If you don't see the connection between food and intimacy, we have more work to do than I thought."

My eyes narrowed in warning.

"Look at the buffet behind me. Take the bread for instance. Notice how the baguettes are displayed upright, with the smaller, round rolls in front. Cocks and balls."

I choked on the coffee I was sipping.

"Check out the fruit. If you don't see the ripe curves of breasts within that arrangement, you're blind."

A reluctant smile tugged at my mouth.

"And the thick sausage links—they're bratwurst size. That's some thick meat. You think that's a coincidence? Not one bit. The whipped cream they're so eager to top everything with? Should I continue?"

"Does everything go back to sex for you?"

He paused. "No. It's not a *me* thing. It's human nature. We're wired to respond to sex on a primal level. It's natural to crave it, be drawn to it, respond to it. What's smart is using that to your advantage, employing it either subtly or overtly to hold someone's attention, even if they don't realize that's why something is aesthetically pleasing. It's the most basic, and effective, of marketing strategies."

"So you're telling me my lessons with you will somehow or another all pretty much revolve around sex?"

He grinned. "Absolutely."

The rest of the week settled into a rhythm. A paper plane found its way to me every morning, whether I ate in the restaurant or ordered room service. I had seven now, a veritable fleet parked in my dresser drawer. I worked out every other day per Theo's instructions, although I never saw Nick in the gym again. I guess he was getting his workouts in some other time. After breakfast, I usually met with Nick for an hour or so, and I had to give him props, he took the mentoring role seriously. Sure, he flirted outrageously when we shared a meal, but when we had our cameras in hand, he meant business and I had picked up some invaluable tips.

I ran two different family-centered campaigns by Grady and he seemed pleased, greenlighting both ideas. And we were finally, finally improving in our dance lessons at night.

Rue had shot back an email three days later about the pictures I'd sent her. While she said she was impressed with the quality of the shots, she had to question my choice of models. Couldn't I find anyone better? When I pointedly told her *not that fit her tastes so perfectly*, she hadn't responded again. Mmhmm. That's what I thought.

I'd been working with an adorable family with three daughters throughout the week for one of my campaigns. The girls were all blond ringlets and big, cornflower blue eyes and matching dimples. When the youngest one went down for a nap Monday afternoon, I put away my camera for the day.

I was past due for some down time.

After making my way down to the water activity cabana, I

stared at the available choices listed on the sign. Jill, the relentlessly cheerful activity coordinator who'd been trying to get me out on the water all week, sidled up next to me.

"You finally ready to take some paddleboards out?"

"No," I admitted. "But I'm going to do it anyway."

"Yay!" She clapped her hands in excitement and I half-expected her to do spirit fingers. "The water's perfect today, super calm, small waves. Let's grab some equipment and get out there before you change your mind." She became a whirlwind, collecting what we needed and shoving it at me before practically pushing me into the surf.

I'd admitted my fear of the water to her the day we met, and she'd promised to go out with me when I worked up the courage. I guess she didn't want to give me a chance to back out.

The ninety-minute lesson blew by. Being able to see through the clear turquoise water went a long way toward allaying my fear of being attacked by hordes of angry sea creatures. And once we paddled out, I wasn't actually *in* the water—I was *on* the water, giving me further confidence that I wasn't in imminent danger. While I wasn't quite as comfortable as Jill, who tried to entice me into joining her in some yoga moves on the boards, I had a fabulous time and promised to meet her again tomorrow afternoon.

By the time we finished, a late afternoon storm was blowing in, the kind that would roll through and be gone after an hour or two, so I headed back up to my room to clean up and change clothes before dinner, wondering if I had time to sneak a nap in before I met Nick and Grady at seven. After stepping off the elevator, I was halfway down the hall to my room when a door in front of me flew open. An older woman with dark, messy hair stepped out, looking flushed. She glanced at me vacantly, a satisfied smile stretched wide across her mouth. Her top had slipped off one shoulder, but she didn't seem to notice.

Pausing, I turned to watch her saunter to the elevator. She was humming as she pushed the button.

Someone had a good afternoon.

When the elevator had whisked her away, I spun back toward my room. I took two more steps and the same door opened. Nick stepped out.

I came to a stuttering stop, looking between him and the elevator behind me. Facing him again, my eyes widened and my eyebrows rose to my hairline. "So *that's* where you've been getting your workouts?"

chapter
seven

H<small>IS FACE WAS BLANK.</small> "She's a *client*."

I opened my mouth. Closed it. Tried again. "So you're an *escort* too?"

"What? No! Not that kind of client."

"That woman—" I jerked my thumb toward the elevator. "—had just orgasmed. She was still fucking glowing, Nick. You're not claiming responsibility for that?"

He smirked and adjusted the front of his pants, not even trying to hide it. "She took care of herself. I watched but didn't touch."

I'm not sure why that shocked me, but it sounded so . . . dirty. More so than if he just admitted to fucking her. Maybe it was because she had decades on him? Could a guy like him—young, attractive, successful—really be aroused by her? She was old enough to be his mother.

Maybe he had Oedipus complex. Of maybe he just liked cougars.

"I have no words." I stared at him, my mind churning to understand.

He held up the camera in his hand. "It was a photoshoot. Boudoir. Dark, sexy, hot—"

"Is this for your campaign? Are you appealing to the horny retirement crowd? I hear that segment of the population has one of the highest rates of STD's these days."

He laughed, loud and long. "No. This is just a side project. Word gets around that I do these sessions, and as long as I'm discreet, Grady turns a blind eye. It seems *well-satisfied* vacationers are a little looser with their wallets."

I glanced down. A slight bulge still pressed against his zipper. "Just took pictures, huh?"

"That?" He grinned, unashamed. "There is nothing sexier than a woman confident in her body. At any age. A woman willing to let go and give in to the moment, and just fucking own it and go for it—that's hot as hell." His bold gaze ran down the length of me, pausing where my wet bikini top had soaked through my T-shirt, plastering the cotton to my chest. He pointed. "Kind of like that look you're rocking right now."

I ignored his lecherous perusal. "I've done boudoir photoshoots." I thought of Aubrey and the photos of her I found in West's nightstand. "None of them have ever ended in a client looking like *that*."

"Maybe you weren't doing it right then."

I huffed out a breath. No, things definitely hadn't gone right with her. "Lemme see, hotshot. Impress me." I reached for the camera in his hand, but he snatched it away, holding it out of reach.

"What happened to customer confidentiality?"

"What happened to professional courtesy?" I countered without missing a beat.

He tucked the camera behind his back. "I'll tell you what. You want to see what my photos in this setting look like, I'll shoot you. No charge. You can even keep all the images."

I chuckled. "You wish."

"I do." His eyes darkened as he met my gaze, then dipped down to where my nipples had beaded against my wet shirt in the air conditioning.

"I'll let you know if I change my mind on that one, but don't hold your breath." I patted his arm and moved around him to head down the hall. "Don't you have something to take care of before dinner?" I waved my hand in the direction of his crotch.

"Worried about my junk now, Sadie? I think I'm making progress. Try not to think about me during your shower." His voice grew louder as I moved farther away. I blushed as I slipped into my own room, my pulse a notch or two higher than normal, as I unwillingly thought about what it would be like to do a shoot like that. Be totally uninhibited, wild, bold . . .

I could never do that.

I'd be too embarrassed, too awkward, too stiff. My body

wasn't terrible—hell, it was better than his client's—but I didn't have the confidence.

Fuck.

Was that it?

Confidence. Was that the difference between me and Aubrey? Was that what it boiled down to on a fundamental level?

I slid down the door until my knees touched my chin, the tile cold under me.

Did I lose to *her*—or did I lose because I *let* her take what was mine? Because I didn't think I could compete with her, did I leave room for her to slip in and sink her gel-manicured claws into him?

I was *not* okay with that.

Not at all.

I PONDERED THOSE questions over the next few days. Examined all my past encounters with both West and Aubrey in painful, excruciating detail. Then went over them again.

She'd intimidated me more times than I cared to admit. And I'd let her. I'd fucking let her. But, even worse, so had West.

He'd stepped away from me after that breathless first kiss in the pool house—when she came into the room.

He'd let her touch him for that stupid ass picture under the palm tree at his grandmother's house, that bold hand on his chest staking a claim without words.

He'd let her climb in his truck at the drive-in, as if she had a right to be there by his side.

He'd fucking let her stay at his house for the night after the BBQ instead of calling a cab and kicking her ass out.

And those damn pictures of her were in his fucking nightstand.

But when I showered, I remembered how he took care of me when I was sunburned.

I thought of him when I saw the pancakes at the buffet in the mornings.

When I shivered at night, I remembered him slipping through my window to spoon until the break of dawn, his warmth surrounding me.

The old beat up maintenance truck on the resort rumbled and rattled like his.

The kids' area at the resort boasted an air hockey table, like the one at the Wreck. Same colors even.

The boat at the activities' shed had a beanbag in the back, like the one I'd slept in on the *Vitamin Sea*.

The sky turned the color of his eyes during the afternoon storms that moved through most days.

And those damn paper planes showed up without fail every fucking morning.

I was staring at them. Twelve of them strewn across my bed. Some were big and basic, the kind a second-grader might make. Others were smaller and intricately folded, mini fighter jets perhaps. Pieces of his angular handwriting peeked through on all of them.

Messages.

Words I'd been too angry, too scared, too raw to read.

Until now.

Tonight, I was tired of being on the tightrope, balancing anger on one hand and love—yes, goddamn it, *love*—on the other. I was tired and I was ready to fall. To let go of it all and just see where I landed. Discover which side was gonna win out in the end.

I ran my finger across the wing of a plane, the one that had showed up the first day. I didn't quite remember the order they'd all been delivered to me—didn't know if that mattered—but I remembered this one.

I had to give West credit. He hadn't given up.

I hadn't called, hadn't texted, hadn't looked at Facebook once.

No contact, yet the planes arrived faithfully each morning with a glass of orange juice.

He was a stubborn bastard, if nothing else.

Anticipation and nerves had my heart thudding heavily behind my ribs.

Biting my lower lip, I tugged apart the folds of the plane, smoothing the paper out as best I could. I didn't read it right away. Instead, I grabbed the next one and repeated my actions. Unfolded, smoothed, added it to the pile.

When I had a stack of wrinkled notebook pages in my hand, I moved higher up the bed, stacking pillows behind me and leaning back against the carved-wood headboard.

My hand shook and my pulse hammered in my throat.

Somehow, it felt like these pages knew the answer. Like I was about to see what my future held.

West or no West.

I picked up the first one, tracing the creases his hands had made. The entire page was covered with the phrase *I love you,* written over and over again. Something shattered in my chest as some of the walls I'd thrown up to protect my heart cracked. A small PS message at the bottom said there was one *I love you* for each day since the morning I'd tried to save him from drowning.

One airplane listed all the parts of my body he wanted to kiss me, and I blushed in places I didn't know I could blush. Another ranked the best places we'd had sex—the stairwell after the BBQ coming in at number one. Several apologized for not being a better boyfriend, not knowing what I needed, and letting me down. He promised to learn, listen harder, communicate more, do better. But he wasn't giving up. He made that abundantly clear. He would be waiting for me when my plane landed, he swore.

But it was the one in my hand that had tears gathering in my eyes. It was the fourth time I'd read it.

> *Sadie,*
> *Even though you'll probably hate the comparison, you remind me of the ocean. See, I love the ocean. I switched addresses just to be closer to it. Moved in with my brother just so it'd be the first thing that I saw in the morning and the last thing I saw at night.*
> *But something's changed. You've changed me.*
> *Now you're what I crave. Need. Live for.*
> *Maybe I suck at showing it. But I feel it. I feel it deep and strong and wide and sure and as far as the horizon. I love you when you're dark and stormy. I love you when you're peaceful and*

calm. I love you when you're wild and unexpected.

I love it when I can still smell you on my skin and taste you on my tongue, hours after you've left.

How I can close my eyes, and feel your nails scratching down my back and your hands in my hair. How your voice is the voice in my head now, arguing with me even when you aren't there.

You've given me a motivation to succeed I didn't have before. Because now I have someone I want to take care of one day, spoil rotten with doughnuts and endless air hockey rematches and Lunchable picnics on my boat.

I just want to touch you, be close to you, in you, near you . . . with you. My world makes sense with you there to ground me. Steady me. Love me.

And I know you do.

I see it in your eyes. Feel it in your kiss. Hear it in your laugh. Know it in my soul.

I won't give up on us. You can't just pretend the ocean isn't there. It's too big, too much to ignore.

Same with us.

I love you.

I should've said it sooner. I've felt it for weeks.

I love you whether you're here next to me or across the sea. In my bed or just on my mind. Today and a million tomorrows from now.

I love you.

I love you.

I love you.

—W

Breathless, I collected the notes scattered around me into one semi-neat stack, then crushed the papers against my chest, a few rogue tears blazing hot trails down my cheeks.

I loved him.

Maybe it should be more complicated, maybe I should protect myself more, know better, run away, play it safe—but I loved him.

And suddenly that wasn't enough.

I scrambled for my laptop, powering it up, impatiently waiting for it to boot up so I could log onto Facebook. I needed to see him—needed to see that he'd been missing me too.

My hands were shaking so bad, I had to type my password in three times before I got it right. I typed in *West Montgomery* onto Facebook's search bar, then faltered, remembering I'd unfriended him. And his page was private—I would need to be his friend to see his pictures.

His friend. That word seemed far too small, too simple to encompass what we were. How my heart ached because I wasn't with him. How my hands itched to stroke his skin, feel his muscles jump and contract under my touch.

No, I couldn't see his whole page. But I could see what public photos he'd been tagged in.

It was better than nothing.

I scrolled through the results. Client photos—proud men holding fish by the base of their tails, grinning like lunatics, West perched in the background. One from his sister Hailey, of West with his two-year-old nephew Cody riding on his shoulders. That one looked like it'd been taken at their grandparents' house, where Hailey and Cody lived.

I paused on that one. He looked scruffy. Like maybe he hadn't shaved since I'd left.

I wonder how that'd feel between my legs?

His brother Wyatt tagged him in one from the house they shared, West asleep on the hammock, three crushed beer cans in a pile below him. Another of West mugging for the camera with Wyatt's oversized hound dog, General Beauregard.

I kept looking, like a junkie searching for her next fix. A series of group shots from the Wreck, the bar Wyatt and West co-owned. My grin faded. I recognized too many faces in that image. Boone, Trevor, Kendra, West, Wyatt, some other girls . . . and Aubrey.

Fucking *Aubrey*.

I checked the date. Last weekend.

I scrolled faster there, looking for more with *her*.

One more—another group shot. It looked like a restaurant. I didn't recognize many of the people, but Aubrey was sitting next to West at the table.

Nice.

Real. Fucking. Nice.

Yeah, try harder my ass.

If he really, truly wanted to make things work between us—wouldn't he have cut ties with her? Avoided her? Because based on this, nothing much had changed for West.

Except the new dark hair highlighting his sculpted jaw.

That *she* was probably rubbing her skanky hand along.

I cut my eyes to the blinking red lights of the clock on the nightstand.

9:47 pm.

The bar downstairs was most definitely open. Open and full of booze. Booze that would make me forget. Make me happy. Make the pain in my heart that stabbed me with each beat just fucking stop.

I was tired of this tightrope act.

And drinking myself into oblivion sounded like the best plan I'd had in ages.

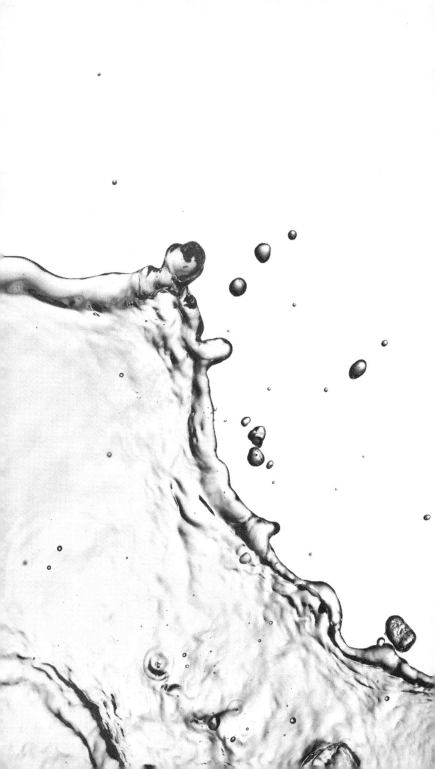

chapter
eight

I MADE A DETOUR ON THE WAY to the bar. That ocean that West compared me to? It could have his damn paper planes. I didn't need them.

Kicking off my flip flops, I walked until I hit the shoreline where the water dueled the sand for dominance. I tried to fold the airplanes back up best I could. The ones I couldn't figure out, I just crumpled into balls. Whatever. They would still fly when I threw them.

One at a time, the sea swallowed his lies, the tide taking them away where they couldn't hurt me any longer.

I stood there, waiting to feel lighter, happier.

It didn't happen.

The waves tickled my feet, soaking the bottom of my jeans.

Something brushed against my toes, and I jumped back. One

of the notes had made its way back to me. I scooped up the soggy paper, wondering if it was a sign. Peeling the edges apart, I held it up, squinting to see which one it was.

I love you. The words covered the page.

He'd said he'd never stop.

So why did it hurt so bad?

I dropped the page. The sand or the sea—either one could have it. I wasn't fighting for it anymore.

THE BARTENDER WAS MY NEW best friend. I frowned. Well, after Rue. And Theo. My third best-est friend. Because she kept pouring me these great margaritas.

I normally hated margaritas.

But Alison? My third best-est friend? She made some *damn* good ones. And there were so many flavors! Lime was okay. Mango was better. Watermelon wasn't that great, but I drank it anyway because I didn't want to hurt its feelings. I was almost finished with blood orange and it might have been my favorite, but I still had two flavors to go, so who knew?

The only thing I needed to decide on was whether pink lemonade or pineapple was next.

Wasn't pineapple supposed to make cum taste sweeter?

Wait—that only worked if the guy drank it. Right?

I couldn't remember now.

And it was fucking glorious.

Alison was my new third best-est friend and blood orange margaritas were the shit.

Best. Night. Ever.

I swung my head around when I heard the stool next to me being slid across the terracotta-tiled floor and almost lost my balance.

But Nick caught me.

Niiiiiick. He looked nice tonight. Tight, dark shirt. Fitted khakis. I could kind of see the outline of his bulge against the fabric.

It wasn't bad.

West had a nice bulge too.

I wrinkled my forehead. No. I shook my head. *No.*

Not thinking about him tonight.

Hey! Nick was here. Maybe he could drink the pineapple margarita and help me remember. I could get the pink lemonade one then.

I grinned up at him, and poked him in the chest with my finger.

"Alison!" I yelled. "This guy—" poke "—needs a pineapple margarita. And I'll take the lemonade one next."

She raised an eyebrow and looked at Nick for confirmation.

Nick with the bulge.

He leaned closer to me. "Why pineapple?"

I rolled my eyes. "Because I can't remember. And this will solve the problem!"

"Can't remember what?"

"If it'll make you taste sweeter."

He stared at me, then coughed. "Do you mean—"

I leaned over and patted his lap. "Down *here*."

He mumbled something and removed my hand from his lap. "Maybe Alison can get you a water if I agree to drink a pineapple margarita?" He shuddered and made a face when he said *pineapple*.

"I don't want water."

Alison slid a bottle of water in front of me, top removed. She was such a good friend.

I drank half of it down in one swallow.

Nick was watching my throat with a bit of a glazed look in his eyes.

Or were my eyes glazed? Could you see if your own eyes were glazed, or just someone else's?

I scrunched up my face and stared at his eyes, trying to puzzle it out.

Alison put a different drink in front Nick. Something dark in a squat glass with a few ice cubes.

"That is *not* a pineapple margarita."

"No." He smirked at me.

"You lied to me. Why does every fucking guy on this planet lie to me? Is it a gender thing? Or is it something about me specifically?" I pushed Nick's shoulder, but he didn't budge.

Nick took a swallow of his drink. I bet it was something fancy. Refined. Scotch. Or whiskey. Some top-shelf shit. He closed his eyes for a moment as he put his drink down. He had a nice neck.

I'd never really noticed before.

"But now I won't be able to answer my question." I frowned at him. It was all his fault.

"How would you have known if it was sweeter?"

I squinted at him. "Tasted it?"

"But how would you have known if it tasted *sweeter*? Wouldn't you have needed an initial taste to compare it to?"

Damn. Nick with the bulge was fucking smart. "I haven't tasted you yet." Something else I failed at. I wouldn't get the answer to my question now.

"Nope."

"Does it taste okay normally?"

Nick choked on his drink. "I've, uh, not had any complaints."

"But have you tried drinking pineapple juice before?"

Handing me the water bottle again, which I obligingly took a sip of, Nick sighed. "Sadie. Why are you down here getting wasted?"

I was not *wasted*. I was . . . close, maybe. But not sloppy drunk. "Because of reasons." I nodded.

"Tell me the main one."

I'm not sure why that did it. Why that little phrase was enough to unlock all the confusion bottled up inside, but it was. The four margaritas probably helped too.

Words tumbled out of me. I told him about West, who wasn't drowning after all. And West who wouldn't let me walk home. And West who drove me home from a party, but I was wasted and woke up in his bed and my thighs weren't sore at all because we hadn't had sex. And West who showed up at a drive-in and let another girl climb in the back of his truck before he saw me. And West who took care of me when I was sunburned, and made me penis pancakes for breakfast. And West who fucked me silly on a staircase, but then let another woman stay at his place that night. And West who flew a kite with his nephew and made me fall in love with him, but had pictures of another girl in his nightstand. And West who then carried that same girl in his arms off his boat, and away to their picture-perfect fucking future. And the West who finally said he loved me, who fucked me in a parking lot, but it was too damn late because I was done, gone, over it, and out of there.

That West.

By the time I was finished, I wasn't as drunk as I'd been when I'd started and two more empty water bottles lay on their sides on the bar. Alison had done last call twenty minutes ago.

I should've been humiliated.

But, *fuck*, it just felt good to let it all out.

"What kind of pictures?"

"What?"

"What kind," Nick repeated, "of pictures were in his nightstand?"

"Oh." I scowled, picked at the hem of my shirt. "Boudoir shots. They were good too. I took them myself. Wasn't that nice of me?"

Nick raised his eyebrows.

"Show me."

"Show you what?"

"Show me the images. Do you have any on your phone?"

I huffed and pulled it out, jabbing at the screen until the thumbnails I was looking for were displayed. "I never showed you these. They're *confidential*." My flat tone had him chuckling.

He studied them, blowing two up to see the details better, before handing my phone back. "Have you ever done any?"

"I just told you. I took those."

"No." Nick smiled. "Have you ever had some taken of *you?*"

I wrinkled my nose and looked down at myself. "No."

"You should. You should get to experience what it's like to pose for a session." Pulling out his phone, he tapped it a few times and slid it across the bar to me. "For the kind of boudoir pictures I take."

I squinted at them, unsurprised to find his technique in this also topped mine. "Why? What's so special about the way you do it?"

He dropped his hand on top of mine, waiting until I met his gaze. "In my sessions, the woman puts me under her spell. She teases me, tempts me, taunts me with flashes of her body, her skin. She lets me look, fucking turns me on just about every time, but she knows I can't touch. It's a strong, heady feeling to have all that power. To feel sexy and wanted and beautiful and to be in control of the situation." He withdrew his hand slowly, his thumb rubbing my wrist once, twice. His eyes were darker than earlier, his voice deeper. "You should let me shoot you, Sadie. Show you what that's like. Remind you that you *are* all those things."

My palms were damp, and when I realized I'd curled my

fingers into loose fists, I forced myself to relax and wiped my hands against my jean-clad thighs.

"The pictures would be yours. You could have the memory card when we finished."

The offer was tempting. "What would you get out of it?"

He chuckled. "You saw me after that session with that lady the other day. Did it look like it was a hardship? And with you? Seeing you in that setting would be reward enough."

I glanced down. His bulge was bigger.

"Let's do it." I wanted that—all those things he described. To feel sexy, desirable, powerful. Not this emotional hot mess sitting at a closed bar.

"Maybe tomor—"

"Now."

"I don't thi—"

"*Now.*" If I didn't do it tonight, before I lost my nerve, I knew I wouldn't. And I wanted to. Wanted to seize the moment, be reckless.

Nick dropped his hand, adjusted himself. *He'd do it.* "You— you've been drinking." He stumbled over his words, belatedly playing the gentleman. "We should wa—"

I put my finger over his lips. "You done arguing?"

He nodded, rose from his stool.

"I know the room. Let me change and I'll meet you there in ten minutes."

I didn't wait to see if he'd follow.

chapter
nine

I WORE RED LACE. THE SILKY sheets, the mountain of pillows, and the filmy panels hanging from the canopy bed were black, the lighting subdued, and the air rich with incense. He'd clearly had this room redone just for photoshoots, because the guest rooms I'd seen, my own included, were all white linen and vibrant, tropical prints. Low, pulsing, bass-heavy music set the tone.

I'd taken a long shower to gather my courage before coming over, and had almost backed out twice. But then it seemed like just another thing Aubrey would have beaten me at. And, *fuck*, I was tired of losing to her.

A bowl of strawberries and a bottle of wine perched on the nightstand. I poured myself a glass because I didn't know what else to do while he set up, and more alcohol sounded like a good idea. I had to give Nick credit; he didn't skimp when it came to good alcohol.

He also hadn't rushed me. I'd slipped off my simple cotton dress as soon as I'd entered the room, knowing the longer it stayed on, the harder it would be to take off. Then I'd crawled across the artfully disheveled bed, which he swore was covered in freshly laundered sheets, and lounged against the pillows, trying to calm my nerves.

Finishing off the wine in my glass and plucking a perfect strawberry from the bowl, I took a second to appreciate the way he'd set the scene. The door to the balcony was propped open, allowing the warm salty air to ripple the fabric draped from the canopy. It was voluminous, partially obscuring him.

It was a clever technique, letting the woman feel less exposed, even though that was the whole point.

"Wait." His voice was husky.

I paused, the strawberry almost to my mouth.

"Slower."

My tongue reached for the fruit, catching the tip and angling it toward my face. I took a bite, savoring the sweetness, tipping my throat back, and licking my lips afterward. Then my fingers.

Nick worked quietly, efficiently. No flash to startle or disrupt the flow.

I finished the berry and flicked the stem back to the bowl.

Squirming against the pillows, I fiddled with my hair, smoothing it over one shoulder. "How exactly does this work?"

He leaned against the mahogany bedpost at the foot of the bed and smirked. "You've done this—you know how it works."

I bit my lip and crossed one leg over the other, unsure how to start, although I could tell the wine was starting to go to my head after all those margaritas earlier.

"You want me to coach you through it? Would that be easier than posing on your own?" His voice was smooth, eyes dark in the dim light.

I nodded and ran my hand through my hair, pushing it behind my back again, just to have something to do with my hands. I'd left it down, the natural waves slightly messy. My eyes were smoky, and my lipstick matched my pushup bra and boy-short set. My metallic gold nails were the only other touch of color. Smooth, tan skin and red lace on black satin.

Before I could wonder how Nick saw me, his voice rasped over the music. "Lay back."

I slid down the sheets, one leg automatically bending at the knee.

"Arms above your head, arch your back." He moved around the billowing fabric to capture me from the side.

"Eyes up, head back."

I tipped my chin, exposing the length of my neck, my mouth partially open. My tongue slipped out, ran along my bottom lip.

"Gorgeous. Raise up on your elbows, keep arching."

I flexed further and pointed my toes, breasts thrusting upwards.

"Look at me."

My head tilted, eyes hooded, and my heart beat loudly in my ears. It was both wanton and glamorous.

Everything about this scene screamed decadence. And he was right—it was a heady feeling.

My eyes dipped. Nick was hard. Already. But he stayed at the edge of the mattress, keeping his distance as promised.

"Relax onto the bed again," he urged. "Get another strawberry. Start at your mouth and trace it down the center of your body. Watch me while you do it."

The chilled fruit slid down my neck, between my breasts, and over my bare stomach, leaving goose bumps and hard nipples in its wake. My bra was thin. I knew he could tell. I loved that he could tell.

The click of the camera was barely detectable as he followed my actions.

"Yes, Sadie. Beautiful. Raise your hand up high and feed it to yourself. Pretend it's a thick, juicy cock. Let your lips surround it. Lick it. Savor it."

My pulse picked up as I mouthed the ripe fruit, and sampled the very tip. A small drop of juice escaped the corner of my mouth, and I caught it with my thumb, sucking it clean.

Nick cursed.

I finished the berry and stretched, arms above my head, tangling in my hair. I rocked my hips one at a time, tightening the muscles in first my right then left leg before relaxing and curling inward on myself.

He moved behind me and part of me knew he was catching the line of my spine, the flare of my hips spreading to the curve of my ass. I pushed it out further, then peeked over my shoulder at him.

His eyes met mine briefly, but it was enough.

The power—the undeniable, primal power a woman held over a man with just her body—it filled me. I was a goddess in that moment. And I reveled in it.

I moved without prompting, slowly twisting and bending my body, displaying my soft curves. I taunted, I teased, I tormented. Warmth pooled between my legs and I wanted more. Never wanted this feeling to stop.

Confidence surged through me and I knelt on the bed, spreading my thighs wide. This—this is what brought men to their knees. The helplessness to resist what hid between a woman's legs. It started battles and caused wars. Civilizations rose and fell from the power of that hidden honey.

And tonight—I owned it.

I traced a finger up my inner thigh, toyed with the edge of my panties.

The sharp intake of breath from Nick made me bolder.

Watching him through half-lowered lids, head held high, I skimmed up my side, pausing to circle one pebbled nipple, and ran the edge of my fingertip along my bra strap. I traced my cleavage, cupped myself, offered up my breasts to the camera.

My eyelids closed as I undulated, rocking my hips. I caressed myself, mimicking all the ways West had taught me felt so good. The ways that made me burn.

Nick blurred and West flooded my mind.

His hands roaming my flesh, kneading me, making me ache.

His mouth licking and sucking at all the right places to drive me crazy. His weight pressed up against me, urging me higher, faster.

One bra strap fell, exposing more skin.

It was West I pictured groaning, reaching down to adjust his hardened length, urging me with his eyes to continue.

I bit my lip and gyrated my hips slowly, performing for him.

He nodded, rubbing himself through his jeans.

I sucked on one finger, then dragged it down my skin, straight to my almost exposed peak. Dipping inside the lace, I pulled on the hard bud, drawing a moan from myself. My other hand dropped lower, teasing the seam between my legs, the scratchy lace providing the friction I sought.

My name shuddered from his lips. Needy. Worshipful.

Closing my eyes, I sank back on my heels.

I shifted both hands to my breasts, feeling them get fuller, heavier, as I played with them. I pinched my nipples until that frisson of pain had me gasping, repeating the action harder, wanting more.

The bed dipped as he moved closer, no doubt wanting a better view.

The air was musky with my arousal, and I remembered how he used to kiss me afterward, and I could taste myself on his tongue, our flavors melding together as we tangled our limbs.

Lowering my hands, my nails scratched a path down my thighs as I unfolded my legs, knees splayed wide. My fingers worked back in from my knees, one heading straight for my damp panties, the other grabbing a fistful of hair and tugging.

My scalp tingled. I'd never told him, but I secretly loved it when he tugged on my long strands in the heat of the moment. When that tiny hint of dominance peeked through and my body submitted to his so beautifully.

I bloomed under the lace, my finger teasing my opening. I was soaked. And it was all for him. All of this, all of me, it was his.

I touched my clit softly, wanting to draw this out, wanting to tease.

His breath came faster, matching mine. I didn't need to open my eyes to register the change in pace.

The hand in my hair slid to my exposed throat, the pulse at the base hammering. I could almost feel his lips there, nibbling the tender skin.

My other hand moved along my slit, forcing the lace between my wet folds.

I moaned, setting a pace meant to prolong the feeling.

My back arched and breasts throbbed. Squeezing one then other, the ache built higher. There was no relief, only more wanting.

I twisted the sheet with my damp palm, abandoning my nipples. My other fingers slipped under my waistband, seeking sweet release.

My fingers slick with arousal, I slid two inside me, pumping slowly. The way he always did when we were making love, instead of fucking. So I felt every hot inch of him rubbing along every tight inch of me.

I writhed, my hips pushing into my hand, impatient, greedy.

He groaned and it spurred me on.

I moved faster, my thumb brushing along my sensitive clit.

My breath caught, and my toes curled. I was so close.

I clutched my breast again, over the bra, the scratch of the lace against my tender nipple zinging straight to the base of my spine, taking me higher.

Someone's voice, mine or his, chanted. "Yes, yes, yes . . ."

My thumb circled faster, pressed harder. Once, twice.

And then I was floating, his name wrenched from my lips as I exploded, suspended in weightless euphoria as my fingers slowed, but didn't stop.

I bucked helplessly through the aftershocks, my skin damp with sweat. They slowed, easing to soft tremors, until I finally withdrew my hand, let it rest on my stomach, just the tips grazing the roughness of the lace. The air, incense and salt and musk, filled my lungs in deep breaths as I came down from my high.

I licked my dry lips and pushed my tangled hair out of my eyes as I sank farther into the pillows. My body felt heavy but boneless, sated for the moment.

The bed shifted. Murmured praise I didn't register, but the tone made it clear he'd loved it.

Of course he had. He loved me.

Something small pressed into my palm and my fingers curled around it automatically.

I yawned, curled onto my side, pulling the slick sheet over my hips. I was so sleepy.

A gust of air as the door opened, a flash of light from the hallway, and then nothing but the sound of the waves crashing in the distance.

I dreamt of his arms around me, his heavy leg on top of mine, and his hand cupping my breast. His breath against my neck, and his voice in my ear.

"I love you too."

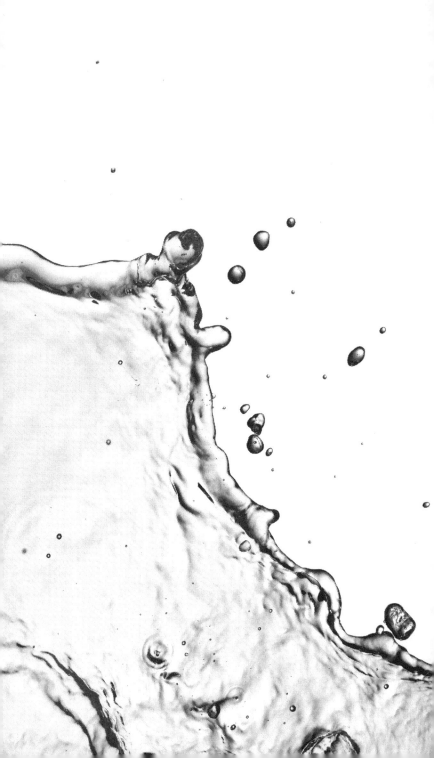

chapter
ten

I BLINKED MY HEAVY EYES, the sun streaming through the balcony door piercing my tender pupils with the agony of a thousand swords. A drumline played a discordant cadence in my skull, and my mouth was sticky and stale. My stomach lurched in warning as I crawled out of bed, still clad in red lace and smelling of sweat and musk.

Hangovers sucked. But at least I'd woken up alone.

Thank God for small mercies.

The journey to the bathroom felt like a million miles, but I eventually collapsed on the floor of the shower, letting the hot water pelt me and the steam hide the rest of the world. Confused thoughts swirled around my head, making the pounding worse. West. Nick. Aubrey. Love. Hurt. Desire. Betrayal. Trust.

Curling up into a ball, I tucked my head to my knees and cried, letting my tears mix with the water running over me.

It wasn't the heaving sobs of heartbreak. It wasn't the silent stream of embarrassed regret. It was tears of frustration that no matter how much my head told me West was the wrong choice, my heart, my body, my stupid fucking soul clung to him, refusing to let go.

Why couldn't I just let go?

Memories of last night seeped in, even as the evidence ran down the drain.

Reading West's words. Sacrificing them to Neptune at the bottom of the sea. Drowning any lingering memories in too much tequila. Spilling my sob story to first Alison—who no longer ranked as my third best-est friend after this morning—and then Nick. Posing for him. Coming for West. Losing myself completely in the moment. Killing any chance Nick would ever be able to take me seriously again. Possibly destroying my chance with this advertising campaign, depending on Nick's reaction.

Fucking men. Always ruining everything.

Because as strong as I'd felt last night, this morning I was a hot mess of indecision and turmoil.

When the warm water threatened to turn cold, I scrubbed myself hastily, wishing last night was as easy to wash away as my smudged makeup. The hotel shampoo had a hint of orange mixed with mint in its scent, and sent me tumbling further down the West Montgomery rabbit hole. I missed his citrus-and-salt smell on my pillow in the mornings.

After shutting off the water, I toweled myself dry, scouring my skin with the terrycloth until my skin was pink. Using the side of my fist, I rubbed at the condensation on the mirror, and peered at my reflection.

My cheeks were pale and my eyes were red, but otherwise I looked the same. Somehow, I thought *slut* would look different on me.

Because as much as last night had been about West for me, Nick had been the one to watch it. Watch me shamelessly fuck my hand and moan my pleasure. Watch me come undone and scream another man's name.

While I recalled the gist of what I'd done, I had no memory of Nick's reaction.

And maybe that was a blessing in disguise.

Hurriedly wrapping my hair in the towel and my body in the white hotel robe from the hook on the back of the door, I gathered up my clothes from the bathroom floor and the small memory card on the nightstand. I managed to make the walk of shame without running into any other resort guests before shutting myself into the sanctuary of my own room.

After dumping the lingerie in the trash can—embarrassment flooding every inch of me—I halted abruptly when I spotted a breakfast tray ready and waiting for me on the small table. Approaching it cautiously and lifting the lid, I found greasy bacon, cheesy scrambled eggs, and loaded hashbrowns awaiting me. Hangover food. And ibuprofen. Nick must have arranged it.

A small paper airplane sat between the tiny ketchup bottle and my glass of orange juice. West still wooing me from across the ocean. Even as he hung out with that bitch Aubrey.

Apparently I wasn't the only one confused about what I wanted.

Pushing them both from my mind, and ignoring the note for now, I swallowed the pills and dug into my food. It was still warm. This resort was fucking magical. And the bacon, my God, bacon did not taste like this on Reynolds Island.

By the time I finished, and my belly settled down and acted like it wasn't going to reject my food offering, I was sleepy again. My head still throbbed, my ears still rang, and the sun was too damn cheerful to handle.

Pulling the curtains shut, I collapsed on the bed, wet hair and all.

A CRACK OF THUNDER startled me from my nap. I tried to check my phone to see what time it was, but the battery was dead. Connecting it to the built-in charger on the nightstand, I looked at the bedside clock. Four-fifty in the afternoon. I'd slept through most of the day like a rock.

Yawning, I took a quick inventory. Head felt better. Eyes were less scratchy. Stomach was growling but okay. And the dark sky and stormy weather outside fit my grouchy mood perfectly.

At least with the rain, it wouldn't seem weird that I wasn't outside interacting with anyone. I threw on some yoga pants and an oversized T-shirt. After opening the curtains so I could watch the storm, I picked up my phone again. It had just enough charge to let me use it while plugged in.

As it powered on, my notifications went crazy. Eighteen messages and seven missed calls. All from Rue.

Alarmed, I opened the texts and read through them.

Call me.

Now.

Why aren't you answering?

We need to talk.

Are you okay?

Don't worry, we can handle this.

Grrrr, pick up already.

Sadie! This is important!

What have you done?

I didn't waste time reading any further.

Punching the icon on my home screen that was my shortcut to call Rue, I waited while the phone beeped and clicked its way through connecting the call internationally.

"Sadie?!" Her normally husky voice was an octave higher than normal, and my heart pounded in my chest.

Whatever had happened, it wasn't good.

"Rue?" My hand tightened around the phone. "What's wrong?"

"Have you looked yet? Seen them?"

I wrinkled my brow. "Seen what?"

She sucked in a deep breath and paused. This time her voice was a whisper. "The naked pictures of you online."

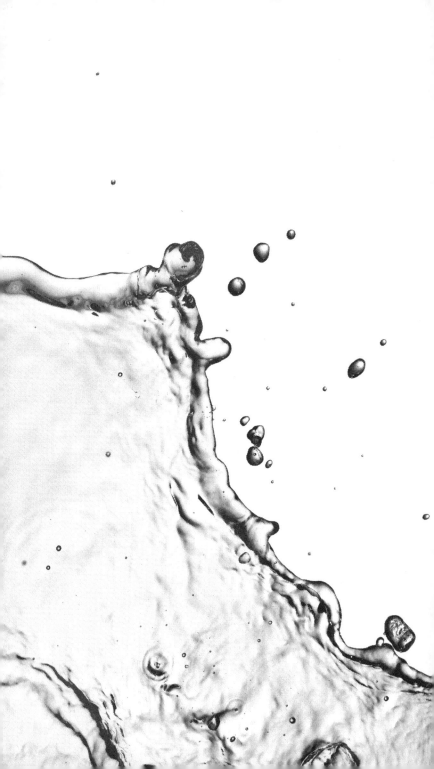

chapter
eleven

I DROPPED THE PHONE. It clattered against the nightstand before bouncing under the bed, still tethered by the cable charging it.

Scrambling to my hands and knees to retrieve it, I put the phone back to my ear, sitting on the floor with my back to the side of the bed.

"What did you say?"

"Check your email—I sent you the link. We nee—"

I disconnected the call. I didn't need to hear anymore.

Nick.

Fucking Nick.

How could he? I'd trusted him. He pressed the memory card into my palm, but technically, the camera itself had some built in memory he could have utilized.

He sure didn't waste any time, did he?

Had those images uploaded and distributed in less than twenty-four hours.

And, hell, they'd already reached my friends?

What the fuck did he do—post them to my goddamn Facebook page?

Pinching the useless micro-SD card in my fingers, I dropped it on the tile floor at my feet. I yanked at the lamp on the nightstand, but it must've been screwed down or something, because it didn't budge. I pulled the clock off instead, slamming it on the chip over and over, shards of plastic from the destroyed timepiece flying in chunks across the floor.

Why did every guy fuck me over?

Why couldn't I ever put my trust in the right place?

Did I have some giant target on me that painted me as an idiot just begging to be taken advantage of?

I banged the largest piece of the broken clock against the floor again, smashing my finger this time. I winced, the skin jagged where a piece of plastic had sliced me. Blood welled up and I sucked my finger into my mouth, tears stinging my eyes.

I gave in to the self-pity this time. I pushed reality away and let the sobs rack my body while the thunder and rain drowned out my gasping breaths and choked cries.

As the storm quieted, so did my tears, until they were a silent, but steady stream leaking from the corners of my eyes. My breath was still ragged as I tried to pull together a few scraps of courage to open the email Rue sent. As if I really wanted to see those private moments splashed across a website for the general public to judge.

That power he talked about? I guess he forgot to mention it transferred to him afterwards.

I climbed onto the bed where my computer sat. Where the evidence of my shame lay waiting to destroy me. The laptop suddenly felt like a viper, coiled and waiting to strike while I was at my weakest.

My eyes burned as I blinked to clear my vision. I powered on my computer, my heart thumping painfully against my ribs. My fingers tapped out a nervous rhythm on the bedspread while it blinked and beeped through its startup routine.

I hesitated with the cursor over the email icon, knowing wherever the link inside led me was going to break me. Shatter me even more than I already was from West.

Biting my lip, I clicked open the program, then followed the link in the email Rue had titled *URGENT!*

A popular porn site loaded on my browser. One of the most popular ones I knew of, its cheesy logo in the corner of my screen.

On the top of the page labeled Top Amateurs, I saw it.

A still of myself, draped across a bed, the paper airplane tattoo on my ankle clearly displayed on the bottom of the screen.

But that wasn't what made my breath catch. Wasn't what made my hand clench into a white-knuckled fist. Wasn't what my made my eyes narrow to slits.

No, the bed on the screen wasn't covered with black silk sheets and surrounded by filmy panels.

And I wasn't wearing red lace.

And I wasn't alone.

Stretched out next to me, eyes out of the field of view, but signature smirk firmly in place, was the one man I hadn't thought about in months. His legs intertwined with mine and he nibbled on my neck, one hand squeezing my ass. My face was visible, tilted toward him, mouth open and eyes pressed closed with pleasure.

The first man who broke me.

Asher Snowdon, the ex-boyfriend I'd left behind when I'd escaped to Reynolds Island. The asshole whose electronic equipment I'd destroyed, dumping it in a full bathtub with laundry soap and bleach. The one who'd planned on proposing to me before I'd discovered that not only was he screwing my photography assistant, but had filmed encounters with both of us.

And shared the videos with his friends.

And, unless this was all just a nightmare, with the whole fucking world too.

chapter
twelve

I BLINKED, MY EYES FLYING OVER the screen. The flickering red-and-yellow banner at the top of the website screaming CONTEST in block letters caught my attention. Ten-thousand dollars would go to the top amateur porn video with the most votes. From what I could tell, the competition had been narrowed down to the top dozen videos.

And I starred in two of them.

Rebecca, my old photography assistant—and possibly Asshole's new girlfriend for all I knew—also made an appearance, in a submission titled *Busty Brunette Likes Anal*.

Classy.

Mine were called *Blonde Girlfriend Can't Get Enough* and *Blonde Likes it Rough*.

Thirty-six minutes and twenty-three minutes long. Almost a

full hour.

Of me.

Naked.

Vulnerable.

Open.

Exposed.

Deceived.

Manipulated.

Violated.

Betrayed.

It didn't feel real. It was like the girl on the screen—the one who undoubtedly moaned Asher's name and shuddered under his touch, leaning into his caresses, demanding more, professing her love—was a prior version of me. Sadie 1.0.

Because the current me couldn't ever imagine a reality that involved this.

Where I would ever welcome strangers to witness the most intimate of acts.

Except that time in the bed of West's truck at the drive-in, his fingers deep inside me.

Or the time in the stairwell when anyone could've walked in.

Or the time in the parking lot, outside of Anchor, just before this trip.

But those were different. The risk of discovery was there, yes. But not outright exhibitionism. Not pimply faced teenagers, jerking off in dirty gym socks, alone in their bedrooms. Or lonely middle-aged men fantasizing about what they'd never have again.

So maybe I lost my mind and my common sense when I was with West. But with Asshole? With our sex scheduled neatly into his day planner and when spontaneity was something *other* people did? No.

I hadn't expected this.

Hadn't really known him at all, obviously.

The same way I didn't know West.

Pushing them both from my mind, I focused on the screen again. I was currently in second and third places. Rebecca's ass ranked sixth. I shouldn't have smirked at that, but I did.

Oh, God. What was wrong with me? Had I sunk so low that I was pleased my illicit sex tapes were more popular than hers? But yeah, if I was going to be stuck at the bottom of the barrel, at least I was still higher than her skank ass.

Take that, bitch.

Hovering over the description, I made yet another disturbing discovery. Asshole had given himself a porn name. While I was relegated to my role as Blonde, he'd upgraded himself to Ben Dover.

I doubted he came up with that himself. Cleverness wasn't his strong suit.

The sheer number of votes cast was mortifying. Five figures of thumbs ups. Pages of comments appeared below each video.

Ride that bitch.

Damn, she's hot.

I bet she'd like a good spanking. Try that next time?

Would you consider a threesome?

Her cu—

I couldn't read any more of them.

The crude words strangers felt entitled to make about my body, my actions.

My worth as a person shriveled. I wasn't Sadie Mullins, the emerging photographer. Or Sadie, the trustworthy friend. Or Sadie, a girl worth loving.

No. I was only a piece of flesh. A pair of tits and a hole to fuck. Some hair to yank, an ass to slap. I wasn't even worthy of a name, real or fake. I was reduced to simply *the Blonde.*

Some chick others could watch, judge, mock, covet, whatever. Just another dumb porn slut, moaning for more.

Numbness filled me, making my limbs heavy and my eyes burn.

I just wanted to get through the rest. See what other parts of me Asshole had given away, parts that no longer belonged to him. If I did it quick, maybe it wouldn't hurt so bad.

Like tearing off a bandage. One quick yank, then it'd be over.

My cursor hovered over the play button of the first video, but I hesitated. I wasn't sure I really wanted to see which nitty gritty details were bared on the videos. Wasn't sure I really wanted to watch myself naively offering my body up to the man I thought I'd marry.

Thank God I'd escaped before he proposed.

My eyes dropped lower, noticing a link below the video.

Interviews with the Stars—Behind the Scenes Facts from the Finalists.

No. No no no no no.

It was bad enough my body was on display. Tell me he hadn't talked about us too.

My hand shook as I selected the one for Ben Dover.

Q: So, Ben. What made you decide to enter this contest?

A: Honestly? I knew had a good chance of winning. And I could use the prize money.

Q: Oh? What do you plan on using it for if you win?

A: I had an unfortunate accident with some of my electronics awhile back. I need to do some upgrading.

Q: Did you make your videos just for the contest? Or have home videos always been a hobby of yours?

A: My girlfriend, the blonde, is obviously hot. And my friends were all single. I made the first ones just to rub it in their faces. Show them exactly what I had that they were missing out on. And then they wanted more. And, honestly, yeah, it was cool knowing they were jerking it to my girl. So I kept filming.

Q: And the brunette?

A: You know, my friends started making some requests. Wanted to see some kinkier stuff. Things I knew my girlfriend wouldn't be down for. Turns out, the brunette was more than willing to help out.

Q: So your girlfriend was okay with everything?

A: She never knew. A man's gotta have some secrets. Right?

Q: Ben, you're obviously a popular man, with three videos in the finals. Tell us—do blondes really have more fun? Or did you prefer the brunette?

A: Well, they were both good in different ways. The blonde, it was deeper with her, ya know? She loved me. Would've done anything for me. Well, almost. You saw the video with the brunette. I had to go to her to get some backdoor action. But, hell, sometimes it's nice to mix things up. Sometimes you don't want to make love. Sometimes, you just want a good, hard, dirty fuck. So I'd say blondes are sweet, but brunettes are spicy.

Q: Yet the entries with the blonde, at the time of the interview anyway, are more popular. Why do you think that is?

A: Because it was real for her. The brunette—she knew what the deal was. We were fucking. For the camera. For an audience. It was still hot as hell, but there were no genuine feelings involved. The blonde? She was my girlfriend. I knew every inch of her body. Knew how to kiss her, touch her, tease her, take her just right to get the kind of reaction I did. The kind everyone seems to like. And I think it's that realness that made the difference.

Q: Are you still with her?

A; Not right now. But I wouldn't be surprised if we ended up together in the end. I mean, seriously, did you see the videos? We're amazing together. She'll miss it and be back. I have no doubt.

I threw up a little in my mouth as white-hot rage filled me.

I'd be back? What planet was he living on?

He'd shown his friends. He'd shown the world.

And now my friends—*wait a minute!*

How did my friends find out?

I scrambled for my phone, hitting the button that was my shortcut to Rue's cell.

She answered on the first ring. "Sadie, we—"

"How did you find out?"

"We have other things to worry about right now. We nee—"

"How. Did. You. Find. Out?" My jaw ached I was clenching my teeth so hard.

"Sadie." Her voice softened. "That's not what matters here."

"Tell me." I had to know.

She sighed and my free hand curled into a fist. "I was at the Wreck, meeting Theo for drinks last night. Aubrey was there with her minions and they were laughing at something on her phone, and I overheard your name so I went to investigate."

"*Aubrey?!*" My screech was reminiscent of a bird of prey. A hawk maybe, screaming as it dove for the soft-bellied animal it hunted. Except, she was the hawk, and I was the helpless field mouse in this scenario.

"If it makes you feel any better, her iPhone met an unfortunate end in a pitcher of grog."

I pinched my eyes shut and huffed out a short humorless laugh. "Thank you for that." Rue would always have my back. Always. At least there was one thing I could count on in my life.

"What we nee—"

"How did *she* know?"

Rue's voice carried a note of impatience this time. "I don't know. She's not important. She's never been important. You are. Now, we need a plan. I've already contacted a lawyer in Nashville, and I have three hacker friends working on getting the videos blocked as we speak . . ."

She kept talking but the words no longer registered.

Fucking Aubrey.

I glanced at my laptop again. The contest had started four weeks ago. I wondered how long she'd known. How many people in Reynolds Island she'd shared the link with.

The place where I'd hoped to start over. Be respected. Maybe build a business. A life.

Fuck, two weeks ago I'd even been imagining starting a family with West one day.

" . . . Are you listening?"

"No. Not really." My mind was spinning a million miles an hour, but going nowhere. A hamster in a wheel.

How the fuck was I going to recover from this?

"Sadie!" Rue's voice was sharp. No nonsense. "Listen. To. Me. I'm not even going to ask why you didn't mention that there were sex videos of you floating around." I hadn't told her because I had been ashamed. I'd simply told her that I'd found out he'd been cheating on me with Rebecca, my assistant at my photography business when I lived back in Nashville. After I'd drowned his electronics, I thought I'd handled the sex tape issue on my own. Could pretend it had never happened. Clearly, I was wrong. " . . . But it's too late to worry about that now. I've already got a plan in place. You're going to be fine. And Asshole . . . he's going down."

The steely determination in her voice fortified me. I borrowed strength from her confidence and certainty. Forcing myself to pay attention as she outlined what steps she'd already taken and what things had already been set in motion, I wanted to kiss her.

Rue. God bless Rue.

She was brilliant.

Evil.

Devious.

And on my side.

Most importantly, she was right.

Asshole was going down.

I didn't know if I'd be okay when the dust all settled after this. If I'd have any friends other than Rue. Any clients who would hire me again. But I did know one thing.

Asher had messed with the wrong woman.

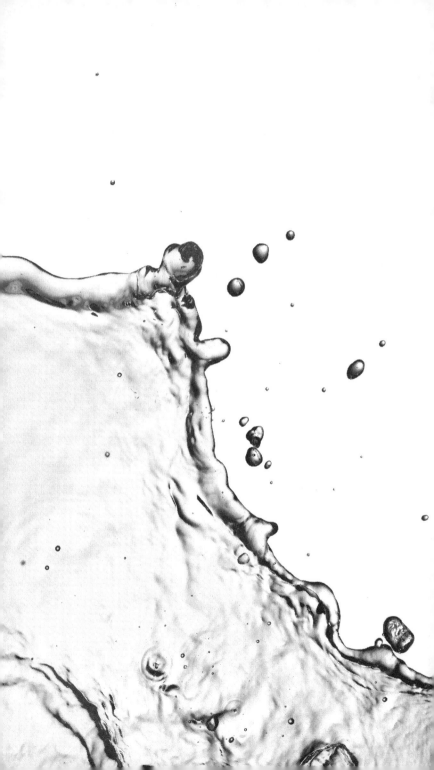

chapter
thirteen

GRADY ACCEPTED MY LIE about a family emergency without a qualm, making me pause and wonder if word of my newfound infamy had reached him as well. But his eyes held no derision, no disgust, no pity. Just concern. He insisted I let him know if there was anything he could do to help, then arranged for a cab to pick me up and take me to the airport in the morning, which was the earliest flight I could catch. I assured him that I had enough photos to cover both campaign ideas we'd discussed, and I'd have the finished product ready the next week.

Assuming he didn't fire me and ban me from the Water's Edge properties in the meantime.

Did my contract have some kind of morality or respectability clause? I knew this project was a big deal for Grady—a potential turning point in his career. And I didn't want my newfound notoriety to reflect poorly on him.

At some point, I'd have to come clean. He took a chance on me and didn't deserve to have his reputation tainted because of it too.

But not yet. Not when everything was still so fresh and sharp. I needed to do it when I could get the words out without reverting to a soggy, weak, broken version of myself. When I could fully accept that I'd been a victim, and the shame didn't belong to me, but instead showed the true character of Asher Snowden.

Predatory. Despicable. Untrustworthy.

Men who preyed on women, especially through sexual domination or humiliation, deserved a special place in hell.

And, with Rue by my side, I was going to make sure he got exactly what he deserved.

I didn't run into Nick, for which I was thankful. I didn't know what to say to him at this point anyway. The last time he'd seen me, I'd been mostly naked, plunging my fingers in and out of myself, moaning with pleasure. To say I was embarrassed would be an understatement. Even more so now after learning about Asshole's deception. There was no way he'd ever look at me with a shred of respect again.

When I'd cleaned up the mess in my room, the small memory card of my session with him was bent and cracked, rendering it unusable, my session lost for good. Those pictures would never be viewed—by him, myself, or anyone. And deep down, I was relieved. I wasn't sure I needed to see them on a screen. See the open vulnerability I'd shown to Nick, when really it had been

West on my mind.

Those moments—they'd been true and pure and unscripted. I knew if I could've seen my eyes in the photos, they would've revealed far too much about how my heart still clung to West. Refusing to let go. And I really, *really* needed to let go of him.

As I boarded the small plane, I pushed him from my mind, letting my anger at Asshole take center stage. When I'd first found out about his infidelity and the sex tapes, I'd felt hurt, used, betrayed. I'd run away like a little girl to lick my wounds.

But he'd underestimated me.

I was done cowering. The woman who'd emerged from the wreckage he'd caused was stronger. Stood up for herself. Knew she was worth more. And was not going to take this shit lightly.

Hell, no.

If he thought some ruined electronics were bad the last time, I was really going to blow his mind when I returned to Nashville.

But first I had a layover in Miami.

Where an early tropical storm pelted the city, canceling flights for two days.

Two days where I sat in a cheap, shitty motel next to the airport because, of course, all the nice hotels were already full of other stranded passengers. Where I stared at the generic palm tree print hanging crookedly on the wall and the carpet that was a weird grayish-brown color probably picked for the way it would hide stains I didn't want to think about, and waited while the plan Rue and I concocted solidified. Phone calls made. Favors called in. Team assembled.

I binged on vending machine junk food and soda, not wanting to fight the storm to find real food. It didn't matter anyway. Everything was tasteless, even the little powdered sugar doughnuts that came in a roll of six and had more calories than anyone needed in a whole day, let alone one sitting. Eating was just a way to pass the time, to mark the hours until I could confront Asshole and fuck him over the way he had me.

My emotions swung like an out-of-control pendulum. Fury at Asshole. Frustration with the whole male gender. Victory when the videos were successfully removed from the website. Disappointment in myself for my taste in men. Confusion whenever I thought about West—my head warning me away, my heart wanting to return to him, refusing to give up.

Rue was a saint. We talked for hours. She listened to my mindless rants, the twisted tangents I took, always agreeing with me, even when I contradicted things I'd said five minutes earlier.

When I suggested we try a lesbian relationship—together— she took me seriously, in true best friend fashion. I wrote down a list of pros and cons on the little pad of stationary I found tucked next to the Gideon's Bible in the cheap nightstand drawer. And there were a *lot* of pros. Except neither of us wanted to have sex with each other. Strap-ons were an option, but we argued over who would top and who would bottom. Naturally, she wanted to top, but I was tired of being second-place in a relationship. If anything, *I* would be the top.

And, typical Rue, who was never satisfied with her partner, even managed to find something wrong with me. If she was going to be a lesbian, she insisted upon Brazilians for both of us. I loved her, but not enough to have hot wax ripped off my lady bits. Our relationship was doomed before it even started.

Drawing a big X across the list, I fiddled with the paper, not realizing what I'd done until I was holding a perfectly folded paper airplane in my hand. Crumpling it up, I tossed it toward the trash can in the corner, and missed by a good foot, which wasn't surprising, since I was failing at life at every turn.

When we finally hung up so Rue could make a few necessary phone calls to ensure everything with our plan was still lined up and ready to go when I arrived tomorrow, I was at a loss.

Television didn't hold my interest. Songs about heartbreak hit too close to home, so I turned off the radio. The Wi-Fi at this motel was abysmal, which was just as well, because I didn't need the temptation of Facebook anyway.

Instead, I pulled out my laptop and scrolled through the photos of my last session on Reynolds Island. The one with West flying a kite with his sister Hailey and her son, Cody. The moment when I realized I could see us having kids together one day. When I realized I loved him.

In the aftermath, I'd never properly edited the images and sent them to Hailey. Guilt and a desire to keep busy had me sorting through them now, picking the best and making small tweaks to enhance the shots.

I smiled as I worked. Cody perched on West's broad shoulders, Hailey's hand reaching up to help steady her son. Cody's wide-eyed smile, full of innocent glee. The carefree grin

West shot me over his shoulder, his eyes soft and warm as they met mine through the lens. West tossing Cody high in the air. Hailey holding his little hands and spinning them in circles until they both fell to the sand, dizzy and laughing, heads thrown back. The look on West's face as he headed my direction, urging me to put the camera down and just enjoy the moment. Lips tipped in a smirk while his blue-gray eyes shone with . . .

I bit my lip.

This one photo. It was all there. It was obvious how he felt about me.

Before I could over think things, I unblocked him and dialed his number, my hands shaking and tears pricking my eyes.

Everything in my life was wrong and upside down and messed up, and damn it all, I just needed to hear his voice.

As it rang, I checked the clock on the flimsy nightstand. It was late. Really late. After midnight. My flight left at 8:40 in the morning, and I should've already been asleep, if only my fucking mind would quiet down and give me some peace.

On the third ring, I was lowering the phone to hang up when his voice came through the speaker.

"Sadie?"

Biting my lip, the first tear escaping from my eye, I lifted the phone back to my ear.

"Sadie."

His voice. Fuck, I'd missed his voice. The way my name rolled off his tongue husky and deep. I could hear so much in just the way he said my name.

Hope. Worry. Relief.

A sharp ache pierced through me, longing so intense my stomach clenched in need and I wanted nothing more in that moment than to be able to touch him, feel his heat next to me. To belong to him again.

I gripped the phone tighter but couldn't answer him. My throat was too thick, the words I wished I could say to him choking me as I fought to swallow them down.

"I'm here. Whatever it is, baby, I'm here. Always."

More tears slid down my cheeks, the first ones blazing a trail the others were quick to follow. I took a ragged breath I knew he could hear on his end, heard the way his own caught in response.

"You don't have to say anything. It's okay. Just don't hang up. *Fuck*, I've missed you." The anguish in his voice had me pressing a fist over my mouth, trying to stifle the sobs that wanted to escape.

I missed him too. I wanted him here, his arms around me, holding me, protecting me from the shit storm my life had become. Curling into a ball on the thin, polyester comforter, I waited, somehow knowing he'd give me exactly what I needed.

"I know I fucked up, Sadie. Not with Aubrey—you have to know that there's nothing between us." His hard tone was insistent, unyielding in his declaration, and I wanted so badly to believe him. "But I fucked up just the same because I hurt you, and that's the last thing I ever wanted to do."

He paused and I could picture him running his hand through his hair the way he did when he was upset.

"I love you." No hint of begging, pleading, or accusation from him. Just quiet sincerity. "I promised myself you'd never have to wonder about that again. I'll tell you every damn chance I get, every chance you'll let me."

My shoulders shook from the silent cries I refused to let him hear, too proud to let him know how broken I was at that moment. My heart echoed his sentiment, but my stubborn head kept my lips from answering him.

Movement on his end. The click of a door shutting. Footsteps. "I'm so glad you called. I check my phone a thousand times a day, just hoping . . ." He trailed off. The rain beat against the window and I strained to hear anything on his end.

"I wish you were next to me right now." Frustration mixed with longing in his voice. A rustling sound mingled with the squeak of bedsprings. I pictured him sliding into bed, the rumpled sheets bunched around his waist. "I miss our sleepovers. The way you burrowed into me and fit so perfectly in my arms, your hair tickling my nose, and your cold feet tucked between my legs." He sighed, the sound cracking another wall I'd erected between us. "My pillow didn't smell like you anymore, so I went to the store and bought some of that watermelon shampoo you use. I thought maybe if I used it right before I went to bed, maybe it'd rub off and it would seem like you'd just been here with me." He blew out a single depreciating laugh. "It didn't work."

I rubbed my palm over my eyes, and licked my salty lips. I wanted to say something, anything to him. But I didn't even know where to start.

"Sadie, don't hang up. Even if you don't say anything back

tonight, just don't hang up, okay? If this is the closest I can get to falling asleep with you, I'll take it. Just knowing you're on the other end, fuck, it's so much better than this emptiness I've felt since you left."

I pulled back the gross blanket, settling between the rough sheets and trying to find a comfortable position on the hard, lumpy pillow. What I wouldn't give to be nestled against his chest, using the crook of his shoulder to sleep on, his solid warmth lulling me to sleep. But I'd settle for his deep voice in my ear instead. Even if I couldn't admit that to him.

"I don't know what finally made you call tonight, but I'm glad you did. I've been going crazy here without you. Even General Beauregard is avoiding me. I guess I've been a moody bastard." He chuckled, then his voice turned softer, more serious. "I hope you're okay. I hope you're happy. Even if that means you're not coming back to me when you come home. That's all I really want—for you to be happy."

We were both quiet. Just breathing over the line, our rhythms adjusting until we were synchronized. I pressed a hand over the ache in my chest.

"I'm just gonna talk, okay, Sadie? Tell you all the stupid stuff I would've told you if you were next to me in bed. About Wyatt making a fool of himself at the bar, and the crazy client I had the other day who wanted to fish a tournament but was scared to actually touch the fish he caught, and about the trouble Cody has been causing Hailey, and . . . and I'm just gonna talk because I'm scared if I stop you're gonna hang up."

He took a deep breath. Then launched into story after story. The words blurred together. The only thing I really listened to was his voice. The way it filled with laughter and twisted with sarcasm and gentled when he talked about his nephew. The way he never stopped talking, never let go of me even as the clock crept past one, then two, then three.

I never saw it reach four. I must've fallen asleep to the lullaby of his words.

When the insistent beep of the alarm woke me at five, I still had the phone in my hand, although it was no longer pressed to me ear.

Texts from him and Rue waited for me.

Helpless to resist, I opened the one from him first.

It was a pic of General Beauregard stretched out on the bed next to him, drool puddling beneath his jowls.

West: He's keeping your spot warm.

I lingered for a moment, imagining West in bed, rumpled and warm and probably shirtless, reaching over to snuggle the oversized hound. Was I jealous of a dog in that moment?

Maybe.

Probably.

Forcing away the bitter sting of longing, I tapped on the message from Rue.

Rue: Everything's in place. Just waiting on you.

I sucked in a deep breath and thought of Asher with his smug, arrogant face I'd once found so handsome. How he'd proven his utter lack of decency as a human being. How he'd broken me, ripping everything I thought I knew about my life to shreds.

A smile cracked the dried tearstains on my face.

I couldn't wait to repay the favor.

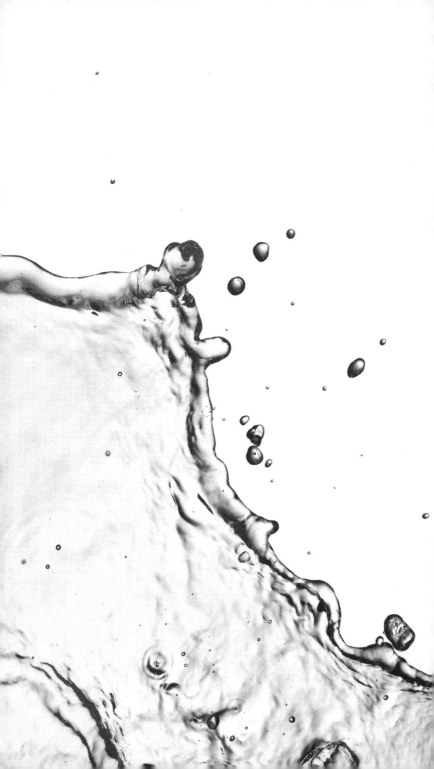

chapter
fourteen

B Y THE TIME THE PLANE LANDED and Rue picked me up from the airport, I only had ninety minutes to prepare myself. When we got to the hotel room—I'd convinced her I didn't want my family involved or to know I was in town until after I had things under control—she immediately set to work on my makeup. No, that's not being shallow. When confronting scum like Asshole, it was important to feel untouchable, invincible. On a level so much higher than him, he could never hope to reach it in his wildest dreams. And part of that was external armor: flawless hair and makeup and a killer outfit. And shoes I wouldn't trip in. Nothing ruined a dramatic exit like tripping over heels that were too tall.

She pulled my hair back into a French braid that somehow screamed sophistication and effortless style, despite its messy-on-purpose appearance. A bright, silky top, black skinny jeans, wedge sandals and fierce eyeliner completed the look.

We argued about whether she would accompany me all the way to my old loft or wait in the car. She didn't want to leave me alone with him. I wanted to show him I was strong enough to confront him solo. We had to watch the time carefully though. Once I showed up, I'd only have about thirty-five minutes or so before the life Asshole had become so comfortable with came crashing down around him.

Because Rue never did anything half-assed and wouldn't be caught dead driving a standard compact car, she pulled the low-slung luxury rental to the curb outside the converted warehouse on the edge of the trendy side of Nashville I used to call home. Turning off the engine, she caught my hand before I could reach for the door handle.

"Are you ready for this? Do you need a moment?"

I licked my dry lips, hoping I didn't smudge my lipstick. "Does it really matter if I'm ready?"

Dropping my cold fingers, she grabbed my shoulders and tugged until I was facing her. "You, Sadie Mullins, are a strong, beautiful woman worth a thousand Asher Snowdens. What he did to you was not only a breach of your trust, your relationship, and basic fucking human decency, but is also a reflection of him. Not you. *Him*. His weakness. His shallowness. His fragile fucking ego that needed his brainless friends to tell him what a stud he was for him to feel remotely like a man. Which he isn't. He's an asshole. Not even a high-production-quality porn asshole. All hairless and bleached and shit. No, he's like a dirty, hairy, I-can't-wipe-my-own-ass-without-help asshole with hemorrhoids. Big, fat, painful ones." Her fingers dug into my upper arms.

"Big ones, huh?" A strangled giggle escaped from me.

"Huge." She nodded, dead serious. "Not to mention his sheer idiocy. Everything's set in motion now. There's no escape for him. He's not getting away with it." She hesitated, before repeating herself. "He's not getting away with it. Meaning, you don't have to go up there and see him at all, and he'll still get everything that's coming to him without you ever having to lay eyes on that scumbag again."

Reaching up, I pulled her hands from my shoulders. "I know. But I need to do this. For me."

"Want me to come up?" She offered one last time. "I could wait in the hall, out of sight, but nearby in case you need me."

I reached across the console and wrapped her in a giant hug. *This* is what true friendship was.

"I can do this, Rue. I have to." My face hardened with determination, and I took a second to just breathe. Thirty-one minutes left.

Show time.

Flashing her a grim smile, I opened the car door and stepped out onto the sidewalk. As I headed for the front door, Rue's voice followed me. "Kick him in the nuts when you're done ripping him a new one!"

I snickered.

As I walked across the limestone floor of the lobby and

waited for the elevator, I kept waiting for my nerves to hit, but my stomach stayed settled. My palms and pits were dry. My jaw set. I was ready. More than ready.

I was a fucking woman scorned, and it was time for him to pay.

Even though I still had a key to the loft on my key ring, I knocked. Besides, I'd left my purse in the car. Just had my phone tucked in my rear pocket in case I needed Rue for back up after all. She'd be at the door in about twenty-eight minutes if I hadn't already reappeared outside. Hell, knowing her, she wouldn't even wait that long. She was probably waiting around the corner to stick her ear up to the door once I got inside, despite promising to wait in the car.

Plus, I'd already hit the button on the phone that would record our entire conversation.

Face blank, I looked right at the peephole. After footsteps from inside approached there was a pause, where I assumed he was checking who it was. Then an even longer hesitation, using another precious minute up, before the chain rattled and the door opened.

And he was right there. In front of me.

Smug smirk firmly in place.

He leaned his forearm against the doorframe, his unwelcome gaze raking me from head to toe.

"Sadie." It was a statement, not a question, and only the faintest hint of surprise slipped through. Almost as if he'd been expecting me.

I didn't fidget. Didn't shift uneasily side-to-side. Wasn't remotely intimidated.

I didn't return the perusal. Had he gained weight, put on muscle, developed a gut? Didn't know, didn't care.

"Asher." I kept the word short and clipped.

His hair was longer than I remembered. Mussed in a way most girls probably enjoyed. Hell, maybe one *had* just enjoyed it. Two days' worth of scruff roughened his jawline beneath the twist of his lips. *Lips that had touched every inch of me in the past.*

I barely restrained the shudder that thought elicited. Ew. Just . . . ew.

Raising his eyebrows, he pushed the door open the rest of the way and swept his arm out, inviting me inside. With a sneer, I moved past him, careful to keep any part of me from brushing against him in the process.

I stalked into the living room . . . which hadn't changed a bit, except it was messier than it ever was when I still lived there. And there was a newer, nicer GoPro sitting on the console table.

Bet he was getting a lot of use out of that.

Following me part of the way, he stopped at the breakfast bar that divided the space, perching on one of the stainless-steel industrial stools I'd splurged on after we moved in, his arms crossed at his chest.

"I figured you'd come back at some point," he started. "But I kind of thought you'd call first."

A sweet, sweet smile broke my stony façade, and I tucked my arms behind my back, to keep him from seeing my clenched fist.

"And what was it you thought I'd be coming back for?"

Running a hand through his messy hair, he chuckled. "Sadie, you can't deny we were good together. We were fucking great together. Especially in there." He tipped his head toward the open bedroom door, where I caught a quick glimpse of the unmade bed before whipping my eyes back at him. "I knew once you got over your little snit and got tired of hiding down on the coast with Rue, you'd make your way back. This is your home. Nashville. Here. This loft. Me."

I blinked at him, hid my shock behind a fake cough. "Tell me again what was so great? The fact that you videotaped me without consent? Shared it with your friends without me knowing? No, wait. Was it the cheating? The lying? Which of those things exactly, Asher?" I rubbed my chin as I thought. "No . . . maybe it was the fact that you uploaded those videos to the internet, again, without my consent, for the whole fucking world to see?"

The longer I spoke, the stiffer his posture became, a muscle ticking in his jaw. He no longer slouched on the stool, but instead stood next to it.

He narrowed his eyes. "I noticed those videos mysteriously disappeared two days ago."

"Did they?" I shrugged.

"Sadie, I was well on my way to winning that prize money. Did you fuck that up for me?"

Inwardly, I cringed. He never used to speak to me like that. Without respect. Like I was beneath him. A part of me couldn't help but wonder what I'd done wrong. This was a man that a year ago, I couldn't wait to marry. Now, I could barely stand to look at him.

I shook my head at him and tsked. "Oh, Asher, I'm pretty sure anything that's screwed up is your own fault."

"Those videos were mine, Sadie. Did you really think destroying my stuff would make it go away?" Confidence seeped back into him, his limbs relaxing, arms dangling loosely by his side, one hand stuck into the pocket of his worn jeans.

Conscious on the recording on my phone, I answered carefully. "I don't know what you're talking about."

"Did you know the renter's insurance covered the cost? I reported a break in, and our policy had an extra clause for electronics." He tapped the side of his head. "I was so glad you insisted we get that added." Taking a step closer, he taunted. "But you forgot about the cloud. Everything was backed up on the cloud."

I took a deep breath, sneaking a quick look at the clock. Twenty-one more minutes and this nightmare was over.

But first, I had to know. "Why?"

"Why what?"

I nodded slowly. "We *were* good together. Or at least, I'd thought we were. So why . . . why mess it all up? Was Becca really worth it?"

"Becca? No, she wasn't. But some of the ones who came before her?" He kept talking but the words washed right over me. In my naivety, I hadn't considered that he'd cheated on me prior to Becca. How fucking stupid I must have been to ignore all the nights he had to work late. To build our future together, I'd thought.

More like, get his dick wet.

Squeezing my eyes shut, I straightened my spine, remembered why I'd come here.

"You forgot something, too. My permission to use the footage."

He sneered. "I didn't need your permission."

Hook, line, and sinker.

"No? See, Asher, I always was the one of us who was more detail-oriented. Those pesky little things like consent and permission? They don't just apply to the sex act itself. It also applies to the distribution of any footage. And sharing it like you did? Without telling me? In a way I would never, ever, *ever* fucking approve of?" I paused, savoring the moment. "There's a name for that."

He snorted, and made a rolling gesture with his finger, telling me to get on with it.

"See, here in the fine state of Tennessee, my *home* as you pointed out earlier, they call that revenge porn." He froze, and I continued. "And it's a felony."

I stood tall in my moment of justice. He may have won a couple major battles along the way, but this, this was a conclusive victory.

"Hey, Asher?" He looked pale, eyes darting around the room, but they moved back to my face when I said his name. "Touchdown!" I whispered the word he used to shout when he emptied himself between my legs and raised my arms like goalposts before heading back toward the front door.

No reason to stay any longer.

Oh, except . . .

"Did I mention the warrant has already been issued? And the police are on their way now?" I shrugged, the very picture of innocence. God bless Rue. With her family's connections, we were able to find a topnotch lawyer who could expedite the warrant and who had a cop friend willing to show up to arrest Asher . . . in seventeen minutes. Hopefully, he wouldn't try anything stupid, like disappearing in the next few minutes. But even if he did, with an active warrant out in his name, it wouldn't be long before he was apprehended.

He lunged toward me, his fingers wrapping around my upper arm. "You won't get away with this, you fucking slut. Do you know who my dad is? There's no way the charges will stick."

I pried his fingers from my arm. "Guess we'll find out." Having gotten what I needed, I reached behind me to end the recording.

With a roar, he turned and punched the wall next to the door, his fist sailing deep through the painted drywall.

The door flew open in the same moment, a reaction from his punch I assumed, the vibration undoing the latch.

Except it was the man who haunted my all my waking thoughts that filled the opening, shoulders hunched, hands clenched, and black fury in his piercing glare.

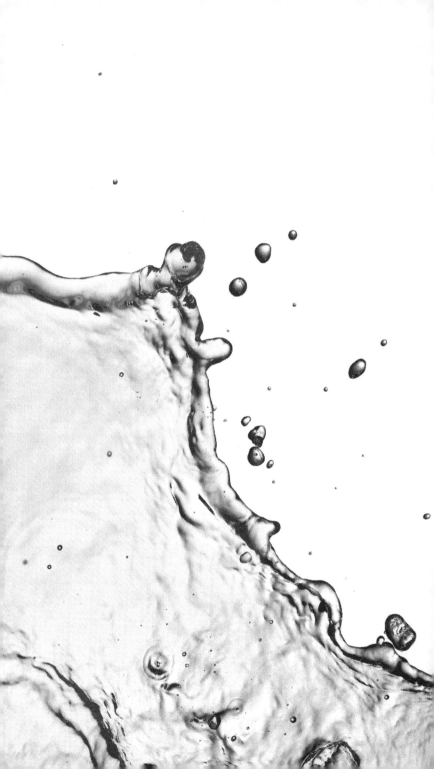

chapter
fifteen

WITH A GUTTURAL ROAR, WEST charged, catching Asher in the belly with his shoulder and driving him backwards until they both tumbled over the couch. Asher's pained cry lingered until they landed in a heap on the other side.

Shock rooted me in place, my hand covering my mouth as I gaped.

Where did West come from?

Thuds and thunks and grunts echoed off the tall ceiling, then a loud crack sounded as the wooden coffee table fell victim to the scuffle.

Rue slipped inside the partially open front door, a satisfied grin stretching across her cheeks. When she reached me, she sucked in a breath, reaching out to softly touch my upper arm with her fingertips, catching my attention. I glanced down. The red imprint of Asher's hand stood out against my tan.

"Did he hurt you?" she demanded.

Everything was happening so fast, my mind was spinning. Who cared about my arm? West was here, in Tennessee?

There was a sudden pause in activity across the room, before West bit out, his voice more savage than I'd ever heard, "You laid a hand on my girl?"

Asher squeaked out a garbled response. Something that sounded like a denial mixed in with, "Who *are* you?"

The sickening crunch of bone breaking split the air and made me wince.

"Who am I? WHO AM I?" West's arm rained down punches, although I couldn't see Asher from where I stood huddled in the entryway with Rue. "I'm the man who *loves* her. Who will protect her from scum like you who dare to even look at her the wrong way. I'm the guy who will never let you get near her again."

I scooted closer, unsure what exactly I'd see. My brain was still trying to wrap itself around the fact that West was in my old loft, battling . . . for me. Another one of the walls around my heart crumbled and fell. He wouldn't be here if he didn't care about me. Right? I bit my lip, wondering if he could kick Asher's ass without getting himself injured in the process. A small, selfish part of me wanted to see that happen. Have Asher know what it was like to feel helpless, hurt, and embarrassed. With no pride left.

A blur of movement jolted me back to the melee in front of me, where both men grappled for the upper hand.

While West was brawnier than Asher, Asher had a couple

inches on West, and he was bucking and twisting for all he was worth to free himself from the onslaught of a furious West Montgomery.

The man who still made my heart beat faster at just the sight of him.

Asher got in a solid jab to West's gut, West's breath whooshing out of him, followed up by a head butt that left them both momentarily dazed.

My stomach clenched when West wobbled, and a cry escaped my throat. I couldn't bear the thought of him getting hurt, of it being my fault.

West shook his head, rubbed his eyes, then landed a hard right hook to Asher's temple.

"How does it feel," Asher rasped, still running his mouth even as he lay sprawled and bleeding on the floor, "having my leftovers?"

"Oh, fuck no, he did not just say that," Rue hissed, darting in and stomping on Asher's ankle with her very tall, very sharp heel at the same time West cursed and put his hands around Asher's throat and started to squeeze.

When Asher's face turned a mottled purple and I started to worry West might not let go, I reached out for the back of West's shirt, fisting the fabric and trying to dislodge him from my dumbfuck ex who didn't know when to shut the hell up.

"Sadie." Rue pointed at the clock on her phone. "We've got eight minutes."

"Shit." I yanked hard twice on the back of his shirt before West glanced my way, his eyes glazed and unfocused. "Hey, we gotta go. The cops are gonna be here soon."

And the last thing I wanted was *both* of them getting hauled off in handcuffs.

West's face contorted as he straddled Asher, muscles bunching as he relaxed his grip only to slam blow after blow into whatever part of Asher he could reach. Blood covered Asher's face, his nose alarmingly crooked, and he tried in vain to block the incoming shots with his arms. He struggled to return a punch or two, until one lucky jab made it through to catch West high on the cheek, forcing West's head around to me.

I reached my hand in his direction again, tugging the torn sleeve of his T-Shirt. "West . . . West, we gotta go," I urged, real fear creeping into my voice the longer this dragged on. "You've got to get up; the cops will be here any minute to arrest him."

This was not part of the plan. I was supposed to get in, say my piece, and get out, and let the police take out the piece of trash I'd wanted to marry a year ago. While there was something innately satisfying watching Asshole get beat up by West, it was a major deviation in a tightly scheduled timeline.

"Just wanted to make sure his going away party was fucking festive," West ground out, landing two more hits before lurching to his feet. Chest heaving with exertion, he stumbled in my direction.

"Where . . ." I faltered. "How did you . . ." I didn't even know what to ask him first.

Rue slipped her hand in the crook of my elbow and started pulling me toward the door. "Not the place for a reunion, guys. C'mon, let's go."

I followed her blindly, not taking my eyes off the spectacle of West Montgomery in full warrior mode. His eyes wild and dilated, they ran over every inch of me, frantic as they drank me up, until he saw the angry red handprint on my bicep.

West's eyes narrowed to dangerous slits and the muscle in his jaw flexed as he ground his molars. He turned back one last time and bent over Asher, who was cupping his nose protectively as West loomed over him. Reaching down, he caught Asher's family jewels in his big hand, then pulled and twisted in a way that drained any remaining blood from Asher's face and had a strangled sound escaping his battered throat. "Keep your balls locked up until you learn how to use them properly, douche bag." West spat in his direction, a final insult, before stalking after me.

Scooping up my hand with his, gripping my fingers so tight I winced, he hurried me out of the building behind Rue. West was pulling me resolutely down the sidewalk when I realized she had stopped at the entrance.

"Wait!" I put a hand on his shoulder, and he stopped in his tracks, swiveling his head back toward me. "Rue?"

She waved us off. "Go on, get him out of here. I want to see Asshole getting put in the back of the police cruiser. Make sure there are no loose ends here."

I hesitated, knowing that was my job, not hers, but she rolled her eyes and pointed at West. "Him! Get him out of here and take care of *him!*"

Mouthing *thank you* to her, I let West haul me down the sidewalk, his stance rigid, and his grip unrelenting.

When we'd turned the corner and reached his truck—the big, shiny dually—I finally yanked my hand free of his as he opened the passenger door.

"Hold on a second, let go. I didn't just confront one man who bullied me only to be manhandled by another." I flexed my bloodless fingers, and shook my wrist to regain circulation.

West turned his stormy gaze on me and crowded me against the open door of his truck with his body. He reached for me so fast I flinched instinctively, jerking my head back. Taking in my reaction, his eyes softened, and when he raised his hands again, the motion was slow and measured, his touch gentle as he framed my face and rubbed his thumb along the slope of my cheek.

He took a deep breath, his chest shuddering as he exhaled, and pressed his forehead against mine, his fingers slipping to the back of my neck.

"I. Would. Never. Hurt. You." He forced each word out through clenched teeth, his shoulders still tense, despite the careful way his calloused fingers tangled in my hair until he cradled the back of my head.

I curled my fingers around his wrists.

"You've already hurt me more than he ever could."

Snatching his hands back, he recoiled as if I'd struck him. *"What?"*

"Asher." I nodded toward the building around the corner. "By the time I found that shit he'd posted online, he didn't have the power to hurt me where it mattered most." I touched my chest. *"He* embarrassed me. He used me. He took what wasn't his to share and gave it to everyone. Destroyed my trust. Sent me running from my home. I thought he broke my heart." West growled, but I continued, my leftover adrenaline fueling my own temper. "But you . . . you worked your way under my skin. Made me feel things he never made me feel. And when I realized I—" My voice cracked and I tried again. "When I realized I loved you, it was different. It was more. It was . . . better. Bigger. More intense than anything I'd ever felt for him. And then to find another woman—to find *her*—in your arms? That hurt a thousand times more than this shit here in Nashville ever will."

Straightening my spine, I stood tall as I admitted my truth and revealed my weakness. I had nothing to be ashamed of.

With either man.

As he took in my words, West deflated in front of my eyes. Wrapping me in his arms, he captured me in a loose embrace. I stood stiffly, not returning the sentiment. The warm breath from his pained sigh brushed across the sensitive shell of my ear. Ignoring my lack of response, he nuzzled into my neck, his lips hot as they skimmed my throat. I couldn't help the shiver that went down my spine, or the way my pulse skipped a beat before throbbing under his searching mouth.

His voice rumbled across my skin. "You scared the shit out of me—when Rue told me you were in there alone. That you didn't wait for the cops. Fuck, Sadie. I was about to come out of my skin."

Pressing my hands against his chest to put some distance between us, I narrowed my eyes. "See, here's the thing. When you realize you can't trust men, you learn you have to take care of the shit in your life yourself. So I did. And everything was handled just fine and dandy before you blew in there and started throwing your fists around like a Neanderthal."

"A Neanderthal, huh?" A thread of annoyance tinged his response, and his arms fell back to his sides, although he didn't step back, staying firmly planted inches in front of me.

Silence fell between us as I mentally rewound the last hour and tried to process his appearance in Nashville and what it meant.

"Wait—Rue . . . she knew you were coming? You were already here when we talked last night?" I cocked my head to the side. "The picture of the dog?"

"It was an old one I had saved on my phone." He winced at the admission before curving his hand around my hip and squeezing. "I meant every word of that text though. You belong in my bed. And that big hound has been the only one to share it with me since you left." He sucked in a breath. "I . . . heard what happened. Yesterday morning, I heard the rumor and called Rue, asking if I could help. I wanted to be here." He hesitated a moment before finishing. "In case you needed me."

"So why didn't you say something to *me*? On the phone last night? Why didn't you ask *me* what I wanted instead of just assuming?"

"You haven't been answering any of my calls!" The accusation flew from his mouth with an intensity that startled me. He took a step back, ran a hand through his hair, and gripped the back of his neck, cursing. He wouldn't meet my eyes, and his voice was so soft I barely heard him. "And I didn't want to give you a chance to say no."

The full impact of his words hit me, almost knocking me on my ass. "Wait . . . did you see the . . ." I couldn't finish the sentence.

"No." He shook his head sharply in denial, eyes blazing. "Rue had already . . . she'd already handled that. That fucker upstairs was damn lucky I didn't see them too."

My heart slammed against my ribs at the thought of him ever seeing those videos. I needed to check with her later about just how buried they were now. "What exactly was the big plan? I assume if you two were talking behind my back, you knew about the warrant, about the cops. Was kicking his ass always on the agenda?"

His eyes glinted a dark, almost navy blue in the late afternoon sun as he reached up to smooth his thumb across my cheek, then back down to brush my lower lip. "Sadie, just the idea of some asshole thinking he had the right to treat you that way . . ." A slight tremor shook his hand. "You're mine. I protect what's mine. And when I heard him threaten you . . ." He lifted my chin until his eyes seared into mine, giving me a glimpse of the turmoil that simmered just below the surface. "I snapped. I acted on raw instinct. As long as I'm around, I will never let anybody hurt you."

I tore my chin from his grip, my fear that something could have happened to him morphing into misplaced anger. "While I appreciate the misguided hero role you were going for, I had things under control."

"The fuck you did."

"Excuse me?"

"I can still see the red marks his hand left on your arm. You'd just told him you were ruining his life and then he punched a wall. Do you think he was just gonna step aside and let you walk out?"

A tendril of uncertainty spiraled in my gut. "The police were almost there—he wouldn't have tried anything."

West full out laughed in my face. "Are we talking about the same guy who didn't think twice about showing the two of you fucking to his friends and the entire goddamn world?"

The sharp echo of my palm slapping his face pierced the air.

chapter
sixteen

MY EYES FLARED IN SHOCK when I realized what I'd done. Putting his hand to his cheek, he slowly turned back to face me, eyes flat and expression unreadable.

"No one," I said shakily, pausing to take a breath and steady my words, "no one will ever talk to me like I'm a cheap piece of ass to be passed around. Not him, and definitely not you."

I tried to scoot past him but there wasn't enough room. Gritting my teeth, I shouldered my way back to the sidewalk, only to be stopped by his hand circling my wrist and stopping me.

"You know that's not what I meant." His voice was adamant. "Not how I would ever see you."

Twisting my arm free, I glared at him. "You're almost as bad as him. Whatever fucked up shit you have going on with Aubrey? If that's how you treat someone you care about, I don't want any part of it."

"Well too fucking bad. You *are* a part of it. You're the only fucking part of me that matters anymore, and I've been busting my ass trying to show you that."

My face wrinkled in confusion. "Beating up my ex-boyfriend? Yeah, you really know the way to a woman's heart."

He stared at me for a long minute, before dropping his chin to his chest and shaking his head. "Is that all you've seen? Did you not get my notes in Grand Cayman? Have you not heard about the changes—" He bit off the rest of his words.

Frustration filled his eyes and pinched his brow when he lifted his head again. "My sister, Hailey, is the strongest, smartest woman I know. And she told me actions say more than words ever will. I'm showing you, Sadie. I'm trying with everything I have to show you that you're my world. Why can't you fucking see that?" He choked out a laugh before turning away from me, stopping next to the open door of his truck. He was quiet, and I watched his chest expand and contract as he took several ragged breaths before he spoke again, his voice flat. "Get in. I'll take you back to your hotel."

"I can get a taxi, you don't ne—"

"Get. In. The. Truck."

"West, I—"

"*Sadie.* Please. Just get in the goddamn truck. I just want to know you got back to your hotel safely. That's it."

Feeling oddly guilty for the defeated slump of his shoulders and the resignation in his voice, I gave in, climbing in his giant beast of a truck without a word. He shut the door for me, before moving around to the driver seat.

He didn't look at me as he put the truck in gear. Didn't turn on the radio. Didn't try to talk. Just kept his eyes on the road and delivered me as promised to the front door of the hotel before I realized I'd never even told him where I was staying. I hesitated before opening the door, looking over at his stony expression as he stared out the windshield, his forearms stiff and unyielding as he gripped the steering wheel tightly with his fists.

His hands . . .

The knuckles were swollen, several of them torn and bloody. I gasped, reaching out instinctively to touch the back of the one closest to me. I hadn't even taken a second to catalogue his injuries—wounds he incurred on my behalf—and I was suddenly ashamed of my selfishness.

"You're hurt!"

"I'm fine."

"Let me help yo—"

"These scratches? They're nothing." He flicked his wrist dismissively, but as I peered at his face in the shadowed interior, I could already see his eye swelling and the purple bruise blooming on his cheek.

"Come inside with me. The least I can do is bandage you up after you defended my honor."

His lips twisted. "Trust me, it was my pleasure." His eyes grew stormy for a moment as he flexed his fingers, but then he glanced at me and slow smirk spread across his face, a gleam entering those eyes that should have been a warning he wasn't going to play fair. "But if you want to play doctor with me, who am I to say no?"

Before I could protest that I wasn't exactly offering up *that*, he shifted the truck back into drive and maneuvered into a parking spot. Ever the gentleman, he opened my door and helped me from his oversized vehicle, his injured hands lingering on my waist after he lowered me down.

"Which room is yours?"

"It's . . ." I faltered, remembering my purse with my hotel key was still in Rue's car. "I don't have my key."

Shaking his head at me, West continued toward the front door. "Guess we're going to my room then." Looking back over his shoulder, he winked at me with his good eye.

"You're staying here too?" I frowned as I hurried to keep up with his long strides.

"Yup."

Of course, he was.

Catching up to him, I took stock of what else I could see. Torn shirt. Scraped forearm. The corner of his lip puffy and crusted with dried blood. Shit, he might have a fracture. Or have a concussion. Were his ribs okay? His back? Maybe when we got upstairs he should take off his shirt so I could—

Yeah, he'd love it if he knew what I was thinking right then. I couldn't help the chuckle that escaped as we crossed the lobby.

"Something funny?" He slanted a glance at me as he pulled the flat, plastic hotel keycard from his back pocket and pressed the button to call the elevator.

No. Nothing about this was funny. Not really.

"Just thinking about a different elevator ride with you," I said finally.

His brow furrowed as he tried to remember, and then his face brightened. "Ah, the night you had the best sex ever?" He leaned closer, his whisper harsh, one part challenge, one part promise. "Until me."

I closed my eyes at his words. *Damn him for being right.*

The elevator doors opened, and I moved to the back. West followed, caging me with his arms against the shiny mirrored walls, crowding me until his chest touched mine. He was giving me whiplash, taking me from angry to concerned to aroused before I could settle on any one feeling. It was overwhelming, not knowing what was going to happen next with him. Not knowing what I *wanted* to happen next.

But, fuck, he made me feel alive and vital and important like no one ever had before.

"Which time was the best, do you think? That first time—in your bed? Or the time in the rain on the boat?" His lips brushed my ear as he spoke and a shiver ran down my spine, a reaction he didn't miss. He ran the tip of his tongue down the side of my neck, and I struggled to contain the moan that wanted to escape. "The stairwell at the barbeque was pretty damn hot."

His hand dropped to my hip, his fingers slipping under the edge of my shirt to caress the skin just above my waistband.

I tipped my neck—turning away from his words, not giving him better access.

Ha. Even I didn't believe that lie.

"Or maybe," he continued, pausing to press a kiss to the corner of my mouth, "maybe we haven't had our best yet."

I bit my lip and couldn't stop myself from putting a hand on his chest. Using every ounce of willpower I could muster, I pushed him back until there were a few inches between us.

"We need to get you bandaged. And talk."

The elevator stopped, the little ding as it opened breaking the moment.

He eased away from me, his expression telling me he wanted to do a lot more than simply talk, and walked down the hall, stopping two doors down from my own room.

Because, where else would his room be? I cursed Rue under my breath for not telling me.

After jamming the key in the slot, he stepped into the doorway and held the door open but didn't move out of the way. My eyes narrowed as I brushed by him, knowing from the look in his eyes that he was forcing the extra contact.

And hell if my traitorous nipples didn't tighten in response.

Trying to keep the upper hand, I snagged the ice bucket from the bathroom counter, flipped the door latch out so the door couldn't close all the way, and slipped back down the hall, needing a minute to just fucking breathe. But really, getting ice from the machine wasn't nearly long enough for me to wrap my head around what West's appearance meant.

What I wanted to do about it.

About him.

About . . . us.

When I entered his room again, he was just pulling his shirt over his head, the muscles in his back bunching as they were exposed. I tripped, almost dropping the bucket in the process.

Was it possible he'd gotten even more ripped in the two weeks we'd been apart?

I stopped in the bathroom and wet a washcloth and collected a clean hand towel. West sat on the end of the bed in all his shirtless glory, a slight smirk on his face as he watched me approach. But he was wrong if he thought I was going to fall right back in his arms, as gorgeous as they were with that Japanese wave tattoo covering the left one.

Since his knuckles looked the worst, I started there, wrapping ice up in the hand towel and gently setting that on his hand. Then I took the wet washcloth and starting wiping the bits of blood from his forearms, his neck, and his face.

As I dabbed around his swelling eye, he sucked in a sharp breath, and I paused. "You okay?"

He wrapped the fingers of his uninjured hand around my wrist, stilling my ministrations. He kissed my palm, then placed my hand over his heart, where I could feel the steady thud. "I am now."

Biting my lip, I tugged free of his grip. He let me go with a sad smile.

Wiping away the last of the obvious blood, I tucked some more ice in the rag and held it up to his discolored eye.

"What exactly do you think is okay now?" I ventured.

"Us."

Us. The word rolled around my head. Such a simple yet elusive concept.

I sighed.

"I'm not sure there is an *us* right now." He opened his mouth to protest so I kept talking. "Whatever did or didn't happen with Aubrey, the fact remains that you should've talked to me more. I get that your history with her is complicated. What I don't get is *why* it's complicated—because you've never bothered to explain it to me past the whole *we're just friends* bullshit you've fed me. And if you think some two-sentence explanation is going to clear all that up, or a couple of punches is going to make that disappear . . . you're wrong."

West lifted the ice from his knuckles, bending his fingers and wincing from the effort. Replacing the makeshift icepack, he kept his gaze lowered, not allowing me to read what was going on in that head of his. I took advantage of his distraction to let my gaze wander over him and drink him in.

He hadn't shaved in longer than normal, his usual two-day scruff replaced with something thicker. It gave him a slightly dangerous look that he worked the fuck out of. I resisted rubbing my palm along it, but I couldn't help imagining what it would feel like against other parts of me.

Like my inner thighs.

I pressed my legs together.

The tug on my arm caught me by surprise and knocked me off balance until I was perched on the end of the bed next to him, our sides touching from shoulder to hip. Scooping up my hand in his, he laced our fingers together and turned his head until our eyes locked.

"Aubrey sees me as her ticket to freedom. Her old-school Italian parents won't let her out from under their thumbs until she's married off to someone they approve of to take care of their precious princess." He rolled his eyes as he said the last part. "And seeing that our parents are best friends, they specifically want that someone to be me. Aubrey isn't interested in *me* so much as what I represent to her. What being with me would mean to her as far as moving forward with her life. And she's desperate to do that."

"Why doesn't she just leave?"

His expression hardened. "Because that Italian princess has never worked a day in her life to earn a paycheck, and her income is dependent on her either living at home or being married."

"So why doesn't she get a job?"

"Because that would actually require her to work, Sadie. And she doesn't want to do that." West sounded exasperated that he was having to spell it out for me. "She's perfectly happy to flit about manipulating people, pulling strings behind the scenes, making people think they owe her favors." He paused. "She really ought to consider going into politics, huh?"

I turned his explanation over in my head, searching for flaws, but only finding an ugly truth.

That I was just collateral damage.

But still . . .

"Why not tell me this weeks ago? And what's that got to do

with her being in your arms in Charleston?"

"I didn't tell you weeks ago because I didn't think she was a problem, and I had better things to do when I was with you than talk about *her*." Frustration colored his tone and his fingers tightened around mine as he spoke. "I've known for months, hell, maybe years, nothing serious was ever going to happen between me and her. I thought that was enough. I didn't realize you were actually threatened by her." He stopped, laughing a little. "I mean, Sadie, have you looked at yourself in the mirror? You're gorgeous. It's like comparing . . . I don't know—a hot Krispy Kreme doughnut to a picture of one. I want the one that's real, that I can touch and bite and lick and get messy with. She's a two-dimensional caricature of what a man wants. You," he let his gaze trail down me before meeting my eyes again, "you're my fucking dream come true."

My heart leapt at his words, pounding furiously within the cage of my ribs. Maybe it wasn't every girl's fantasy to be compared to a pastry, but when he started using words like *lick* and *get messy with*, I could get on board with the analogy. Lord knew I liked the way he devoured me.

"Hell, you're the dream I didn't even know I had until it happened. I'd never cared about waking up next to a girl, or trying to figure out how to make her smile, or wanting to show her all the things I loved until you tried to rescue me out in the waves that day. You did save me. I just hadn't realized it yet." He freed his hand to cup my cheek, and I leaned into his touch without thinking. I was drowning in his words. He ran his thumb across my lower lip and my tongue snuck out to steal a taste, pulling a tortured groan from West.

"And Charleston . . ." His fingers trailed down my neck before intertwining with mine again. "I hate to say she planned to sprain her ankle on my boat, but I wouldn't necessarily put it past her either. Regardless, once it happened, she milked the situation for all that it was worth. Her piece of shit dad couldn't be bothered taking his daughter to the clinic and slipped me an extra hundred to take care of that little chore for him. I'm sure he saw it as a way for us to get closer. Maybe he was hoping I'd feel protective or something, I don't know. And as much as she makes me crazy with her little stunts, I wasn't so heartless that I was just going to abandon her at the marina when she couldn't even walk."

He wasn't. And the way he loved his friends, was there for them when they needed help, was one of the things that made me fall for him in the first place.

But fucking Aubrey could take a long walk off a short plank and I wouldn't miss her.

A drop of water dripped from the rag I was still holding to his eye, tracing an icy path down my forearm. I shivered and lowered my arm.

His eye looked terrible, and bruises were starting to purple his torso and jaw beneath the scruff. I'd never had a man actually fight on my behalf before.

And it was fucking hot.

But I'd trusted Asher with my whole heart once, too, believed every pretty lie he'd spouted at me. And look where I'd ended up.

Even though I knew West wasn't Asher, it didn't make trusting him any easier.

I ghosted my fingertips over his injuries, wincing as he pulled away when I brushed a tender spot on his ribs. "You should probably get some x-rays or something," I murmured. "Or at least some decent painkillers."

He rolled his shoulders, all those delicious muscles flexing and moving under his tanned skin. "I'll live. I'll be a bit stiff tomorrow, but it's nothing you can't nurse me through tonight." He snuck a hopeful glance at me when he said that last part.

Through the night?

I couldn't help my eyes from straying to the mound of pillows on the king size bed.

Or the way my palms grew damp.

Or stop my tongue from darting out to slick my parted lips.

I can't stay.

I repeated the phrase like a litany until my thighs relaxed from the way they were pressing together.

"You know you want to." His voice was a husky dare.

I do . . .

"I can't."

"You can."

"No. I don't know exactly what we are—if we're anything— but staying the night isn't the solution."

"It'd fix one of my problems," he said, glancing at the obvious bulge in his pants.

Holy hell.

I rubbed my palms over my jeans and he cursed softly, watching the motion.

"Sadie." My belly fluttered at hearing him say my name. "I've missed you. I haven't seen you in two weeks. Are you really going to make me sleep here alone—knowing you're two doors down the hall?"

"I think . . ." I took a measured breath. "I think I just left from cleaning up the mess that happened the last time I trusted a guy. And I'm not sure I'm ready to trust another one yet. Not the way you want me to."

Disappointment flared in his eyes, the brightness that was there a moment ago dimming. "I'm not *him*." Conviction threaded his declaration.

"I know. And while your wounds are visible, that doesn't mean I don't have some too. I need some time." Tears burned my eyes, and I blinked rapidly to hold them at bay. Rising from the bed, needing to escape, I gestured at his battered-but-still-beautiful body. "Do you want me to at least find you some ibuprofen before I go?"

His laugh held no humor. "No. Ibuprofen isn't what I need." The stark need in his eyes rooted me to the spot. "You are."

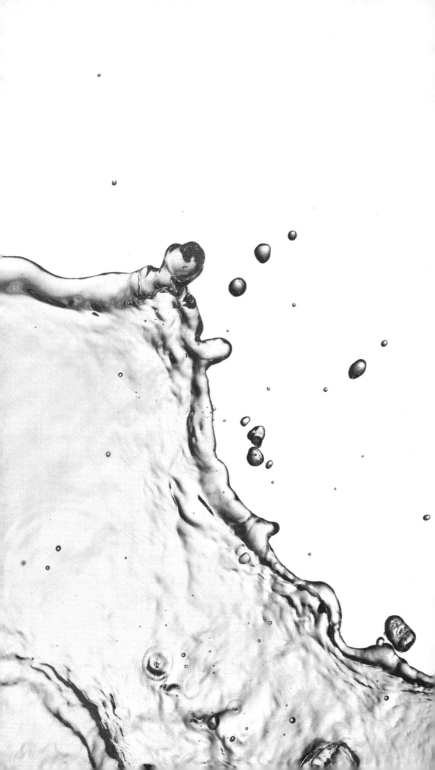

chapter
seventeen

MY FINGERS WERE WRAPPED AROUND the door handle when the heat from his chest pressing against my back seared through my thin shirt, his palm shooting out to keep the door closed.

"One last thing before you go." Hot breath fanned my neck, and my nipples tightened.

I dropped my head down, resisting the urge to turn around and throw myself into his arms, but I couldn't help leaning into him just a little. He removed his hand from the door and traced a finger down my bare arm.

"What?" I whispered.

Gripping my waist, he nudged me until I gave in, slowly spinning me around until my spine was against the door and his hips were snug against mine, his arousal hard against my stomach.

"I need you to look at me when I tell you this—so you know I mean it. So you know this isn't some game to me."

I lifted my eyes, peering at him from under my lashes.

He chuckled, tipping my chin up further. "Stubborn."

A helpless grin came and went, because it was obvious from the affection in his tone, he meant it as a compliment.

When we were face-to-face, inches apart, his expression turned solemn, but his eyes stayed soft. "I love you. And I'm never letting you out of my sight again without telling you. Without you knowing how I feel."

I swallowed down similar words clawing at my throat—needing for once to play it safe.

"You can leave, I won't stop you. Just know you're taking a piece of me with you." He leaned closer, tugging me against his chest. "You're running because you're scared. Just like you are with the damned ocean. I know trusting what you can't see isn't something you do easily." His lips were so close, the words fell against my mouth. "You're worth waiting for. You're worth everything."

He erased the last millimeter separating us, but I turned my head, my heart beating so hard he had to feel it against his own. He kissed the corner of my mouth, lingering—the moment so achingly exquisite I wanted to cry.

My fingers curled into his chest and held him against me, neither of us moving. It was too much and not enough, and I was torn between needing to escape and never wanting to let go.

With a cry, I jerked free and slipped out the door, not allowing myself to look back. Rue should be back with my purse and room key by now.

I needed time.

To break down.

To breathe.

To think.

To quiet my mind and feel my heart.

I couldn't find my way back to him until I sorted through the broken pieces inside me and reassembled myself. Separated the anger and the hurt from the embarrassment and the pain. Gave hope and truth a chance to repair the foundation and see if it was still strong enough for love to stand on, or if the damage was already irreversible.

CONDENSATION COVERED THE mirror and the bathroom was thick with steam by the time I finally emerged from the shower, my tears washed down the drain along with my cheap watermelon shampoo. While my time in there hadn't magically produced all the answers I sought, I felt cleansed clear down to my core.

I'd forgiven myself.

For loving with my whole heart, even when Asher couldn't see that for the gift it was. For letting that same trust in him blind me to what was really happening. And for running away when I found out the truth.

I stood a little straighter as I toweled off, realizing that this whole trip to Nashville was really about me—not him. It was about regaining my own self-respect by not allowing him to walk all over me, continue to use me for his own selfish gain. And I'd done that.

Well, Rue had helped.

And West had pounded the message home for good measure.

But I'd done it.

I'd closed the chapter of my life with Asher's name in the heading and accomplished it with decisiveness and confidence.

And, most importantly, on my own terms.

But this was the kicker. The realization that knocked me on my ass.

I could trust *myself*.

I wasn't broken beyond repair or unlovable or only destined for heartbreak.

I'd made a choice, invested my all, and when it turned sour, I'd saved my own damn self.

And I could do it again.

The mistake would be in living half-heartedly. Running scared. Letting fear hold me back. Not experiencing the full range of emotion life was waiting to clobber me with next.

My nerves hummed with excitement, and my mind jumped repeatedly to the room two doors down, where West waited in a room identical to this one.

After pulling on the first clothes my hands touched from my suitcase, I twisted my hair into a messy bun, not wanting to waste valuable time trying to dry it with the crummy hair dryer attached to the bathroom wall.

Adrenaline rushed through my veins, making my nerves sing, as I slipped on some rubber flip flops.

West.

I had to see him. Talk to him. Touch him and see if my pulse raced and my breath caught and my skin prickled. Let down my guard and see if he still sparked that part of my soul where it felt like I could never get enough and he was the only thing who could make it better.

The addiction and the cure rolled into one potent package.

I wanted to listen to the rumble of his words, run my hands over all that new scruff, and taste his sincerity.

I wanted to explore new beginnings and rekindled passion.

I wanted to believe that tomorrow would be better.

After jotting down a quick note for Rue, who'd left to get some dinner to give me some space when she discovered me sobbing in the shower earlier, I slid the extra room key I'd gotten from the front desk downstairs into the back pocket of my jeans and hurried down the hall.

Eager. Smiling. Ready.

I knocked impatiently, somehow surprised he hadn't read my mind and flung open the door when I stopped in front of it. I strained to hear his footsteps, but only silence greeted me.

Wrinkling my brow, I reached down to jiggle the door handle, and that's when I first noticed it.

The paper airplane with my name scrawled across the wing wedged between the handle and the doorframe.

I don't know why, but this plane, its mere presence outside his room, waiting for me, seemed ominous.

Cradling it in my hands, I sank against the locked door.

My fingers traced the edges, hesitant to know what kind of message was delivered by hotel stationary and an empty room.

I bit my lip as I unfolded it, smoothing the creases on my thigh.

It was short—just four lines.

> *Sadie—*
> *I couldn't stand being so close and having you push me away again.*
> *I knew sleep wouldn't find me—not without you in my arms.*
> *The open road and hours between us seemed the best way not to make a bigger fool of myself.*
> *Find me when you're ready—you know where I'll be.*

He'd signed it *Yours. Always.* Two separate promises, underlined with a harsh slash, the line so deep it dug into the paper, leaving indentations I could trace.

He'd left.

He'd left.

He'd *left.*

I closed my eyes against the painful constriction in my chest.

I'd told him I needed time. And he'd given it to me. My fist crumpled his words.

"I'm trying to show you . . . Hailey said actions speak louder than words . . ."

He wasn't the only one who would have trouble sleeping

tonight.

Pushing to my feet and numbly returning to my own empty room, I formulated a backup plan.

Drinking my way through the mini-bar.

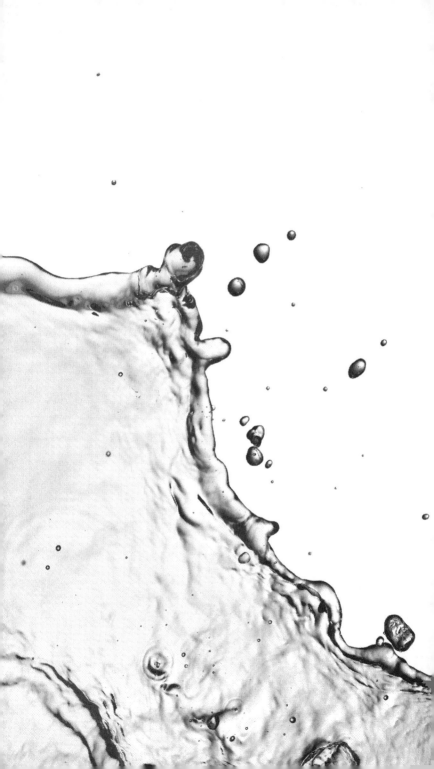

chapter

eighteen

THEO GRUNTED HIS DISAPPROVAL. It had been two days and I was back on Reynolds Island, trying to lose myself in some semblance of normalcy. And even though I was sweating like a pig, he still wasn't happy.

"You slacked off while you were gone, didn't you?" He pressed his palm against my back, pushing me lower into the plank position I was shaking to maintain. "Right there. Hold it. Thirty more seconds."

I called him every dirty word I could think of, including a few I made up, in that half a minute. He grinned the whole time.

"It wouldn't hurt so bad if you'd kept up with the workouts I sent you."

"I was *busy*." I collapsed on the mat and glared up at him as I gasped for air like a fish out of water, sweaty tendrils of hair plastered to my face.

He shook his head in annoyance. "Excuses, excuses. Roll over. Russian twists, thirty on each side."

I groaned, my ab muscles protesting every movement as I turned on my back and forced my way through the reps.

"Come on, faster, you're better than this. Watch your form."

"What the hell, Theo? Is Chelsea the redhead gone? Are you not getting laid and taking it out on me?"

He crossed his arms as he watched me struggle through his evil torture of my midsection. "She left two weeks ago. And, yes, I've hit a bit of a dry spell."

"Twenty-nine, thirty," I muttered, falling back and crossing my forearms protectively over my stomach. I was dizzy from the exertion, and my heart pounded against my heaving ribs. "And I haven't gotten any action either, but you don't see me punishing you because of it."

He squatted next to me. "And we're gonna talk about all of that over breakfast. The one you're not getting until you finish your workout."

I lolled my head in his direction and squinted up at him. "You know I hate you right now, don't you?"

"Did I mention we're having Krispy Kremes on the beach?"

I closed my eyes and sighed, already tasting the warm sugar melting in my mouth. "Did I say hate? Hate's a strong word. And I might have misspoken. Love—love might be what I meant to say."

He chuckled. "That's better." Reaching down, he hauled me to my feet and steered me by the shoulders to the dreaded treadmills.

I stopped mulishly in front of them.

"One mile, whatever speed you want. But the faster you go, the quicker we get to eat." He raised one eyebrow and smiled, knowing he'd won this round.

I grumbled under my breath as I climbed on and punched the buttons to start the machine. "You know it's really not fair that you use my weakness for doughnuts against me like this."

"Life isn't fair. Get moving."

"Slave driver."

"Your ass will thank me later."

"There's nothing wrong with my ass," I fired back, legs aching with every stride. The slow jog I attempted was all I could muster.

"Because I work your tail off."

I huffed at him, annoyed that he'd gotten the last word in, but I didn't have a good comeback. Theo really was an excellent trainer, the arrogant piece of shit.

Twelve excruciating minutes later, I slowed the machine to a crawl for a five-minute cool down. The towel I used to wipe my face and neck was already damp from my sweat earlier and didn't do much to dry me off. "I'm gonna need a shower first."

"Hell, yeah, you are. I'm not getting in a car with you smelling like that."

The smirk on his face disappeared when I threw the terrycloth towel at him and nailed him right in the face. "Nice, Sadie. Real mature." He plucked the towel off him by the edge and held it away from him like it was contaminated as he carried it to the laundry basket in the corner to get rid of it. "Just for that, you're paying for the coffees."

Coffee. I swallowed back a moan. The sweet, sweet taste of Starbucks and caffeine. And *Krispy Kremes.* This early in the morning, the HOT NOW sign would still be lit.

Theo pointed across the gym to the locker rooms. "Go get your shower and I'll run down the street to get the doughnuts. I'll meet you next door at Starbucks."

I didn't need to be told twice. After a quick fist bump, we headed our separate ways.

The shower area was empty, so no one witnessed my contortionist moves as I struggled to undress. Was there anything in the world harder than removing a sweaty sports bra? Especially when the end of my ponytail got tangled up in it while I tried to yank it over my head.

After washing off the stink and spraying some product in my hair that promised miraculously frizz-free beach waves, I threw on an orange oversized T-shirt I paid way too much for in Grand Cayman, some Nike gym shorts, and my trusty rubber flip flops.

My stomach growled in greedy anticipation as I walked as fast as my sore thighs would carry me to the coffeehouse next door. No sign of Theo yet, but that was fine. He always ordered the same thing, so I knew what to get. A tall, black coffee. Plain. So boring.

By the time I had my caramel latte with whipped cream, his coffee, and a bottle of water for each of us, Theo was pulling into a parking spot, the familiar green and white box visible on the passenger seat. I handed him the drinks and climbed in, settling the box on my lap before taking the holder with the coffees back. I started to lift the lid to steal a glazed one en route, but Theo reached over and smacked it closed again.

"Nuh-uh. No doughnuts until you spill the details about what happened while you were gone. And what the hell is going on with you and West?"

"Nosy."

He glanced over at me and I could see the concern etched across his boyish face. His hair was a bit longer, the dark curls giving him a sweet puppy dog look. "Don't even try to play that card. Rue already told me she couldn't get much out of you, but that you've cried more in the last two days than you did in the first week after Asshole . . . you know. Last Christmas. When you first came down here."

"So you and Rue are ganging up on me?"

"Yup. She tried being nice cop. Time for me to pull out the big guns." He let go of the steering wheel with one hand and flexed, showing off his admittedly impressive bicep.

I rolled my eyes. "Oh no, not the big guns."

We both laughed as he dropped the cheesy pose.

Biting my lip, I stared at the swaying palm trees lining the road as we headed toward the quiet section of beach we preferred for our sugar-laden breakfasts. While I didn't like involving other people in my love life, talking it out with Theo might not be the worst idea ever. A guy's perspective might help me see things more clearly.

Or not.

Guys were fucking weird, after all.

But Theo was coming from a good place. He wasn't fishing for gossip. I knew he genuinely cared about my happiness.

I sighed. Plus, he was serious about withholding my beloved doughnuts if I didn't talk to him.

Damn doughnuts.

I'd blame this beachside confessional on them.

Theo let me stew in my own thoughts until we were comfortably settled on an old striped quilt halfway between the dunes and the foamy edge of the water, coffees in hand and the still-closed box of heaven nestled between us. I kicked my flip flops off and dug my toes into the cool sand, stalling.

"You're really gonna make me talk, aren't you?"

"Yup."

I grumbled. "Where do you want me to start?"

He turned his head, his expression neutral. "Where do you need to start?"

"You're not really cutting me any slack here, are you?" I twisted my lip in annoyance as I tried to appeal to his soft spot for me.

"Nope. You need to work through this shit, for your own peace of mind, if nothing else." He met my gaze, raising his eyebrows. "And we both know you're avoiding doing that."

I fought the urge to stick out my tongue at him like a child.

"Fine." Unable to look at him while I laid myself bare, I recapped the few days before I left for Grand Cayman. The photoshoot with West, Hailey, and Cody. Realizing my feelings for West had tipped from like to love. Aubrey appearing half-naked on West's balcony and her pictures tucked in his nightstand. The week of shitty communication leading up to my trip to Charleston, where I watched my worst nightmare come true. West cradling that skank in his arms as he walked along the dock, completely oblivious to the way he was shattering my heart.

I hit the highlights of our confrontation outside Anchor, glossing over some of the more naked details from the parking lot. Then I admitted to not being able to read the paper planes right away during my trip. Saving them for almost two weeks before I could bear to look.

The photoshoot with Nick I omitted, choosing to avoid that memory as much as possible for now. Guilt niggled at me whenever it crossed my mind. Guilt that, I reminded myself, I shouldn't feel since I'd told West it was over before I left.

When I haltingly brought up the videos Asshole had uploaded, Theo's cheeks blazed with color and he stared fixedly at the water in the distance.

"You saw them, didn't you?"

The noncommittal noise he made was answer enough. I groaned, burying my face in my hands.

"Let's just say, I didn't need any further clarification about what he did."

Taking a deep breath, I snaked my hand out and popped open the box, snagging a warm glazed pastry and taking the biggest bite I could. Theo didn't say anything as I chomped my way through the first treat, barely tasting it over the bitterness that rose in me whenever I thought of Asher.

"Can I just say, on behalf of decent men everywhere, that what he did was beyond shitty. Utterly reprehensible. And I'm so fucking glad you escaped from that mess before he put a ring on your finger."

Theo wrapped an arm around my shoulder and squeezed me in an awkward side hug.

Memories of dumping Asher's beloved electronics in the tub and giving them a bubble bath flitted through my mind. One of my better moments, if I did say so myself.

"Yeah," I agreed. "Marrying him would've been a mistake of epic proportions."

"So, Rue told you about the . . ." Theo coughed and waved his hand between us. " . . . the thing. And then what?"

I sighed, picking up another doughnut and taking a small nibble as I continued my analysis. We covered my frantic departure, my moment of weakness where I called West in Miami, the showdown at my old loft in Nashville, and West's unexpected arrival to finish the confrontation with Asshole with a bang.

My words got slower as I recounted the events from the hotel. My epiphany after I bandaged West. The note I found when I'd sought him out.

The fact that we hadn't spoken since.

"Why not?" Theo asked, wrinkling his nose as he tipped his head at me, the angle of the morning sun making him squint. He took a doughnut for himself and studied me as he joined me in our carbohydrate lovefest.

"Because," I started, then hesitated. "Because now I've had too much time to think about things. To *over* think them. To wonder if maybe it's all too little, too late. Or if, despite what he says about me, I'm not really what he needs right now."

"What the hell is that supposed to mean?"

"I mean, as much as I hate to admit it, Aubrey's right. My reputation, whatever positive image I'd started to build here, it's in the gutter after this. I'm an internet slut with no morals in the eyes of most of the island, I'm sure. West comes from old money. He's trying to build a respectable business for himself. Who am I to latch onto him and tarnish everything he's worked toward? And we both know how much he cares about his family. There's no way they'd ever accept me after this." I paused to take a long swallow of coffee, relishing the way the hot liquid burned my throat. "Plus, who knows if I even have a job anymore? I have to call Grady tomorrow and see where I stand with the resort. If I'm lucky, I'll be able to finish out the season as a lifeguard. I seriously doubt I'll be booking any photography jobs."

I tore off another bite, barely chewing it before I swallowed it. My movements were stiff, jerky. Fucking Asher. Fucking Aubrey.

And, hell, while we're at it—fucking West. Why couldn't he have been just some normal guy trying to get his shit together? Instead of being practically island royalty? Even if it was a title he didn't embrace. Maybe then, none of this would matter. Or at least, not as much.

"You're nuts."

I whipped my head to glare at Theo. "Excuse me?"

"You. Are. Nuts," he repeated, enunciating each word slowly, and pointed at me for emphasis. "Do you really think West gives a shit about any of that? That any guy who's gone to the lengths he has would? You could try giving the guy a little credit. Give him a chance to make up his own damn mind instead of you trying to do it for him."

"I'm just trying to be honest with myself. And do the right thing, even if he doesn't see it."

"Since when is breaking the guy's heart ever the right thing to do?" I started to protest, but Theo waved my words away. "Okay, okay, okay. I'm not saying West is perfect. That he didn't make some missteps along the way. The dude definitely could've communicated better, and I don't know what the fuck to tell you about those pictures in his room—but I know him. And I've never seen him this way over a girl before. Not until you." Theo took another doughnut, biting into the soft pastry. He wagged it at me and talked around a mouthful of sugar. "You need to give him a chance. You owe it to him and you owe it to yourself. Don't screw yourself out of the best thing that might ever happen to you."

I bit my lip, my eyes hot and stinging at his words. Damn it with all the tears the last few days! I pretended the wind kicked some sand up, and surreptitiously wiped at my face.

Maybe Theo was right. I needed to find West.

And have a seriously long overdue conversation with the man I couldn't get off my mind.

Or out of my heart.

chapter
nineteen

I COULDN'T FIND HIM.

Not at the Wreck. Not at the beach house he shared with his
brother, Wyatt. Not at the marina. Although, the charter fishing
boat he owned and captained, the *Vitamin Sea*, was missing from
its usual spot at the dock.

I wanted to find him in person.

The stuff I wanted—no, *needed*—to say, it wasn't the kind of
thing I wanted to deliver over text, or a cut-off voicemail message.

I wanted to see his face when I said the words. Touch his skin.
Hear his reply. Maybe even jump in his arms.

And I couldn't do any of that through electronics.

I glared at the empty expanse of water where his boat normally
bobbed. The ocean, my eternal nemesis, had stolen West from me,
whisked him out of my reach. With a sigh, I left the little present

I'd brought along. I tucked it under the edge of the heavy-duty, two-inch rope that wrapped around one of the dock pilings, and prayed it wouldn't blow away before he found it. It was the first paper airplane I'd ever made for *him*. The folded design was pretty basic, nothing like some of the intricate ones he'd crafted for me in the past. And the message was short. Only three words.

I miss you.

But they cut to the heart of what I wanted him to know until we could meet face-to-face.

That night, I tossed and turned for hours, restless to my core from the unfinished business I had with West. I wanted us to hash things out so we could move forward, whether that meant together or separately. My mind was adrift with memories of us—good memories. I'd pushed the bad from my head for now, choosing to believe that we'd earned this chance at happiness together.

Aubrey wouldn't tear us apart. Or Asher.

Or my own fucking insecurities.

Now, if I could just find the man haunting my thoughts and dreams, maybe I could finally find some peace.

I didn't know what time it was when the bed dipped beneath the weight of his body settling behind me, but the stars had been out for hours, and silver slices of moonlight through the wooden blinds made stripes across my patchwork quilt. Heat from his bare chest warmed me through my thin tank top, my back arching to meet him, nipples already hard and aching. I started to turn, but his arm slid around my stomach and tightened, holding me in place. His citrus-and-salt scent surrounded me, welcoming me home.

A sense of peace flowed through me. A feeling of completeness. My bed didn't seem so empty anymore.

"No. Just like this." His lips brushed my ear as he spoke the words and my whole body shuddered.

Biting my lip, I ran my hand over his arm, loving the way his corded muscles rolled and flexed under my palm and his sun-bleached arm hair tickled. He groaned softly and flexed his hips forward until he was flush with my ass, his arousal nestled against me. I pushed back against him without thinking, just wanting to get closer to him.

Warm lips teased my ear and then meandered down my neck, nibbling and sucking, a trail of goose bumps lingering in their wake. My spine undulated beneath his teasing touch. Part of me loved it when he took it slow, but the other part of me wanted to be taken, fast and hot and hard and *now*. I snaked my arm between us and gripped him, squeezing and stroking along his considerable length once, twice.

"Fuck." He hissed, reaching down to cover my fingers with his own, tightening my grip. He bucked his hips and groaned low against my shoulder, before pulling both of our hands away from his throbbing cock. "I won't last if you keep that up. I've missed you too much."

His teeth sunk into my shoulder without warning and I gasped, squeezing my eyes closed in surrender. *Yes!*

He slid his callused hand under the hem of my shirt, stroking the soft skin of my stomach before inching higher. His thumb brushed the underside of my breast, and I squirmed within his embrace, eager for him to continue its upward journey.

I murmured his name, a feverish plea for more.

"I've got you, Sadie. And I'm not letting go again." His husky words melted me. All that was left was the pool of desire he created.

He cupped my breast, and I was happy for once that my B-cups weren't any larger. I filled his hand perfectly, my sensitive flesh responding to every stroke of his sea-roughened palm. I copied his move from earlier, covering his fingers with my own, making him squeeze me harder, give me more.

"Mmmm, impatient?" Laughter lurked in his teasing words.

"For you? Always." Admitting that didn't make me feel weak like I thought it might. Instead, I felt freed. Lighter. I rolled my hips against his shaft, backing up my words with action.

When he let go of my chest I wanted to cry out from the loss, but he moved quickly, pushing my back flat against the mattress and making himself at home between my parted thighs. Stitches ripped in my tank top, he tore it off me so fast. My underwear disappeared in the same fashion.

And I fucking loved it.

When the heat of his mouth settled over one nipple and his fingers pinched the other, I almost came unglued and arched wildly into his touch, my mouth opened in a silent scream. *Yes yes yes yes yes!*

My nails scratched erratic lines up his back, wrenching a

muffled curse from West, and I clutched at his hair. It'd grown out some and was just long enough for me to grip now. The scruff on his jaw added another layer of roughness to his caress as his tongue swiped at my pebbled bud, sucking it hard between his firm lips.

I wrapped my legs around his hips, digging my heels into the small of his back, and panted like the bitch in heat I was at the moment. He surrounded me, covered me, and I never wanted him to leave.

He switched sides, his sharp teeth nipping at the other peak just to the edge of pain before soothing the sting with his tongue, then starting the process over. His other hand squeezed and molded my swollen flesh, his fingers teasing the already sensitized nipple he'd left behind.

My head thrashed against the pillow and my hips jerked helplessly against his length of his cock where it slid along my wet seam. He rubbed against me, coating himself in my slickness, the broad head of his arousal bumping into my clit on occasion, stealing a sharp cry of bliss from me each time he did.

I pushed on his shoulders, and he took the hint, licking his way down my stomach, stopping only to explore my hipbone, before following the dip inward on a beeline to the small bundle of nerves that so desperately wanted his attention. Without preamble, he latched on, sucking my clit like it was sweet, sweet candy and he couldn't get enough.

My eyes shot open at the initial stroke of his tongue, then slowly drifted closed again, my hips matching the rhythm he set with his mouth. He lifted my thighs over his shoulders and buried his face between my legs, feasting on me like he wouldn't be satisfied until he'd had seconds or thirds. My breathing turned ragged, catching as the tension built higher within me.

"West!" Two long fingers buried themselves in me, twisting and curving to seek the one spot guaranteed to curl my toes.

Was there anything more erotic than a man bent on pleasing a woman with every ounce of concentration he had? The sight of him, tongue slipping out to tease, hand thrusting, shoulders bunching, his dark hair between my fingers—it was almost enough to send me over the edge.

My hips bucked when his fingers caressed the most sensitive spot inside me, and everything tightened in response. I bit my lip, and fought the tide rising within me threatening to crest. I never wanted this feeling that zinged up my spine and built higher and higher to ever end. As if he knew what I was doing, he doubled his efforts, his fingers pumping in and out of me, the smell of my musky arousal filling the air, and his tongue trying out a new tempo. The unfamiliar roughness from his scruffy chin brought a surprising new element to the act, one I thoroughly enjoyed. I rocked higher, needing just a bit more, and he sucked hard, swirling his tongue at the same time.

It was as inevitable as a wave crashing onto shore. I peaked, screaming his name, pressing him to me as I rode out my orgasm. He didn't stop, didn't slow. When it got to be too much, and I weakly pushed him away, he rose over me, fingers weaving with mine, and slid inside with one sure thrust, his firm lips capturing mine at the same time.

The solid weight of his chest crushing my breasts anchored me to the moment, and brought me back down from the clouds I'd been floating in. He demanded my attention, here, now. All of me, stretched out under all of him. The urgency of his movements told me he wasn't done with me yet, and a delicious shiver ran down my spine. I moaned as I rubbed my toes against his calves, unable to get close enough.

While his arms pinned mine above my head and our hips dueled, his wicked mouth claimed me. Marked me. Devoured me. And I surrendered, my body more than happy to be owned by his.

His tongue licked deep, seeking mine in a frenzied dance, then retreated to trace my bottom lip. I'd forgotten the thrill that came from just kissing him. That slide of lips and clash of teeth and the lingering taste of myself on his tongue and the way he barely paused to steal a breath before coming back for more, like any second apart was too long.

My senses were overwhelmed in the best way and I clung to him as we moved together. His chest rubbed my tender nipples as he rocked above me, sinking to the hilt with each plunge. I followed his lips where they led and met his hips with my own and when a second orgasm began to rise even as the first still retreated, I gripped his tight ass and moved faster, chasing it.

He tore his lips from mine and buried them against my damp neck, sucking the soft skin just below my ear.

"Sadie." He chanted my name as his motions lost finesse, his coordination forgotten as he sought his own release.

And then he froze, taut as an arrow, the ecstasy written in the pinch of his brows and open mouth and slack jaw. He pumped softly a few more times, before slipping a finger between us and flicking my clit, sending me overboard with him.

I had no doubt my nails left crescent-shaped indents behind, one hand clutching his nape, the other his shoulder blade.

He sank onto me, and his weight should have smothered me, but I loved his heavy solidness along my hypersensitive skin after I came apart so hard. I sighed with contentment when he nuzzled farther into the crook of my neck, his dark scruff tickling me. My hands roamed his broad back, happy just to feel all that hot flesh, to stroke it and have his muscles respond to the caress.

His arms stole around me, shifting to hold his bulk so he didn't crush me. His softened member was still in me, still connecting us.

"I love it when I come to your bed, and you smell like that watermelon shampoo you use, but then we do this," he paused to roll his hips against mine, "and you smell like *us* instead."

"You like us?"

"No. I *love* us."

A beeping sounded in the background, soft but insistent. I ignored it. There were more important things we needed to worry about.

"West, I need to tell yo—"

He lifted his head up and squinted into the pale light of dawn beginning to fill the room.

"What's that noise?"

The beeping was louder now, harsh and grating. I rolled my eyes, then snagged his chin and tugged until he was looking at me again. "I don't know. What I'm trying to say—"

"Is that yo—"

Noooooo.

My eyes flew open, my *own* hand buried in my wet panties, fingers slick with arousal.

But it was.

It was, indeed.

My fucking alarm destroyed the best dream I'd had in weeks.

I buried my head in my pillow and screamed my frustration. A pillow that smelled only of watermelon shampoo.

The clock made a satisfying crunch as it shattered in pieces against the far wall, found guilty of the crime of simply doing its job.

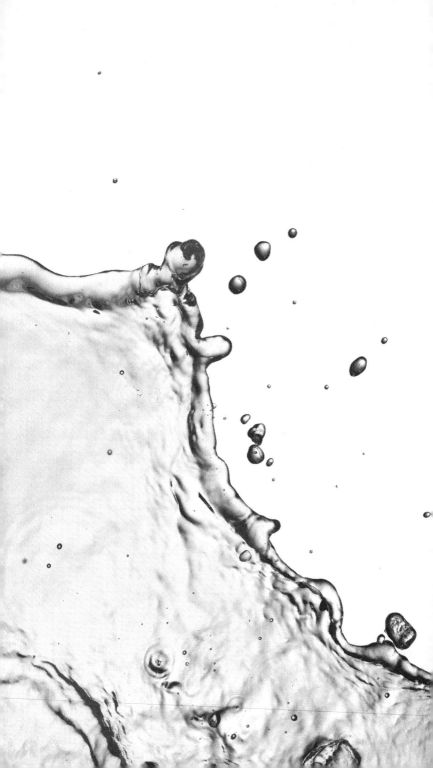

chapter
twenty

I TURNED INTO THE PARKING LOT of the Wreck and checked the display on the dash of my Wrangler. Just a few minutes before three. Made it with time to spare. After setting the brake, I ran my hands over my hair. The unruly strands refused to lay sleek against my scalp no matter how many products I used, the humidity once again winning the battle of the frizz. When Hailey had texted me earlier in the day and asked me to meet her here this afternoon, promising the bar West owned with Wyatt would be empty except for a few diehard regulars, I'd been hesitant to reply at first. I didn't want my first run-in with her brother to be in a public place if I could help it.

Hailey: He won't be here. He's in St. Augustine for two more days in a big tournament, if that's what you're worried about.

Me: That hadn't even occurred to me.

Hailey: Suuuuuuure, it didn't. You have no excuse. I'll see you later today.

No doubt, she was rolling her eyes as she saw right through my feeble denial. But here I was, unsure exactly why West's little sister had summoned me. I checked the small mirror on the visor one last time, just in case this was a trick and he really was waiting inside.

West was sneaky.

I wouldn't put it past him to use his sister to arrange a surprise meeting. Although, his boat had been missing from the marina yesterday, lending some credence to the fishing tournament story.

I sighed, knowing the only way to discover who was waiting in the bar was to just go into the ramshackle building and find out. I'd missed the ambience of the place in the weeks I'd been gone. The casual hominess of the picnic table seating, the Coleman coolers of peanuts and the children's sand buckets to scoop them out with, the graffiti on every flat surface, and the dollar bills covered with Sharpie-scrawled pick-up lines pinned around the bar itself. It was the type of place you could relax and just be yourself.

I tugged on my loose navy tank top and fingered the frayed edge of my cutoff shorts as I picked my way over the crushed oyster shells that covered the parking lot. Pausing outside the weathered door, I took a deep breath, well aware that my pulse had picked up its pace simply because I was at a place I associated with West.

Straightening my spine, I pulled open the heavy door and

slipped inside, my eyes needing a minute to adjust to the dim interior after the harsh glare of the Lowcountry sun. Peanut shells crunched under my flip flops as I wove past the tables to the bar, where I spotted Hailey cutting up fruit behind the counter for the Wreck's signature grog. With her sandy hair pulled back in a simple French braid and no makeup on her face to hide her freckles, she looked far too young to be manning a bar, let alone be the mother of a precocious two-year-old son.

Hailey smiled a silent greeting and pushed a cutting board, paring knife, and a bag of apples across the bar to me, making me grin as I remembered the last time we cut up fruit together, when I'd worked to pay off the shot I'd downed before realizing I didn't have any money with me. Fishing a Granny Smith out of the bag, I began to methodically dice it, wondering what this whole meeting was about.

"How was your trip?" She shot me a huge smile as she sliced grapes in half. "I've missed you!"

I hesitated, hope bubbling up inside me. Was it possible she hadn't heard of my internet porn fiasco?

"I mean . . ." She rolled her eyes and waved her hand dismissively through the air, still holding the knife. " . . . besides that fucked up stuff your ex did."

I deflated. Of course, she'd heard about it.

Everyone knew, apparently.

I opened my mouth then closed it again, unsure what to say. Certain parts of my tropical adventure didn't need to be shared—with anyone. "The island was beautiful. I even went paddleboarding a few times, if you can believe it. And the photos I took there were some of my best work yet, but I don't know if any of that matters. I haven't talked to Grady yet . . . I'm not sure if he still plans on using them. I doubt it."

"Why wouldn't he?"

"My name . . ." I scowled. "Asher did a pretty good job of screwing me over." Hailey froze in the act of chopping, and I mentally replayed what I just said. "Oh, God. Not like that. That's not what I meant." I buried my face in my hands, unable to meet her eyes.

When she giggled, I peeked through my fingers at her. "Sorry. But that word choice was priceless."

I attacked the apple in front of me a little harder than was necessary. "It's just . . . I was starting to find myself again, ya know? And then he swooped back in and destroyed me. For a second time. Who the hell does stuff like that?"

"Assholes," she said solemnly. "Assholes who don't deserve to ever call themselves men."

I nodded and we worked in silence for a few minutes, with me ignoring the questioning looks she kept shooting my way. Finally, I dropped my knife and threw my arms up in the air. "What is it? You obviously brought me here to talk about something. Let's talk."

Pushing her wooden cutting board aside, she leaned over the bar, resting on her elbows and propping her chin on her hands. Her face lit up with excitement, and her eyes shone with unbridled curiosity. "Is it true? Did West really show up and kick that guy's ass? I know he went up there, but he won't talk about what happened. At least, not with me."

My jaw fell open in shock. "*That's* what you want to talk about?"

"One of the things." She shrugged, looking sheepish. "I'm just trying to picture West riding up there to rescue you, all knight-in-shining-armor style."

I narrowed my eyes. "While I'm not denying that he did give that piece of scum the beat down he deserved, let the record show that I had the situation firmly under control before he arrived."

Hailey dropped her arms to the bar and her eyes widened. "*You* were kicking his ass?"

I tipped my head to one side then the other, then smiled with satisfaction at the memory. "Even better. I had him arrested. Let's just say I wanted to give him the gift that would keep on giving, the same way he did to me with those videos."

She stared at me, frozen as she absorbed my words. "I think you're my hero," she finally managed.

I threw back my head and laughed, a loud, genuine belly laugh. "That's a girl's secret weapon—the one men never seem to expect. Revenge."

With the ice broken between us, I turned the conversation back in her direction, and she caught me up on the antics of Cody. Ever since I'd pulled him from the bottom of her grandma's pool earlier in the summer, I'd felt a bond with the adorable red-headed two-year-old. Hailey had me in stitches over an incident where he wanted to help feed his Jack Russell, Edison, and kept refilling the bowl every time the dog emptied it. Only, Cody was feeding the dog Froot Loops. By the time Hailey discovered what had happened, the box was empty . . . and Edison puked all afternoon. Which she also didn't realize until she found Cody covered in dog vomit. Rainbow-colored dog vomit.

She glared at me as I covered my mouth to hide my mirth. "I have a childproof cover over the pantry door handle now."

A tear slipped down my cheek and I hopped up from the barstool. "Oh God, I gotta pee. I'll be right back."

I hurried past picnic tables and dodged my way around the games on the side, air hockey, foosball, and pool tables. Three guys were shooting pool and gave me a passing glance as I rushed by. I pushed open the door marked Ladies and slid into the first stall, barely making it in time before my bladder released. Taking a deep breath, I looked at the walls in confusion.

Last time I'd been in here, scrawled messages—declarations of love, snarky comments about unfaithful guys, and, most memorably, a life-sized drawing of West's erection—had covered the painted walls. But now, they were blank. Just a fresh coat of warm turquoise paint.

Finishing my business, I ducked my head into the other empty stalls.

No writing. Anywhere.

I washed my hands, mulling it over. I wasn't exactly heartbroken to have all the scribblings of the West Montgomery Fan Club gone. It'd always made me uneasy to see how many girls lusted over West—or claimed to know him intimately.

Pensive, I paid more attention as I returned to the bar. The graffiti out here still covered the walls, but all the picnic tables had a new coat of whitewash. The old markings still showed through, they were just faded now. Newer doodles darkened the surfaces here and there, but it had all been toned down a notch while still maintaining the same casual, lived-in atmosphere.

Hailey eyes sparkled as she watched me look around, a knowing smirk pulling on her lips. "You finally noticed, huh?"

I scrunched my eyebrows together. "West and Wyatt made some changes?"

She paused a beat, watching me. "West did. Wyatt went along with it."

"But . . . why?"

She raised her eyebrows at me pointedly and plucked another strawberry from the pile to slice. When the silence stretched, she sighed, putting the knife down on the cutting board. "You," she said simply.

"I don't understand."

"It's—" She waved her hand toward the bar. "—a sign. He wanted the crap all those chicks throw his way gone. But more than that, he wanted to show he wasn't available. Maybe they got the message, maybe they didn't. But, mostly, he did it out of respect for you. To show you he was serious."

Unable to meet her intent gaze, I carefully sliced the rest of the apple into precise, equal pieces.

I've tried to show you. West's words echoed in my mind.

"Did he tell you that?" I didn't look at her as I asked the

question. My focus stayed on my task, as if her answer didn't matter.

As if my heart wasn't slamming against the cage of my ribs, threatening to escape.

When she didn't answer, I finally stole a quick glance at her. She was smiling softly at me.

"He didn't have to."

Hot tears burned the back of my eyes, and I bit my lip.

"Have you talked to him yet?" She pitched her voice low, hesitant with her question.

I shook my head, and swallowed the lump in my throat. I hadn't expected this. It was just paint, but it felt so much bigger.

The wisest person I know, my sister, told me actions speak louder than words.

"Did you tell him to do it? Was this remodeling your idea?"

"No, Sadie. This was all West. I might have suggested that he needed to up his game where you're concerned, but that's it."

I nodded, relieved, and slid the apple chunks over to her. Without a word, she handed me four mangoes. We worked in silence for long minutes, the only sounds the clink of the pool balls and the steady *thwap* of our knives on the cutting boards. She was waiting me out, letting me turn all this new information over.

"You knew," I said. Two of the mangoes were done and I was halfway through the third. "You knew and that's why you wanted me to meet you here today. So I'd see this."

She looked offended. "Can't a girl just miss her friend? And want some help chopping up all this damn fruit? You did such a good job with it last time, I figured you wouldn't mind."

I snorted. "Riiiiiight."

Her face twisted as she worked to hide her smirk, until she lost the battle and it broke free. "Maybe I just thought you needed a little nudge."

"Real subtle, Hailey."

She shrugged, unconcerned. "If you guys would just open your eyes and see what the rest of us do when you look at each other, I wouldn't have to scheme. It's so damn obvious."

"It's just . . . it's just not always that simple." I sighed, frustrated. "And I haven't even been able to find your brother to talk to him."

She made a face at me. "You lose your phone again?"

"No, I didn't *lose my phone again*," I mocked her, my aggravation making my voice rise a little at the end. "But some conversations deserve more than a just a phone call."

She dipped her head in reluctant agreement. "He'll be back in town Saturday night, the same night as the gala." She looked at me meaningfully, as if daring me to come up with another excuse. "You are still going to the gala, aren't you? I already told Cody you'd be there. He's excited to see you again. Grandma is too."

My heart melted a little at the thought of seeing Cody again. And her grandmother was pure gold. A true Southern lady, proper when necessary, steely when needed, and blinded by love when it came to her own family. I adored her too.

"You're not gonna let Aubrey's bullshit keep you from showing up, are you?"

I bit the inside of my cheek. I *had* considered bailing on the event. As much as I'd hoped to use the Sailing Regatta Gala as a chance to network my budding business, Paper Plane Photography, now I wasn't so sure. Aubrey had made sure to spread the news of my videos among the island residents of my generation. I wasn't sure how far her poison had reached though. An evening of people laughing at me, either behind my back or directly to my face, wasn't exactly my idea of a good time.

Letting Aubrey win this round wasn't really an option either, though. But beyond the concern for my own business, was how my actions might reflect upon both Grady and West—and hell, even Rue for that matter. Although, I had no doubt that Rue would be happy to stand by my side and give Aubrey a great big middle finger if she tried to pull any shit to my face.

"Actually," Hailey hesitated, twisting her engagement ring on her on finger. Her fiancé was a U.S. Marine currently deployed overseas. "She's the other thing I wanted to talk to you about."

I tipped my head to the side, unsure where she was going with this little detour. "Oh?" I wiped any expression from my face, bracing myself for bad news.

"Look, I don't like to gossip or get in the middle of other people's relationships or whatever it is you've got going on with my brother," she said in a rush, not quite meeting my eyes. I think she was watching my chin as she pushed the words from her mouth, like if she did it quick, like ripping off a bandage, maybe it wouldn't suck so bad. "But I was working here last weekend, filling in for West when he took off like a bat out of hell to go to Tennessee, and Aubrey was here with her friends—you know, the hard plastic looking ones with perfect teeth? Anyways, they must've had too much grog, or not known I could hear them, or hell, maybe they just didn't care, but Aubrey started talking about West."

She paused again, and peeked up at me from under her lashes, her eyes big and pleading, like a puppy's. "And you. She was bragging about how she'd finally sent you running and West was hers again. Something about … some pictures? At his place? Does that mean something to you? I wasn't sure what that was about. But anyway, something about planting some pictures and you finding them at the perfect time. And then she was cackling about you appearing out of the blue at the marina when she sprained her ankle. That the timing couldn't have been better."

She took a deep breath and poured me a shot, top shelf, and slid it across the bar. I drank it down in one swallow, face blank, and then rolled the empty glass between my palms, absorbing her words. I stared at one of the pinned dollar bills over Hailey's shoulder. The currency tacked behind the bar all had pick-up lines scrawled on them. I was fixated on one I hadn't seen before. *Do you live on a chicken farm? You sure know how to raise a cock.*

Hailey reached out, the woven nautical bracelets I knew she'd made herself sliding down her wrist, and gently took the glass from me, setting it in the bin with the other dirty ones; then she placed the knife I'd been using earlier behind the counter, out of reach. Taking precautions, I guess. "I don't know if what she said makes any sense or not, but I don't trust her, and if I'm going to possibly have one of you as my sister-in-law one day, I'd pick you a million times over her."

Her words buzzed faintly in the background. I barely heard her. Instead, I was back at the beach house West and Wyatt shared, the day I realized I'd fallen in love with West. The day I pictured a future with him.

With us.

And then *she'd* been there, wearing only one of West's shirts, looking all rumpled. And West had sworn she'd just been drunk and sleeping it off on the couch, and I'd wanted to believe him, but then I saw the pictures in his nightstand. The boudoir pics I'd taken of her. Glossy image after glossy image of her more naked than clothed, tucked right next to his bed.

Where there's smoke, there's fire, right? So I'd rushed out, not looking back.

My dreams crushed.

And he hadn't chased me.

But since then he'd told me he loved me, and sent me love notes, and driven twelve hours to save me from Asshole, and given me space.

And he'd fucking painted the bathroom.

I swayed on the seat, eyes unfocused, pulse tripping as it tried to keep pace with my whirling mind. I loved him. I did. But at the same time, he scared me.

I didn't want to be hurt again. Could you love without risk? I didn't think so.

The room blurred around the edges, and I exhaled the breath

I hadn't even known I'd been holding.

And I realized.

He made me want to believe in the magic of paper airplanes.

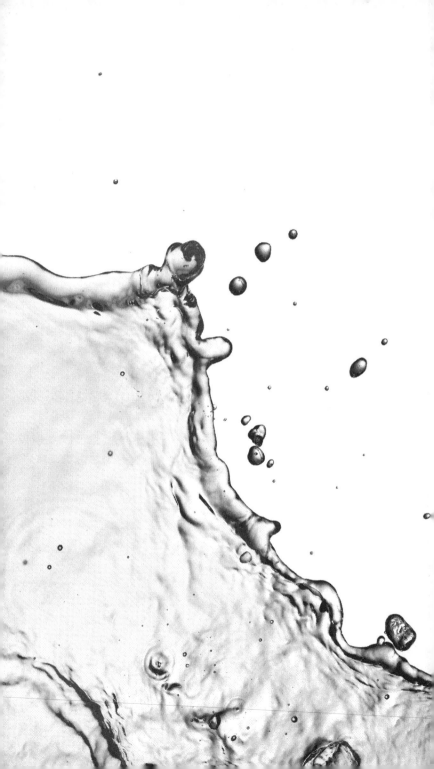

chapter
twenty-one

My NAME. SOMEONE WAS SAYING my name.

"Sadie? You okay?" Hailey waved her hand in front of my face. Her brows dipped in worry and she pushed another glass across the bar to me. Water this time.

I snatched up the glass too fast, splashing some over the rim as I took a long swallow. Drops splattered across the front of my cotton shirt, but I ignored them.

"He'll be back in two days?"

She nodded, a slow smile spreading across her face. "You're gonna talk to him, aren't you?"

I lifted a brow. "If things go right, I'll do more than just talk to him."

"Ew." She threw a towel at me. "You realize he's my brother, right? I don't want to think about his . . . extracurricular activities."

I mopped up the mess I'd made on the worn, wooden bar top and dabbed at my shirt, sopping up the worst of it.

"So he gets back the same day as the gala? Dammit, I'm gonna have to try to corner him beforehand. Or on the way there. Or something." I was thinking out loud, forming my plan.

"Oh." Her voice trailed off and Hailey spun around, busying herself with the fruit in the cooler. She dumped in the rest we'd cut up and poured a whole bottle of Everclear over the top.

"Hailey?"

"Mmm?"

"Why won't you look at me all the sudden?"

She shook her head. "I'm sure it's nothing. Just something I overheard at the house the other night, during one of the planning meetings Aubrey came over for."

I rolled my eyes. Could she drag this out any longer?

" . . . and?"

She stirred the fruit with a wooden spoon, studiously avoiding my gaze.

"What'd you hear?"

Reluctance and apology colored her voice. "Aubrey was whining about how hard it is to drive in heels and Grandma sorta kinda volunteered West to go pick her up." She mumbled the last part, and it took me a second to process what she said.

I pursed my lips and my knee started bouncing in irritation. "So your brother is taking Aubrey to the gala." It wasn't a question. It was me acknowledging Aubrey worming her way between me and West. Again.

"I mean, I don't think they're going together like, a date or anything. I think he's just ... picking her up," she finished, looking at me helplessly. "Honestly, she set the whole thing up. Grandma fell for it, and West was stuck looking like a jerk if he refused. It's only a mile away."

"And Aubrey is incapable of driving in heels? When I don't think I've ever seen her in flats." My sarcasm wasn't lost on Hailey.

"I'm sorry," she whispered. "I'm sure you're the one he hoped to take as his date."

I drummed my fingers to the same rhythm I was bouncing my knee. "Yeah? I don't know."

"I'm sure he just—"

"You know what? I'll see him there. I'll drive myself. In heels, no less."

THE NEXT DAY, I STOOD outside of Grady's penthouse office at the Water's Edge resort, fighting the nerves that had my stomach rolling. I'd requested the meeting, hoping to apologize and find out where I stood with the company. If I still had any employment at all—as a photographer or a lifeguard.

My expectations weren't very high on either count.

I picked a piece of lint off the pale pink shell I'd paired with slim black pants and pointy-toed flats. I'd pinned my hair back off my face too, trying to exude a professionalism I certainly didn't feel as I waited for Grady to answer my knock.

A minute passed. Shit. Maybe he didn't hear me? I'd knocked more timidly than I meant to, my anxiety showing through the too-soft action.

Or ... maybe that was his response? Maybe not answering the door was the message he was sending me. That I wasn't welcome here any longer.

But, no. The Grady I'd come to know, the one who'd taken salsa lessons with me on the island and surfed with abandon, he would never be so rude. He'd at least hear me out before he sent me packing.

I raised my hand again, and squared my shoulders. My knuckles had almost met the dark, solid-wood door when it whooshed open. My hand continued its arc, not meeting the expected resistance, and rapped Grady's shoulder, hard enough to make him take a step back.

"Oh, God!" I cried, taking a step forward, my hand reaching out to him.

He retreated hastily. "Woah, there, killer. I was coming, no need to attack." He rubbed the spot where I'd thwacked him, rotating his arm at the shoulder.

"Grady, I'm so sorry, I was just trying to kno—"

"I'm fine," he interrupted. "Trust me, I've survived worse." His face clouded momentarily and his eyes went a bit hazy as he massaged the spot one last time. "Much worse." Shaking his head, he moved around behind the mammoth desk that dominated the room. The wall behind him was floor-to-ceiling glass, much like the main room at his beachfront mansion. From here, he had a bird's eye view of most of the resort, like a king surveying his kingdom.

He lowered himself into the plush leather office chair and pointed at the two upholstered armchairs arranged in front of the desk. "Why don't you have a seat and catch me up with your progress?"

"My progress?" I sat on the very edge of the seat, legs pressed together. "You mean . . . with the . . ." I trailed off. Was he asking about the emergency I'd told him I had to rush off and handle?

"Not that." He shook his head. "It seems to me that you got that nightmare in Tennessee handled just fine."

My face burned. "You know."

He swiveled in his chair, and gazed out the window for a minute, his hand coming up to rub across his mouth. His face appeared more drawn than I remembered, even though he looked as impeccable as ever in his charcoal gray suit with a pale silver shirt beneath. His eyes seemed more tired, heavier somehow, than they had in Grand Cayman. Working his jaw back and forth, he turned back to face me, his eyes both sincere and formidable. "What I saw was a beautiful young lady, who has nothing to apologize for, and a smug fool who, frankly, could stand to learn a few new moves, let alone some better personal grooming habits. I also noticed that said video has disappeared from the internet, and that the Nashville police blotter showed the arrest of one Asher Snowden. Well played, Miss Mullins." He dipped his head in my direction, a pleased smirk playing around the edge of his mouth.

I collapsed back in the chair, relief and shock making me forget my posture all together. "Am I . . ." I tried to swallow past the dryness of my mouth.

"Fired? Is that what you came here to ask me?"

I nodded, mutely. Miserably.

"Why would I fire you? Your work has been more than satisfactory and your coworkers sing your praises, in your roles both at the pool and behind the camera. That said, I do expect an update on the family-centered campaign for the new resort." He raised his eyebrows expectantly.

Numb with relief and gratitude, I was speechless as I searched through my purse, before emerging triumphantly with a thumb drive. I leaned across his wide desk to hand it over. "Right here. Finished, edited, and ready to go."

He opened the sleek laptop and front of him and started to insert the small device when he paused. "You sure these are the right images?"

I flushed and looked away, nodding.

"Too soon?" He winced at my reaction.

I bit my lip. "Just a bit." His joke helped though, awkward as it was. Some of the stiffness left my shoulders, and I scooted back to sit properly in the chair, instead of perching on the edge, ready to flee. No, now my nerves centered on what he thought about my work. My first big commercial campaign.

As weird as it sounds, those shots almost felt more personal, more revealing, than anything Asshole had uploaded.

Long minutes ticked by, broken only by the sound of Grady

clicking through the pictures. Needing a distraction, I studied the room. The oversized desk was a dark, rich wood. Not mahogany, something darker. Probably exotic. A sleek, low-slung olive-colored couch anchored one wall, with two offset armchairs boasting an unexpected botanical pattern facing it. A thick rug with an abstract pattern topped with an oval coffee table lay between them. Square sepia-toned photos of desolate docks backing up to frothing seas marched along the wall above the couch. I recognized the prints. It was a series Nick had done. The other wall had a shallow bar set up, with crystal decanters placed precisely along the top. A huge nautical map of the Caribbean took up the rest of the space. No curtains hung from the windows, as if he didn't like anything to block his view of the sea's endless attack and retreat along the beach.

Finally, he leaned back from his computer, steepling his fingers as he looked at me. It took everything in me not to fidget under the weight of his gaze.

"I love them," he said simply. "Your eye is excellent. The brightness, the innocence. Joy radiates from these shots. It's exactly what we want our customers to feel. What's more, it provides an excellent counterpoint to Nick's work. The contrast between the two campaigns is going to work beautifully. In fact, this one here," he spun the computer around to where he had stopped on a shot of the youngest tow-headed child with a look of absolute glee on her face, jumping in a tidal pool, the moment captured mid-splash, while her sister was shrieking and spinning away, "can we get it blown up by the gala tomorrow? Water's Edge will have a sponsorship display near the entrance, and I'd like to have this shot and one Nick has already sent set up."

Shocked, but in a good way for a change, I released the breath I'd been holding, and for the next hour we discussed the logistics of size, price, and delivery for the rush order. After I'd tucked away my notepad where I'd jotted down pertinent information, I rose from my chair, sure that this concluded our meeting.

"Grady . . ." I hesitated, knowing what I wanted to say applied to both Grady-my-boss and Grady-my-friend, but not wanting to overstep. "I just want to thank you for your support and understanding. I wasn't sure . . . I wasn't sure how today was going to go."

Grady nodded and got to his feet as well, moving around the desk toward the door, but he paused halfway, turning back to assess with me with a calculating gaze. "You do plan on attending the gala, correct? It would be hard to show off my talented new photographer to the larger community if she wasn't there."

I nodded, a bit unsure if the timing was really right for that networking, but trying to draw from his confidence. "I am."

"West is taking you, I assume?"

I laughed once, a dark, bitter sound. "No. No, I believe he's escorting Aubrey. It seems she has difficulty driving in heels, and West will once again be coming to her rescue. In any case, he hasn't asked me."

"Can't drive in . . ." Grady furrowed his brow as his voice trailed off. He crossed his thick arms over his chest and tipped his head slightly as he regarded me. "Sadie, it would be my honor to escort you to the gala tomorrow."

Surprise widened my eyes and froze me in the act of pulling my purse strap up my shoulder. "That's generous of you, but certainly . . . not . . . necessary." My voice betrayed my confusion.

"Oh, I know it's not *necessary*." He smirked. "But I think it's time West got a taste of his own medicine, don't you? I know he's crazy about you, but I'm not sure he always thinks things through where women are concerned. He's never really had to before."

This was a side of Grady I hadn't seen yet. The troublemaker. And yet, I couldn't help but appreciate the deviousness of his plan.

I had just opened my mouth to answer him when he spoke again.

"Unless you'd prefer Nick to take you?"

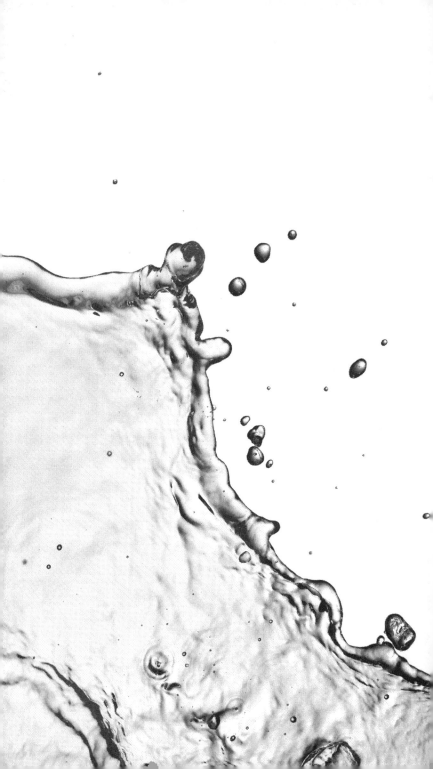

chapter
twenty-two

I SMOOTHED THE DEEP BLUE dress over my hips, then twisted to check how my ass looked in the mirror. Not bad. In the front, a scalloped lace overlay met in a V deep enough to show just a hint of cleavage, and in the back, the lace dipped all the way down to my waist. Short, fluttery sleeves lifted and flirted with my every move and the skirt fell to my feet in a whisper of chiffon that was light enough to keep me from melting in the humidity at the outdoor gala at West and Hailey's grandmother's oceanfront mansion. I'd curled my hair and piled it up into a messy-on-purpose updo, knowing the back would just turn into a sweaty mess if I left it down. I skipped jewelry altogether except for some diamond studs that Rue loaned me.

But when it came to my makeup, I'd gone all out. Dark, smoky eyes, fake eyelashes that were trickier than I'd expected to apply, and pouty, pink lips. It was my armor, my war paint in my battle against Aubrey. Also, it ensured that no matter what happened later that night, I couldn't cry. My eyes had taken me close to an hour to perfect, between the fucking lashes and getting the winged edges of my eyeliner to match. God bless YouTube tutorials. I'd had to start over after my first try, but the second run had gone much smoother.

And Rue had insisted I wear her delicate champagne-colored, strappy heels. They were tall enough to make a statement, but not so tall I feared for my life while wearing them.

She'd left twenty minutes ago to pick up Theo, her date for the evening. She loved Theo, but hated his beat up car, so she was driving them. The golden bangles lining her slender wrist had jangled as she'd air-kissed me goodbye, careful not to smudge our makeup, saying she'd see me there shortly.

I was just checking that I'd remembered to tuck my phone into my small clutch when the doorbell rang. Taking a deep breath, I plastered a smile on my face and opened the door, knowing it wasn't West on the other side, no matter how much my heart wished it was.

"Hey," Grady said, his eyes automatically drifting down my body. "You look breathtaking tonight. You ready to go knock 'em dead?" His formalwear fit him in such a way that I knew it was custom made, not just off the rack, and he pulled off a bowtie well, unlike most men. It was a real one too, no doubt hand-tied himself, not one of those cheesy clip-ons. I imagined he would be quite devastating with the bowtie hanging loose around his neck, a few buttons undone near his throat.

"I was thinking of letting everyone live tonight, actually." I laughed and locked the door before following him down the steps. "Well, mostly everyone. There is this one person . . ."

He shook his head. "I don't think you're going to have anything to worry about tonight. I know I'm looking forward to it more than I expected."

"And why's that?" I slanted a curious glance his direction.

"Let's just say I'm expecting some fireworks." He winked at me, then opened the car door and ushered me safely inside his low-slung, matte-black sports car. It probably cost more than my college tuition and was exactly the type of car I expected him to drive. Powerful, but understated.

The conversation flowed easily between us on the ride, reminding me of our time together in Grand Cayman. The normalness of it all helped me relax, helped me push the red, jealous thoughts of Aubrey riding to the same destination next to West from my mind. Did he open her door? Did he help her climb up into that monstrosity he called a truck? Grip her waist and hold her hand? The traitorous image lodged in my mind, but I turned to the handsome man next to me and focused on him instead. Tonight, he would be my lifeline if I needed one.

The quiet strength he emanated, the cool confidence that flowed through all his subtle movements as he handled the car, I wanted to absorb it all during our ten-minute commute. Let it wash over me until I was calm as the sea at slack tide. Incapable of being ruffled by anything less powerful than the moon.

Once we parked, he turned off the ignition and let me sit for a moment in quiet, gathering myself. It was as if he could tell I needed one more minute to prepare myself for battle. I took a deep breath, and he seemed to recognize it as the signal he'd been waiting on, that I was ready to go.

After squeezing my hand reassuringly, he came around to open my door and escort me to the entrance.

I tucked my fingers in the crook of his arm as we walked, my heels sinking slightly in the loose, sandy soil beneath the perfectly manicured grass. I knew from listening to Hailey and West talk about the logistics that a wooden dance floor and pavilion would be set up, so my footing shouldn't remain a liability much longer.

And then I could see them. Up ahead. All lined up in a reception line of sorts. First Aubrey, then Margaret Montgomery, the family matriarch and West's grandmother, her husband, Charles, and West, devastating in his tuxedo. The black material fit him a little snug around the shoulders, as if it had once been custom made for him, but then he'd put on more muscle.

I shivered a little.

I was all too familiar with his muscles.

We paused in front of Aubrey. Ignoring Grady, she pointedly looked me over, her lips already curling into a sneer. Not to be outdone, I returned the favor. She'd gone for beauty pageant chic, was all I could conclude. A tight black dress with slashed cutouts and beading over what material was left, caked-on makeup, and the tallest hair I'd seen outside of a TLC television special. I grudgingly gave her a few points for her shoes. They were killer.

As in, they would've killed me if I tried to walk in them.

"I didn't expect to see you here." She sniffed, tossing her head back. Not one strand of her hair budged with the motion. It was kind of creepy.

"And yet here I am." I smiled sweetly, but my nails dug into the arm I was still clinging to.

"I just figured after . . . everything . . . you'd have wanted to be a little less *visible*."

"Aubrey!" Margaret's voice was sharp with rebuke, but dangerous in its softness. "Stop it at once! Sadie rescued my sweet Cody and will *always* be welcome at my house. Is that understood? And beyond that, you only make yourself look classless when you attempt to belittle another woman in public. I'm ashamed of you." The razor edge to her voice seemed to make Aubrey shrink several inches.

Cutting me one last nasty look, Aubrey turned to the couple approaching farther down the drive, her Miss America smile once more firmly plastered to her lacquered exterior.

I reached forward with my free hand to shake Margaret's in greeting, but was immediately pulled into a warm hug instead. As she embraced me, she spoke in my ear, soft enough that the words didn't carry to those around us. "My dear, West has spoken to me about you several times now. I expect to start seeing you around here regularly, and moreover, I couldn't be more thrilled to see him settle his affections on you." Pulling back, she continued at a more normal volume. "You look exquisite tonight, Sadie. I do hope we'll have a chance to talk more later." She squeezed my shoulders before dropping her arms from around me.

I'm not even sure how I responded, my mind still in a daze from her words.

West has talked about me? To the point that he's shared his feelings with her?

I murmured a greeting to her husband, forced a perfunctory smile, and then I was there.

In front of him.

I blinked.

He was beautiful. The tux hugging the breadth of his shoulders, his untamed hair, and the sexy scruff on his strong jaw. His eyes smoldered as they ran down me, before flickering warily to the man at my elbow.

"Grady." West nodded, his eyes jumping between us, a question clear in the way he said his best friend's name.

"West," Grady replied smoothly, moving forward to do the fist-grab, half-hug, black-slap combo that guys did when they met. They sized each other up for a moment, and then Grady stepped aside. Smiling broadly, he tipped his head in the direction of the bar. "Now that my work here is done for the moment, I'll be over there if either of you needs me." With a quick wink to me, he melted away into the crowded backyard.

chapter
twenty-three

"WEST." I HADN'T MEANT to whisper.

Emotions chased over his chiseled face. Desire, uncertainty, determination, tenderness. Blatant want. Capturing my hand in his larger one, he pulled us back a few steps, giving us some semblance of privacy.

He tucked a wayward curl behind my ear. "Sadie." My name was a caress on his lips.

Our eyes clung, trying to determine where the other stood. Where we stood.

"You didn't call," he said.

I shook my head. "No. But I looked for you."

"I found the paper plane. At the dock, when I got in this afternoon."

My eyes widened. I'd forgotten about that.

He hooked my pinky finger with his. "Did you mean it? Did

you miss me?"

I nodded and bit my lip, suddenly shy now that he was standing right here in front of me. He took another half step, until my breasts rubbed his chest, and he wrapped one strong arm around me, his fingers spreading wide on the bare skin of my back. I swear I felt his breath catch just a little when his hand met nothing but warm flesh. He dipped his head, murmuring in my ear. "You made me crazy, not hearing from you. But then, I've been crazy about you since you pulled me from the ocean."

I sagged against him a little, my hand slipping up to clutch his hard hip.

"I don't even care that he brought you tonight. You're mine, and we both know it."

I moaned softly at the feel of his lips against the rim of my ear, and the tip of his tongue stole a quick taste.

Determined not to let him distract me, I pulled back. "He only brought me because you brought her."

"Her?" His eyebrows knit with confusion.

"Don't play games with me. Aubrey. Hailey told me you were bringing her."

"Ahhhh, so that's what this is about. You're trying to make me jealous." He tugged me closer. "It's working." I tried to jerk back to glare at him but he wouldn't let me put any distance between us. "Sadie, I didn't bring her. I didn't bring anybody. I got delayed in St. Augustine and only got in a few hours ago. I barely had time to get myself here. Besides that, I never had any intention of bringing her, no matter what story she told to my grandma."

"But Hailey sa—"

"I also don't run all my plans past my sister."

Relief, thick and heavy, poured through me, and my tense muscles relaxed. He'd come alone.

His hips pressed against mine, and the thickness of his growing arousal was impossible to miss. "I have to mingle for a while, shake hands, do the obligatory networking. But then I'm finding you, Sadie. And we're going to talk." His finger trailed down my spine, awakening every nerve ending in its path. "You look gorgeous tonight. No man will be able to keep his eyes off you." He sounded slightly disgruntled.

"I'll be waiting," I promised him, pulling away reluctantly as I sensed the presence of another couple waiting to greet West behind me.

EXCEPT, I BARELY SAW HIM for the next two hours. He'd gotten involved in several longwinded conversations with paunchy men who had too much money and time on their hands, and I hadn't been able to get to him. Not that I'd just been standing around spying on him.

No, Grady had kept his word, and I'd made the rounds myself, meeting community leaders and making new connections. Not one of them batted an eye when they heard my name, no one gasped or pulled away in disgust. Aubrey's campaign to destroy my reputation hadn't spread as far as I'd feared.

And Nick was there. He found me hovering by an empty table near the edge of the dance floor, taking a moment to clear my head, and handed me a blood orange margarita with a look of pure innocence. "Really?" I'd chided.

He dipped his chin. "In remembrance of a great night. What can I say? The salt air and humidity are bringing back memories."

"Memories we're never going to speak of again," I said pointedly, taking a long swallow of the frozen beverage before setting it down on the table.

He winked, and mimed zipping his lips while I glared at him. "I met with Grady yesterday." He waited for me to react and when I didn't, he continued. "He showed me your finished campaign. I'd like to commend you. The images were stunning." He tipped a slight nod my way. "Almost as good as mine, even." I rolled my eyes at his ego but he kept talking. "Seriously, Sadie, I wanted to say good job. I'm proud to have my work next to yours for this project, and I'd love to work with you again in the future."

Slightly stunned by his unexpected praise, I could only gape at him.

Setting his drink down, he scooped up my hand. "Dance with me?"

Glancing around, I finally spotted West sequestered with a small group near the corner of the huge white tent that dominated the yard. Aubrey was next to him.

"Sure," I gritted, following him to the dance floor. The live band had been playing a wide range of favorites all night, from the

Beach Boys and Jimmy Buffet to more current Top 40 hits. While we danced, I couldn't help but glance at West from time to time. He had shifted positions so he was facing me. The weight of his gaze tracked my movements, but Aubrey was still next to him, so I did my best to ignore him.

"That's him, isn't it?"

"Huh?"

"The guy staring daggers at me. It's the idiot we talked about on the plane. The one who lost you."

I'd forgotten we'd talked about that. "Yeah. That's him."

"Are you still lost? Or has he found you again?"

I wasn't sure how to answer. Our status was nebulous, murky, awaiting that big bang that would solidify us into being.

"What about you?" I countered instead of answering. "Has anyone claimed you yet?"

He threw back his head and laughed. "Not for more than a night or two."

I shook my head in mock disgust as we wove around each other, finding an easy rhythm. He didn't crowd me or try anything inappropriate. In fact, considering our previous encounters, Nick was actually being quite . . . tame.

"Why not?" My question was serious.

His eyes darkened and shifted away from mine uneasily. "Despite my appearances of chasing every hot woman whose path I cross, yours included, I'm not an easy man to get close to."

"On purpose," I guessed.

"On purpose."

The song came to an end, and we both turned to retrieve our abandoned drinks. I started to follow up the question, but he shook his head sharply. "Just leave it, Sadie. You passed on your chance to dig deeper." His face softened, tipping his head toward the corner of the pavilion where West was still locked in conversation. "And the idiot doesn't look like such a bad guy."

I snuck a quick peek at West, whose face had turned stormy and tight as he tracked our movements. "He's not." Aubrey twisted to follow his gaze and scowled, stepping forward half a step to block his view.

"Should I be worried for my safety?"

"Maybe." My lips twitched.

His eyebrows rose. "Duly noted. And with that warning, I think I'll leave you to your drink. It was good to see you, Sadie. Keep up the good work."

I laughed as he retreated and pretended to keep a wary eye on West. Picking up the half-melted margarita, I joined Hailey, Rue, and Grady at the edge of tent. "Did I miss anything?"

"No," Hailey mused, looking quite sophisticated in a strapless, tea-length emerald dress. "I'd say things were just getting good."

I giggled. "What does that mean?"

"Have you talked to West yet?"

"When I first got here. He's been tied up since then."

"He might be tied up, but he's been watching you."

"Well, yay. How can I untie him?"

Grady spoke up. "I think I can help with that. Sadie, would you care to . . . salsa?"

chapter
twenty-four

I WASN'T ENTIRELY SURE WHAT Grady's plan was—with West or on the dance floor. On the island, we'd practiced to a more authentic Latin beat, but tonight we were making do with a Marc Anthony song. I'll admit, if I was going to put myself out there on display, I wanted to look damn good doing it. If West was gonna have his eyes on me, I wanted to put on a show he wouldn't forget. And the selfish, shallow part of me—the petty devil on my shoulder I wasn't proud of—just wanted to fucking show Aubrey that, for once, it wasn't all about her.

Even if it was for just one damn song.

After two weeks apart, the first several measures of the song were rusty. I couldn't find the one beat and was throwing off our rhythm. Grady improvised, adding a little twisting spin to focus my concentration back on him. And purposefully face me away from West.

"You forget," he murmured as our feet finally coordinated, regaining the syncopated fluidity of the dance, "that there's someone here I might want to impress as well." He spun us, dipped me low, and continued on. "Concentrate. We're only gonna get this one shot."

I smirked and donned my game face. "Bring it."

The beat took up residence in my chest, the 4/4 cadence becoming a natural extension of my feet as I followed his lead. We ran through several of the combos we'd learned, with an emphasis on the ones with the flashier moves we knew we can handle.

My face lit in a smile. We. Were. Owning. It.

Grady spun me again, and I must have done something wrong, because my wrist was captured at an awkward angle, keeping me from completing the movement. I lifted my gaze, brows dipping low in confusion, and clashed with the blue-gray storm clouds rioting in West's eyes. I followed the line of his shoulder down his bicep, past his strong forearm to where his fingers clasped the thin bones of my wrist, not painfully, but enough to make a point.

"West," I exhaled.

Not lifting his piercing stare from mine, he tipped his chin at Grady, the words somehow both heated and icy at the same time. "You don't mind if I cut in, do you?"

I tore my eyes from West's long enough to glance over my shoulder, where Grady tried to smother the mirth threatening to overtake his face. He acquiesced with grace, ever the Southern gentleman. "The lady is all yours."

The storm clouds erupted, West's eyes flashing dangerously as they ran over my face, searching for something. A signal? Whatever it was, he seemed to find it and his fingers threaded through mine, tugging me closer, until he was all I could see, all I could feel. I caught a whiff of his salt-and-citrus smell, and my knees weakened a bit, a slip he took advantage of to bring me snug against his broad chest. "Yes. Yes, she is." He shifted me fully into his iron embrace, molding me to his hard contours. "If you'll excuse us, I'm going to remind her."

My eyes widened and my breath caught, even as I instinctively followed his movements. It wasn't a salsa anymore. No, it was dirtier, slower, but just as sensual, the way his hips rolled and mine followed, our bodies flush and his solid thigh thrust between mine.

The other times we'd danced at Anchor flashed through my mind. The first night we'd been intimate together, when he'd stolen me away from the boy with the British accent. And then again, before I'd left on the trip a few weeks ago. How dancing with him had always been foreplay to wild, frenzied lovemaking

It reminded me of the last time. When love and anger had sparred for control, fighting for the upper hand. Because looking in his eyes, I didn't doubt that both of those emotions simmered in him tonight as well. The intensity coated the air between us like molasses, thick and dark and sweet.

I lifted my chin in challenge. He wasn't the only one whose feelings were threatening to boil over. I wasn't sure if I was more inclined to beat my fists against his chest or yank him closer until

I could claim him as mine, publicly and irrevocably, polite society be damned.

If there were other people around us, I was oblivious. It was just him and his touch and the sticky humidity and my pulse hammering so hard, I was sure he felt it in his own chest.

His hand dropped until it rested dangerously low on my back. The other crept up until his fingers tangled in my upswept curls, tugging until I raised my eyes to his, the sting in my scalp skipping down my spine and pooling low in my belly.

My tongue slid out to wet my lower lip, capturing his gaze with that small action. He groaned, his eyes dilated in the waning evening light as they focused on my mouth.

"Sadie." His voice was harsh, demanding, at odds with the vulnerability I saw lurking in his eyes. "Take a walk with me?" His grip tightened fractionally, as if he was scared I'd refuse him.

I lifted an eyebrow. "Took you long enough to ask." Honestly, at this point I didn't care. He'd blown me off again all evening, and I didn't really want to have another conversation about Aubrey. But I made no move to escape from his arms as he maneuvered us to the far corner of the dance floor, where the twinkling lights dripping from the live oaks along with the Spanish moss didn't penetrate. "Will Aubrey be following us? She seems rather attached to your hip." I spoke flatly, wanting to sound uninterested in his answer but knowing I failed.

He dipped his head, murmuring against my ear. "My hips are only interested in one girl here tonight, if you hadn't noticed." He ground against me, the hard length of him evident through his tailored pants. His mouth stole a taste from the tender flesh of my neck, dissolving any remaining arguments on my tongue.

With a quick glance over his shoulder to make sure no one was watching, he nudged me into the shadows beyond the party boundaries.

I wasn't sure what I felt. Arousal, yes. Frustration, definitely. But did I want to tell him with words—or with my body? We edged around the pool, his grip on my hand firm and steady, as if making sure I wouldn't try to slip away.

When we got to the pool house, he pulled me inside, then pushed me back against the door and covered my body with his larger one. His heat warmed me right through my dress, awakening my nipples, which promptly beaded a hard hello as he rubbed against me.

"You've been trying to make me jealous tonight, haven't you?" He pinned my wrists above my head with one hand.

The lights were off, the only illumination coming from the very last of the sun's deep orange rays peeking through the windows. His free hand cupped my cheek, tilting me up to face him, his thumb tracing my lower lip. "First, you were with that guy, the one you let bring you a drink."

"Nick."

He gripped me tighter. "You know him then."

I nodded best I could. "We met in Grand Cayman. He was the other photographer for the campaign."

West turned my head, and pressed open-mouthed kisses along my jawline, his thumb still teasing my lip. I couldn't resist licking the rough pad, pulling it into my mouth and biting down. He groaned, then dragged his hand down, pushing the edge of my dress aside until his wet thumb softly rubbed my pebbled nipple, just enough to tease, but not enough to ease the ache. I arched my back, silently asking for more.

"And you spent so much time together that he knows what you drink?" He spoke against my throat.

I tipped my head to give him more access. "He—" I gasped when he nipped the tender skin where my neck met my shoulder. "He mentored me."

West reared back with eyes so dark they looked feral. "Did he now? And were you a good student?"

I was glad the light was all but gone, twilight bathing us in a purple glow. He couldn't see the way my cheeks burned, both from embarrassment and anger. "I might know a few new tricks." If he was going to believe the worst about me, I'd fucking let him.

He cursed, and his grip around my tender nipple bordered on cruel. "You're mine." He gritted out the words from behind clenched teeth, the muscle in his jaw pulsing.

"Then act like it." My words had the effect of a slap. He dropped his hands and stepped back until a few inches separated us, his face slack with disbelief.

"Grady was the one who introduced me to everyone tonight, not you," I pointed out. I bit my lip, hating how catty my next words would sound. "And she's been the one by your side all night, not me." I didn't have to use her name for us to know who I was referring to.

He shoved a hand through his hair impatiently and stepped forward again, crowding me so I had no choice but to look at him. "Tonight was an opportunity. One I've worked all summer on. I needed to network with those men out there, the ones who could help expand my business to the next level, but instead I'm in here with you, arguing." He laughed, but there was no humor in the sound. "What did you want me to do when she walked up? Pout like a little kid? Walk away like she had cooties? This was business. My business. She wasn't my concern, those men were."

His hands bit into my hips, as if he was trying to keep himself from shaking me. "Do you still not get it? Why I want to succeed so damn bad? Why I've been busting my ass?"

I frowned at him, not sure where this conversation was going now. "Why?"

"I want to take care of you, damn it! I want to make enough money to spoil you and pamper you and give you everything I know you deserve." He leaned his forehead against mine and squeezed his eyes shut. My heart pounded inside my chest at the intensity of his words. "I want to be worthy of being yours."

I quit breathing.

"Actions, right?" His fingers twined with my damp ones, and he pulled them against his chest. "Tonight was about securing *our* future. Her walking up on a conversation was not important enough to deter me from my goal." Pulling back, he narrowed his eyes at me. "However, you continuing to taunt me by dancing with other men? Men who weren't me?" He looped my arms behind his neck, and my fingers tangled in his thick hair. "I found that very,

very distracting."

He nudged my legs apart with one of his, forcing his thigh between mine, then palmed my ass and pulled me close. He kneaded the flesh that filled his hands, and I wondered if he could tell I wore nothing beneath my dress. The filmy fabric of the skirt bunched between us as he tugged it up, until his hand cupped me, one finger sliding easily between my slick folds.

"Is this for me, Sadie?" His thumb circled my clit, and I sagged against him, his other arm slipping behind me to hold me up, my head pressed into his shoulder. "Or is this for your mentor? Or Grady?"

He stilled, waiting for my answer, his fingers touching me but not giving me what I so desperately wanted. I twisted my hips, seeking friction, and his arm tightened, not allowing the movement.

"You, West." I met his eyes with my own, knowing he could see the tears pooling. "I'm yours. But you don't feel like mine."

chapter
twenty-five

PAIN, SHARP AND DEEP, SLASHED across his face and he withdrew his hand from my aching core, righting my dress until it once again swirled at my ankles. I swayed from the sudden loss of his touch, and he steadied me, but didn't pull me close.

Taking a jagged breath, he pulled my arms from around his neck, breaking our connection.

"Fuck!" He turned from me, pacing the length of the small pool house. He passed the bathroom doorway, where we'd had our first kiss. It was hard to believe that only a season had passed since then. That four short months ago, he'd just been a surfer I'd thought was drowning, and now I was the one in over my head, hoping to be rescued. Knowing that without him, I might never recover.

On his third pass, he stopped in front of me, one hand

clenching and unclenching, the only outward sign of his agitation. His face was carefully blank. "How can you say that to me? How can you look me in the eyes, and say that to me?" His voice was tight, controlled. "I begged you to stay, sent you paper planes, dropped a client last minute to rush to Tennessee on the off chance you might need me, painted the fucking bathroom myself after hours, bared my soul to you, then gave you the space you said you needed. I loved you every way I knew how."

He lifted his hand as if to stroke my cheek, but then let if fall to his side limply, defeat slumping his posture. "What more do you want from me?" His eyes were glossy, voice raw.

I bit my lip, because all those things were true, and yet . . ."I don't like feeling that *she* can replace me every time I'm not there. That she *does* replace me. And that you're okay with that." Despite my best intentions, my voice cracked as I finished, and a few traitorous tears slipped down my cheeks.

"Aubrey?!" Incredulity made his voice higher than normal. "She's an annoyance I tolerate for the sake of my grandparents. And she could never, ever come close to your level, Sadie. I thought you understood that when we talked in Tennessee." His thumbs wiped the wetness from my face and tipped my chin up, refusing to let me hide.

Leaning in, his lips brushed mine, the barest imitation of a kiss. "You're the sun, and she's a firefly, flitting around trying to get everyone's attention with her shiny ass while you paint the sky yellow and pink and dazzle everyone with your light. Sadie, there's no comparison."

"So you notice her ass?" The words came out wobbly, insecurity bleeding through, even as a small smile cracked my lips.

He shook his head, nipping my lower lip hard enough to sting. "Sadie, you're not listening to me. You've blinded me to everyone else. I'm yours. Only yours. For as long as you'll have me." His hand cupped my neck, thumb settling over my pulse running wild at the base. "I love you."

I licked the spot he'd bit, and his eyes darkened. Swallowing hard, I looked into his eyes, knowing this was the pivotal moment. That whatever I said next would determine where we went from here. Closing my eyes, I took a shaky breath, taking a moment to just feel. To quiet my brain and listen to the whisper of my heart, where his name echoed with every beat. When I opened them again, he hadn't budged, but his muscles were flexed, braced for my decision.

His eyes traced over my features like he was memorizing them. As if he worried this might be the last time he might ever get the privilege. I put my hand on his chest; his heartbeat unsteady against my palm. He covered it with one of his own, holding my fingers to him, pressing me close.

"I love you too." It wasn't so much an admission as a truth I could no longer deny. A truth he deserved.

He closed his eyes and took such a deep breath, his chest brushed mine, our hands still caught between us. When they opened, his lips twisted into a wry smile. "So are we basically fighting over the same thing here? That we belong together?"

I opened my mouth to argue, then stopped and frowned.

"Yeah. Yeah, I think we are."

Swooping me into his arms and spinning me around, he crushed his lips to mine, stealing my breath and my heart and my tomorrows in one smooth motion. When he finally pulled back, he framed my face in his hands, scattering kisses over my cheeks, my nose, and my forehead. "Do you trust me? God, Sadie, I need you to trust me. Deep down, you have to realize I'd never jeopardize what we have for someone like her."

"I do. I trust you, West," I whispered, the conviction in my words even surprising me.

I let go of the last of my lingering misgivings. Let go of the past and wrapped my arms around him and embraced the future. He nuzzled close, whispering all the dirty things he wanted to do to me later, all the things he'd been dreaming of doing to me for weeks. And my heart was so full it threatened to burst, happiness and heat seeping through my veins and settling low in my stomach as I listened to his voice describe all the ways he'd touch me, pleasure me, fill me.

The sharp knocking on the door caught me off guard.

Wary, I clung to West, looking at him as if he knew who dared to disrupt our reunion. The one I kind of hoped to consummate on the couch I'd spied against the wall.

With one arm tucking me close to his side, he pulled open the door a few inches.

"There you are!" The unmistakable and unwelcome sound of Aubrey's voice spilled into the room, and I couldn't keep the snarl from forming on my lips.

"Did you need something?" West was brusque, bordering on rudeness.

She tried to push the door open farther, but his foot blocked it.

"Just you," she purred.

"Enough!" West snapped. He didn't yell. He didn't need to. The innate authority in his tone silenced any retort she might have had. "This fucking charade has gone on long enough. Whatever pity I once felt for you, whatever façade I tried to keep up for the sake of family harmony—it's over. I'm not yours. I was never yours. I'm Sadie's."

"She's in there with you, isn't she?"

I tried to push my way into view, but his arm was like a steel band, keeping me from launching myself at her.

"Yes, and you're interrupting." He sounded impatient and started to inch the door closed again.

"I can't believe you'd choose her over me. Have you seen us together? We're the perfect all-American couple. And our families would be thrilled. And—"

"Not happening. Ever," West injected. "Accept it and move on."

She shrieked. "Did that skank say she's pregnant? Is she trying to trap you so you can't leave after she embarrassed you with that vid—"

"Here's how this is gonna work," he cut her off before she could spew more venom. Pushing his way fully into the doorway, he faced her head on, but blocked the opening with his shoulders, hiding her from my view. "You will never mention Sadie again. To anyone. You aren't fit to speak her name. And if I hear *any* whisper of anything I *think* might have started from you, those naughty little pictures you so kindly stuffed in my nightstand will find their way to your daddy. I'm guessing it was his money that paid for them? We'll see what he thinks of his perfect little princess then."

"You wouldn't!" She gasped. I could imagine her clutching her throat dramatically. "We have a history, West! We grew up together and—"

"Then quit acting like a spoiled brat and actually try growing up like the rest of us." Rue's voice joined the fray, and I took advantage of West's surprise by slipping past him to stand in the doorway. "Get a job. Pay your own bills." She glanced at me before smirking at Aubrey. "Find your own man."

Aubrey's eyes bounced between us uneasily, perhaps sensing she was outnumbered but clearly not wanting to back down. Her cheeks were flushed, and she had a hand propped on her hip, attitude radiating from her.

Grady strolled around the corner and took up a position behind Rue, not speaking, but staring at Aubrey impassively, making it obvious what he thought without having to say a word.

Turning, she fixed her bright eyes on me, desperation lending a shrill edge to her voice. "You've ruined my life! All of my plans. What does he even see in you?"

"Everything." West laced our fingers together. "I see everything in her."

"She's not even pretty!" She threw her hands up in the air, as if that was the worst of it.

With a growl, I took a step toward her at the same time West yanked me back, turning furious eyes her direction. "You. Don't. Speak. To. Her."

"Who's gonna stop me? Looks like you have your hands full. You might need a leash for that bitch."

"Me." Rue stepped closer, and drew her fist back. I watched, wide-eyed, as everything seemed to happen in slow motion.

Rue's arm flew forward, her hips twisting to put full power behind the punch, but then Grady was there, stepping between them, and her fist connected solidly with his face, his head jerking back with a snap. I gasped, my hand covering my mouth.

"What did you do?" Rue squeaked, as she rushed to Grady's side, where he stood hunched over, his hand cupping his eye. "Why did you do that?"

Grady groaned. "Who taught you to punch?"

"My brother!"

"He did a damn good job." Grady grunted and ignored Rue's attempts to pull his hand away to see the damage.

"She tried to hit me!" Aubrey yelled. Everyone ignored her. She stomped her foot. "I'm pressing charges. That's attempted assault."

"*That's* why I stepped in," Grady said dryly, squinting at Rue through his uninjured eye.

"No one's pressing charges." West glared at Aubrey. "You're going to go back to your little party and keep your mouth shut, and if I hear anything, *anything* about my friends or Sadie, or see you near my bar, you're going to find out there're worse things than not existing to me. Trust me, Aubrey, I'm one enemy you do not want to have."

She drew herself up to her full height, and searched his eyes. He never wavered. Whatever she saw there must have convinced her, because she wilted in front of us before slinking around the pool house, pausing only to give me one last scathing look.

I exhaled, the pain that had dug its claws into my ribs relaxing once she was gone. He'd done it. He'd chosen me—*us*—over her.

But Rue. And Grady. I turned to them, but they were focused on each other, arguing about whether he was fit to drive himself the three miles down the road to his house. Rue was insisting on going with him, in case he'd gotten a concussion, and he was denying that she'd hit him that hard.

"It was a good punch! You're going have a black eye at least."

Grady shook his head, but then staggered a step to the side from the motion.

"That does it." Sticking her hand in his front pants pocket, she withdrew his keys, dangling them triumphantly in there air. "I'm taking you home. Let's go."

"Rue," I called after her as she tried to wrap an arm around Grady.

"You punched my eye," he snapped. "There's nothing wrong with my feet."

She shook her head and looked back at me, shooting me a small grin. "Don't worry about us. I've got this one under control.

Now that you two seem to have worked things out, shouldn't you be having wild make-up sex or something?" She winked.

"Under your control," Grady muttered, stalking toward the long driveway where the cars were parked. "You wouldn't know what to do with me if you had me."

"I could think of a few things," she said, right on his heels. "I might surprise you."

He snorted as they rounded the corner.

Stunned, I turned to West. "What just happened?"

He watched them, amusement curling his lips and crinkling his eyes. "Nothing that hasn't been brewing for a long time."

I hesitated, unsure what to do next. "Do you need to go back to the gala? Will your grandparents be upset? Do you need to schmooze some more?"

He wrapped his arms around me and placed a soft kiss on my upturned lips. "Fuck the gala. I got everything I need right here."

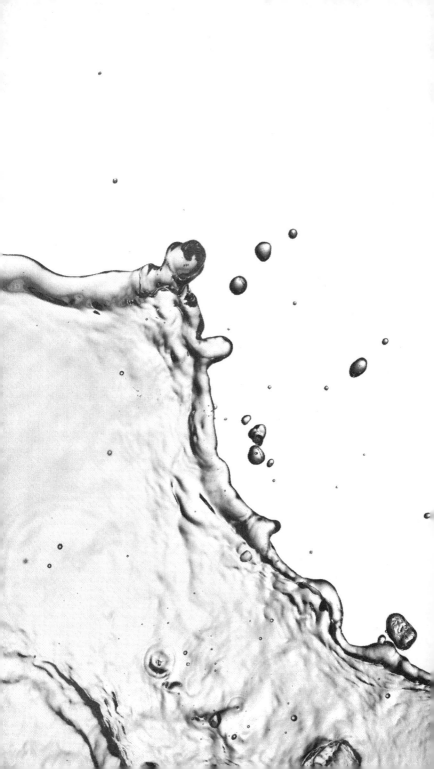

chapter
twenty-six

WE LEFT THE GALA AND went straight to his bedroom. We did not pass go, we did not collect two hundred dollars. But for all our rush to get there, he changed speeds once he got me alone.

He unwrapped me slowly, deliberately, as if each part of me was a gift meant to be savored and treasured.

First, my shoes. I held onto his shoulders for balance as he knelt in front of me while his hot breath teased my already damp core. Then, the tiny hidden zipper that ran along my lower back, his lips welcoming each newly exposed inch of skin.

Once my dress was loosened, he lifted the right sleeve off my shoulder, letting it dangle. My nipple barely had a chance to pucker before his palm covered it, lifting and squeezing, molding it to fit his grasp. I gasped, and pushed my chest out further, eager for more. His mouth followed the curve of my jaw, before wandering with painstaking thoroughness down my throat. When he licked the hollow at the bottom, I melted, putty in his skilled hands.

I'd expected him to hurry. For the clothes to fly and the bed to squeak within moments of entering his room. But he seemed intent on reminding me what we'd been missing out on while we were apart.

The slow, sweet heat that came from a long-banked fire.

My hands were restless, unsure if they preferred the solid muscles of his shoulders or the thick softness of his hair, unable to settle in just one location, but instead seeking to touch as much of him as possible. He'd slipped off his jacket and discarded his tie on the way over, but his torso was still hidden from sight. When I tried to push him back so I could get to the buttons of his shirt, he shook his head, dipping down until he could suck on my aching nipple. I forced my hands between us, opening the buttons blindly while he tormented me.

The other sleeve of my dress slid free while I worked on baring his chest, and I dropped my arms long enough to allow it to slither to the floor, a whisper of fabric forgotten in an instant when his hand came up to cup my other breast, rolling my nipple in a mimic of his lips. I inhaled sharply then pressed him closer, my nails scraping his scalp. A soft moan escaped me when he bit down before he switched his attention to the other side.

He might have been content to take it slow, but I needed more. Grabbing both sides of his partially opened shirt, I yanked hard, scattering the remaining buttons around the room, the pings of them bouncing over the hardwood floor sounding like muted applause for my impulsive action.

He smirked, swatted my ass in acknowledgement, but refused to be rushed. He licked the lower swells of my breasts and kneaded my ass, ignoring the way I leaned against him, trying to get some friction, hell, any kind of attention, where I wanted it most.

When I tugged on his dark hair in an effort to speed him along, he leaned back on his heels, and captured both my wrists. Placing one firmly alongside my thigh, with a pointed look that told me not to move it, he lifted the other in front of him, massaging each part in turn—the heel, the palm, the length of each finger, and the tender spaces between them, and the base of my thumb. He kissed each fingertip reverently, then the delicate skin of my inner wrist where my pulse throbbed. The other hand received the same meticulous attention, and it was all I could do to keep my knees from buckling by the time he finished.

Who knew my hands would be my erogenous kryptonite?

Unable to wait a second longer, I cupped his jaw and yanked upwards, meeting him halfway in a kiss that I felt all the way to my soul. He rose to his feet, taking over control, slanting my head so he could stroke deeper into my mouth.

His tongue was a sin I would happily burn for.

We tangled, fought, dueled, and surrendered, each taste more drugging than that last. There was only his warm lips and his hands in my hair and his breath mixing with mine. Hair pins scattered, and my curls fell around us, as untamed as our kiss.

I shoved at his shirt, until it finally joined my dress on the floor. Finally, my hands were free to roam his torso unfettered. I traced the grooves of his abdomen, smoothed over the broad planes of his chest, and sought out his dark, flat nipples. Tearing my mouth away from his, I flicked one with my tongue, peering up at him through my lashes to see his reaction.

He exhaled harshly in surprise, curling his hands around my shoulders to hold me back and twisting away from me. "That tickles." Nudged partially off balance, I caught myself on his forearms, grinning in triumph at catching him unaware.

Following the line of his arm from his shoulders down over his tattoo that seemed to dance with his flexing biceps, my gaze stuttered on his wrist.

My royal blue hair tie.

It was still there. A bit faded and stretched out, like he never took it off, it quietly proclaimed his unwavering intentions. I rubbed it with my thumb. Had it been there this whole time? Back at Anchor, before I left? And in Tennessee? I hadn't looked, hadn't noticed.

My amusement faded, and I looked back at his face, at the hungry intensity in his eyes. My eyes filled as emotions flooded me. Guilt for doubting him, relief that we'd moved past our obstacles, a fierce joy to be able to call this gorgeous man in front of me mine.

We stared for a long moment, making promises without words.

And then stillness was no longer an option.

I hitched my leg over his hip and attacked his mouth with a

new fervency that bordered on anguish, needing to apologize for my part of our separation these last weeks. With an appreciative growl at my initiative, he took the hint, lifting me so I could wrap my legs around his waist, giving me a slight height advantage. As he moved us toward the bed, I forced his head back, turning into the aggressor, unable to get enough of his mouth.

I delved deep, nipping his lower lip, and chasing his tongue until I was panting for air and had to draw back, keeping my forehead pressed to his, unwilling to let even that much space separate us. His eyes glowed fever-bright, hot lust mixed with dark passion.

He leaned forward at the hips, lowering me to the bed. When he started to rise, I made a sound of protest, trying to pull him back to me, but he shook his head.

"You first. Always."

And then he settled between my legs, raised my thighs over his shoulders, and nuzzled into the crease where my hip met my leg. His scruff tickled there, the thin skin extra sensitive. He followed the path to my slick core, continuing to tease me as he kissed up one side and down the other, without delving between my swollen folds.

I lifted my pelvis, impatient words falling from my lips. His name, curses, pleas, anything I thought might work to speed him along, but they all fell on deaf ears. His hands smoothed up my stomach until they cupped my breasts, rolling my nipples between his fingers while he ghosted a kiss right over my entrance, refusing to be rushed.

STACY KESTWICK

I squeezed my legs, trying to keep him there, press him closer, but he pinched one tight peak in warning, and I relaxed my thighs reluctantly, starting a slow grind of my hips instead.

"West." His name was both a demand and a request wrapped in one.

He tongue made teasing forays, quick dips, soft passes. I dug my hands into his hair and tugged restlessly. He mouthed my lips, sucking on first one and then the other, before flattening his tongue and dragging it right up my center, finally giving me the pressure I craved.

He lifted his mouth just slightly, so when he spoke, I felt the words against my heated flesh. "Fuck, I've missed the way you taste."

I almost came right then.

Lowering his head, he devoured me in earnest, his lips and tongue a beautiful torment. And then he did what I wanted most, what I needed. He focused his attention on my clit, sucking it into his mouth, flicking it with the tip of his tongue, plying me with his lips until I lingered right on the edge.

My breathing was ragged at best, grabbing just enough oxygen to keep from passing out. I fisted my hands in his hair and urged him closer, lifted my hips, arched my breasts into his palms.

I was so, so close.

And when he plunged two fingers inside of me, twisting when he was fully embedded, I imploded.

Thighs squeezed and hands fisted and spine curved, all trying to keep him right there right there right there *oh God yes* don't stop don't stop *don't stop!*

I didn't breathe, didn't blink, couldn't move.

It was just waves of pleasure, battering my taut form, pulling me under to a deep oblivion where nothing else existed, just me and him and utter bliss.

And I willingly drowned.

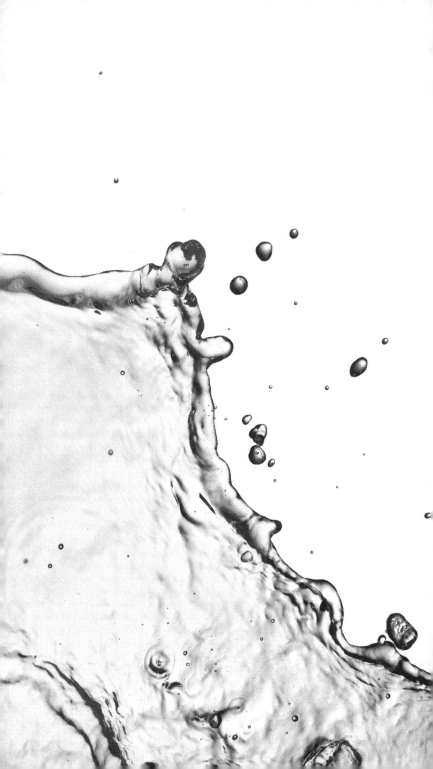

chapter
twenty-seven

West

I BARELY REMEMBER TAKING THE REST of my clothes off before I climbed over her, pulling her up the bed and covering her with my body until we were skin to skin everywhere. I don't think she realized she was still whispering my name, but hearing her shout it as she peaked was the hottest thing I'd ever heard. I wanted to hear her scream it again, this time while I was inside of her.

As I balanced over her on my forearms, looking down at her, I knew this was it. The sight I wanted to wake up to every morning and go to bed seeing every night. Her face was flushed, limbs loose, her gorgeous green eyes unfocused as her body trembled with the aftershocks of her pleasure.

I couldn't help the surge of raw possessiveness that swept me, knowing *I* did that to her, put that satisfied Cheshire-cat grin on her face. It took all my self-control not to plunge balls-deep right then, to force myself to savor this, to savor her, the way she deserved.

I nuzzled into her neck, breathing in her watermelon shampoo, and when her arms curled around my waist and her legs bent until she was rubbing my calves with her feet, I thought my chest might explode. I couldn't understand how I'd survived without this connection while she was gone, without feeling the satin of her skin on mine, her taste on my tongue.

I knew one thing. We'd never be apart for that long again.

She hummed in contentment and I gathered her closer, my arms slipping under her back. She lifted her legs higher, wrapping them around my hips, and my cock throbbed at the feel of her wet heat. Fuck, she tempted me. I rocked gently, unable to stop myself. I'd jacked off in the shower to her memory for the last three weeks, but nothing compared to be being wrapped between her long thighs, ready to sink home.

"West." Hearing her husky voice whisper my name in my ear had my balls tightening, pulling up higher. Her nails scratched a path up my back and I flexed my hips, unable to resist sliding against her a little harder.

"I'm here," I murmured against her damp skin. "We have forever. No need to rush." Except for the overwhelming urge to slam into her over and over, mark her in the most primitive way as mine.

I nibbled her ear and filled my hands with her sweet ass, torturing myself with the way her hips tilted to meet my gentle thrusts. I spent long minutes just moving against her, loving the little sounds she made when my cock rubbed her greedy clit.

Her heels dug into the small of my back and she wiggled lower, until the head of my cock hovered, nudging at her opening. She tugged my hair impatiently, growling when I lifted my hips higher, keeping her from pulling me in.

"I need a condom." I started to roll toward my nightstand but she stopped me, catching my outstretched arm.

"Nothing between us. Not anymore." She pulled my hand to her tit, distracting me when her nipple beaded against my palm. "And I'm on the pill."

My blood ignited at her words. *Nothing between us.*

I swallowed hard, and then dipped down to lick the sweet, pink peak calling my name. Some guys might prefer a girl with bigger boobs, but hers were perfect. I could cover them fully with my outstretched hands and the way she bucked when I scraped one with my teeth was addicting. I sucked hard, and she shuddered beneath me, a greedy noise vibrating her chest.

"I need you so much, baby. Need to feel you everywhere. Squeezing my cock and scratching my back and yelling my name." I leaned up to capture her mouth in a demanding, ravenous kiss, tracing the seam of her lips until she opened up and let me in.

She matched my every move, fighting me for control, and wrapped her arms around my neck. As if I had any plans to escape.

But I loved it when she got aggressive, showed me how hot my touch made her and asked for more.

I'd always give her more. I'd give her everything.

I needed to bring her to the brink again before I entered her. I wanted her pulsing around me with a second orgasm when I finally released inside of her. Sliding a hand between us, I tested her readiness with one finger.

She was fucking soaked.

My cock jumped, and I quit denying myself. Grasping myself at the base, I lined up at her entrance, and nudged inside the first inch, pinching my eyes shut at the sensation.

"Tell me how you want it, Sadie." I tore my mouth from hers long enough to ask. "Fast or slow?"

She moaned. "Slow. But hard."

Fuck me, this woman was perfect.

Holding her still with a hand on her hip, I seated myself in one sure thrust, and I swear my vision turned black around the edges with how tight she was.

I pulled her legs up higher around my waist, then withdrew until only my tip was still in her before plunging deep again and again. Her snug walls hugging every inch of me was heaven and hell blended together. I never wanted to leave, but I'd go up in flames if I stayed.

I rose up partway on my knees, changing my angle so I could hit that one spot inside her that made her bear down against me and squeeze tighter. Every time I bottomed out, I rolled my hips, knowing I pressed against her clit with that move and it made her crazy. Her teeth dug into the meat of my shoulder, and I groaned, the slight sting of pain shooting to the base of my cock in the best way.

"I love you." My voice was strained, but I couldn't stop the words as they tumbled out of me. "I love you so damn much." I licked her neck and the tender spot below her ear. Her breath hitched and she began to meet my thrusts erratically, driving the pace faster. "That's it, baby." I wrapped some of her curls around my fist, tugging until her face wasn't buried in my shoulder, so I could see the moment when she found her release. "Come with me."

She cried out, a long string of words that settled into a chant of just my name, over and over, and my balls pulled up tight, those familiar tingles growing at the base of my spine, and I knew this was it. I pushed my hand between us, circling her small bundle of nerves with my thumb, once, twice, and then she stiffened beneath me, her inner muscles clamping down, and I was lost.

I pumped deep one last time and filled her, her name a guttural roar on my lips, and a primal satisfaction spread through my chest as I squeezed her tight, unable to get close enough to her.

My hips pumped slowly, softly, while her walls pulsated around me. I couldn't quite seem to stop. She felt too damn good.

"West," she grunted, breaking me out of my daze, pushing her palms to my chest. "You're crushing me."

I rolled us over, switching positions until she lay sprawled on top of me. "Sorry." I loved the weight of her on my chest, the solidness of it, the realness of all her softness pressed close.

Gathering her mass of curls in my hands, I drew her back until I could see her face. "Are you okay? Did I hurt you?"

She shook her head, cheeks flushed, and she almost would've

looked shy if it weren't for the wicked gleam in her eyes. "I imagine I'll be sore tomorrow, but it'll be worth it."

I groaned a deep noise of agreement before kissing her nose and letting her readjust her position. She slid to my side, using my shoulder as a pillow, but kept one arm across my chest and threw her thigh across my hips. My dick stirred hopefully beneath her leg.

"Down, boy," she laughed. "I think you'd had enough for now."

My bicep muscle flexed beneath her in denial. "I'll never have enough of you, Sadie." I stroked her hair and her breath fanned across my skin.

While part of me wanted to close my eyes and drift off to sleep with her cuddled next to me, a bigger part wanted to stay awake and just watch her, smooth my hand over whatever parts of her I could reach. Maybe it made me a pussy, but nothing felt better than holding her close, knowing she was floating in a post-orgasmic haze delivered by me.

She shivered, and I pulled the blankets over us. I pressed a kiss to the top of her head, and whispered to her to get some rest.

Because I'll be waking you up for more in a few hours. I grinned in anticipation.

"I love you," she murmured, nuzzling closer and pressing a kiss to my chest.

"Love you too."

And I would. I'd love her every day for as long as she'd let me. I relaxed, knowing I'd found my peace in her. After everything we went through over the last three weeks, we were solid. She was here and she was mine. She finally believed in me.

Believed in us.

The soft slide of her blond waves over my calloused hands was addicting, and I continued to sift through her hair, letting the silky strands slip through my fingers. Long minutes passed as her breathing slowed down, and then evened out.

She filled my arms and my heart and all my fantasies. She'd wake up in my bed in the morning, the sheets still smelling like us. And I'd make love to her all over again.

I didn't need sweet dreams with a reality like that.

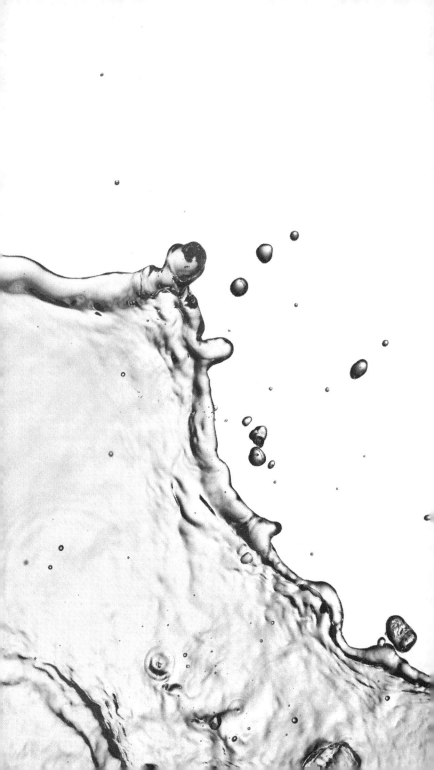

chapter
twenty-eight

Sadie

T HE BREEZE WHIPPED THE tails of West's white button down shirt around my thighs as I sat on the steps outside his bedroom that led down to the beach. The sun was just rising over the watery horizon, pinking the sky as it fought back the purple of the night.

A new beginning.

I raised the coffee cup to my lips, watching West and General Beauregard play catch on the sand below me.

He was way too cheerful for a man who'd barely slept after waking me up twice more during the night with his tongue between my legs. My thighs ached after three rounds, but damn, the discomfort was worth it.

Rising from my spot, and only wincing a little, I descended the stairs toward the man I hoped to wake up next to again tomorrow.

I paused long enough to snag his hand, and continued on toward the gentle waves lapping the shore. The ocean was the most patient of lovers, wooing the beach day after day in a constant tug-of-war neither would ever win. Demonstrating the perfect harmony that could be achieved when both sides learned to give and take in equal measure.

A lesson most of us were too blind to ever appreciate.

West walked next to me, puzzled, but playing along. When the water kissed my ankles, I stopped and turned to him.

"You'll always keep me safe, right?"

He pinched his eyebrows in confusion. "Of course."

"And I can trust you?"

"Always and forever." He didn't hesitate with his answer.

I took a deep breath then slid the mostly button-less shirt off my shoulders. I was naked beneath.

"Sadie, what are you doing?" Concern mixed with amusement filled his voice.

"Going skinny dipping. You coming?"

epilogue

Several months later
Sadie

"OH NO, HE DIDN'T!" RUE clapped a hand over her mouth and almost fell off the barstool laughing.

"Yup. And then he disappeared."

"Bastard."

I nodded and took a sip of my drink. West had warned me what would happen if I continued to send him naughty photos while he was out of town for a tournament. But we'd always had communication issues, so I'd ignored him and kept on texting him pics. Completely innocent ones. Like the one where I was holding the beer bottle between my thighs because I needed my hands to answer his message. Or the shot of my cleavage, when I'd accidentally spilled that same beer down my shirt. And I figured, just to be thorough, he'd need to see that I'd had to remove my shirt because of the beer, and I was stuck lounging on my bed in just my lace bra and cutoffs.

Just normal pictures of my day.

But, sure enough, when we Skyped last night and got frisky, and I was seconds away from coming, one hand down my panties rubbing furious circles around my clit and the other holding the phone so I could watch him jack off, he disconnected.

A few minutes later, after he presumably finished taking care of business, he'd messaged me a reminder that sending him dirty pics when he wasn't there to see me in person was torture and that he hoped I liked a taste of my own medicine.

He had a point. My impending orgasm had fizzled to a lackluster finish without him sharing it with me, and I'd gone to sleep feeling grumpy and out of sorts.

I really hated it when he was right. Not that I'd ever admit to it.

So when Rue had suggested a girl's night at the Wreck, I'd been happy for the distraction. West wasn't due back until tomorrow, and I needed something to take my mind off him and all the sex we weren't having with him gone. But I hadn't been able to resist sending him one quick photo of me in the strappy coral sundress I was rocking. I'd lifted one side, showing off a generous slice of thigh, and added the simple message *hurry home.*

It'd been three hours and he still hadn't responded, so I'd pushed him from my mind for now and was focusing on Rue and the fruity goodness of the grog in my cup. My second cup.

"What about you?" I raised my eyebrows expectantly. "What's going on with you and Grady?"

She rolled her eyes and started to answer when a deep voice from behind me spoke up.

"Excuse me, miss. On a scale of one to American, how free are you tonight?"

I whipped around and eyed the gorgeous man leaning his hip against the bar behind me.

"For you, I'm a damn patriot." Smiling like the lovesick fool I was at his surprise appearance, I threw my arms around West's neck and that familiar spark shot down my spine when he pulled me close. He buried his nose in my hair and I felt every muscle in his body relax as he breathed me in.

"Fuck, I missed you." He pressed a kiss below my ear, and his hand slid lower to cup my ass, snugging me tighter against him.

Rue coughed. "I think I see Theo . . . that way . . . yeah, I'll be over there."

I hummed an acknowledgement. Pulling back slightly, I gripped the back on West's skull, my thumbs resting along his scruffy jawline. "I thought you didn't need a line."

He pressed his lips to mine and stole a kiss that managed to take my breath away despite its brevity. "With you? I'm not taking any chances. I even pinned a dollar bill above the bar for the first time last week."

I squinted at him in confusion, noticing the hint of vulnerability in the flush on his cheeks that I might have dismissed as sunburn if I didn't know him so well. Scrawled pick-up lines covered the currency tacked above and behind the bar, and, earlier this summer, he'd told me he'd never once added one of his own. My eyes flitted over the bills. "Where?"

"Down here." He tugged me down to the end of the bar, weaving us past the other patrons, his hand firm on mine the whole time. "Look, right there on the end." He pointed to a crisp bill, folded in the shape of a paper airplane, tucked along the end of the top shelf. His strong script trailed along one wing.

I drowned.

My eyes flew to his, trying to understand. "You weren't drowning. You were floating."

He nuzzled the side of my neck, then dragged his lips up to my ear. "Maybe. But you saved me just the same. I just didn't realize it at the time."

I melted into his arms, turning my face until our lips met. He didn't waste time, tracing the seam until I opened for him, then delved inside to chase my tongue. I gave it to him on a moan and buried my hands in his hair, pulling him closer. His mouth slanted over mine again and again until the catcalls around us filtered through my lust-fogged awareness.

I pulled away slowly, reluctantly. He relaxed his hold until his arms circled my waist loosely, my hips still pressed to his, but allowing some space between our upper bodies. I shook my head to clear it. "What are you doing here anyway? I thought you weren't due back until tomorrow?"

"My client had an emergency back home and had to cut his trip short. And I couldn't resist a chance to get back to my girl a day earlier."

I smiled at the way he claimed me as his. Because I was. Totally.

"But how'd you know I was here?"

He smirked. "Was I really supposed to believe you were just gonna hang out at the cottage with Rue wearing this sexy-as-hell little dress?"

Oh yeah. I'd forgotten about that.

I glanced over his shoulder at the exit and he twisted to follow my line of sight. He chuckled and leaned down to press his lips against my forehead. "I like how you're thinking, but I thought we might hang out here for a bit. I saw the guys over by the games, and I haven't seen them in a few weeks." He must have seen my crestfallen expression because he squeezed my hips and bent his head to whisper in my ear, "Don't worry, I'll make sure you're well taken care of before you fall asleep tonight."

"You better," I muttered, slightly mollified.

After helping himself to a longneck from behind the bar, we made our way over to where our cluster of friends were watching a furious game of air hockey between Theo and Wyatt. The boys called out their greetings, and then West rapped on the side of the machine after Wyatt scored a goal amongst the distraction of our arrival.

"Hey, Sadie and I have next game."

I turned to him, eyebrows raised. "We do?"

"Yup."

"Are we playing for a certain prize?" I asked suggestively,

bumping his hip with mine.

He laughed. "You have no idea."

After Wyatt squeaked out a narrow victory over Theo, who demanded a rematch later in the evening, we took up our places on either side of the table. A sense of déjà vu washed over me as I remembered the first time we'd played together.

I leaned down as I retrieved the puck from the slot, making sure West was watching. Sure enough, his eyes immediately dropped to the neckline of my dress.

"Ready?"

"Wait. Don't you want to know the stakes first?"

I cocked my head to the side and blushed. "I mean, are you really gonna just say it in front of all our friends?"

Keeping his gaze locked on mine, he reached into his back pocket and pulled out a small velvet box, and delicately balanced it along the side of the game. My breath caught and I froze as my eyes ping-ponged between him and the box.

I couldn't force any words, but my pulse skipped before damn near pounding out of my chest.

Rue, on the other hand, didn't have the same problem. She went to snatch up to the box to sneak a peek, but West was faster, pinning it to the table with the flat of his palm. "Nope. If she wants to see what's in this box, she has to win."

Rue pouted and the comments from the guys grew louder as they punched West on the shoulder and ribbed him for being so cheesy.

I licked my dry lips. "What if I'm not ready to win? What if

I'm . . . not good enough to beat you?"

"Mmm, I thought about that." His face was serious. "If I win, you get this instead." From his other pocket, he withdrew a key, and placed it on the other side of him from the velvet box. Wyatt was faster than Rue and snagged the key, holding it up to the light.

"What's this to, bro? It looks like a house key, but it doesn't look like the one to the beach house."

"Because it's not."

I stared at him in bewilderment. Then what was it for?

"Heads up, Wyatt." West spoke to his brother but watched me like I was a skittish filly that hadn't been broke yet. "Consider this my two-week notice. I got a new place closer to the marina."

Wyatt whistled and put the key back down. "Damn. Is this for real? You're playing for either a ring or a key?"

West glanced at him briefly and lifted one shoulder in a lazy shrug. "I figure it's really a win-win situation here." He tapped the surface of the table with his mallet. "Ready, Sadie?"

Was I ready? Hell, no, I wasn't ready. I hadn't been expecting any of this. Wildly, I turned to Rue, who had a huge grin on her face until she cut her eyes to Grady who was standing on the other side of Wyatt, and the smile faltered momentarily. Theo sidled up next to me and nudged me with his shoulder.

"So what's it gonna be? You aiming to win or lose?"

I lifted the mallet, studying it intently as if it held the answers. "I don't know." I placed the puck on the playing field, and drew back, slamming the mallet into the puck and sending it ricocheting across the table, catching West off guard. He scrambled to guard his goal and return the volley. The puck zipped between us, pinging sharply off the bumpers and our mallets. "How about you, West? You looking to win or lose over there?"

"Doesn't matter to me, baby. Either way, you're mine."

He was right. But I hated to lose.

And air hockey was my game.

I wasn't worried though.

Aubrey was gone. She'd taken a one-way trip to California to visit her cousin.

Asher had taken a plea bargain, making him a registered sex offender and leaving him with a hefty fine and a restraining order against him. He'd also been fired from his dad's company, and I'd heard from my brother in Nashville that my old assistant had dumped his ass like yesterday's news.

My photography business had taken off after the release of the Water's Edge campaign, and Paper Plane Photography was booked solid for the next three months.

And I had a brand new set of sheets, the nicest ones I'd ever had, on my bed.

All the background noise had faded from my life, leaving behind the important stuff.

Work. Friends. This gorgeous island I called home now.

And West. The guy who'd shown me how to trust in love again.

Plus, there were the side benefits.

His fingers.

His tongue.

His cock.

Bending down lower, I wielded my mallet like it was a weapon, intent on scoring, confident of my impending victory. When the buzz of our game reached Hailey across the bar, and she squealed and came running, not stopping until she barreled right into her brother, I saw my chance and took it.

A perfect shot, dead center down the field, straight into his goal. One to zero.

"You're going down, West."

"Every night of my life if I'm lucky."

Yeah, I admit that threw my concentration, when images of him between my spread thighs flooded me, heating me right down to the already damp core. I wasn't going to last much longer. He'd been gone all week, and I was dying to get him alone to welcome him back properly. The puck bounced off the wall and into my goal, the rattle as it slid home jarring me back to the present.

The score was tied, one to one.

But instead of retrieving the puck, I threw my mallet at Theo, who scrambled to catch it.

West paused, watching me as I made my way down the table until I stood in front of him. Nothing had ever felt more right than standing in front of him in this moment, surrounded by our friends.

"What are you doing? We're not done." He pointed to the other end of the table.

"Yes, we are."

"We are?"

"We are." I nodded.

"So who's the winner?"

"It's a tie. We both won."

His lips crushed mine as he gathered me in his arms, spinning us around slowly before letting me slide back down his body to the floor, his laughter ringing in my ears and filling my heart. "Yes, we did."

Other books by Stacy Kestwick

Wet

Stay in touch! I love hearing from readers!

www.facebook.com/stacykestwickauthor

Twitter: @stacykestwick

Instagram: @stacykestwick

Visit www.stacykestwick.com for a current list of books, book

signings, and to sign up for my newsletter.

PS—ask me about my secret reader group, The Wreck!

Acknowledgements

First off, I'd like to thank my husband for tolerating my time spent in author world.

To Erin Noelle, for being not just my best friend, but my critique partner, cheerleader, and general ass kicker, depending on what the situation called for. I haven't had a friend like you in years (or ever?), and now that I've found you, you're stuck with me. At least until we're too old to skip.

To my Masta Betas—you're my #squad. Alison, Allison, Jenn, and Michelle, thank you for accepting me into your fold and partaking in the cheerleading and ass kicking.

To Ashley Jasper, Mariah Rice, and Yessi Smith for keeping it real, chapter by chapter.

An extra special thanks to Alison for listening to me ramble, providing me with links when I got stresed, and being the best damn admin I could've ever hoped for. Thank you for doing all the million little things I asked you to do, because it adds up to be a really big deal. If it weren't for Canada trying to keep us apart, I'm sure we'd be inseparable. Dallas, February, me and you, it's a date!

To Jill Sava, for keeping it real and telling me what to do—for any given situation. You're my hero. I can't wait to meet you in Miami!

To Melissa Petersen, for being the best PA ever, especially when I'm indecisive, which is always, right? Your graphic skills astound me and the fact that you didn't cuss me out when I sent you 2500 magnets or kill me while designing the banner shows our love is real.

To Hang Le, for knocking this cover out of the park. To Kay Springsteen for polishing my words. To Jenn Van Wyck for finding the rest of my mistakes. And Alison and Lindsay for double and triple checking.

To all the authors out there who taught me something about author world—Erin Noelle, Aly Martinez, Brittainy Cherry, Meghan March, Lex Martin, Rachel Van Dyken, CM Foss, Yessi Smith, Brooke Blaine, Rachel Blaufeld, Ahren Sanders, Geneva Lee, Jessica Prince, Sierra Simone, Emily Snow, Whitney Barbetti—and all the authors in FTN and the Hideout. Y'all are the best!

To Stephanie Rose, for the steady supply of Stephen Amell pics. Don't stop.

To Hazel James, for sending doughnuts and being awesome. And Ashley Christin for thinking I'm cool. I'm glad someone does.

To every blogger of any size who read my books and helped spread the word—I'm beyond grateful.

To every reader who found me and left a review or told your friends about the book—you're the very, very best kind of reader in existence.

And lastly, this book is dedicated to the Wreckers. Your endless support, enthusiasm, and patience while I worked on this project astounds me. I have the best readers and you guys prove it to me every day. (You may ask, if this is the dedication, why is at the end? Because I know the Wreckers will read this sucker to the very end, and they'll see this. 'Cause that's the kind of rock stars they are.)

I probably forgot somebody. If I did, let me know, and I'll name a character after you. Best I can do.

*** Authors Note: Revenge porn laws are real, but at the time of publishing, vary widely from state to state. Some assholes are being brought to justice under them and serving very real jail time.

About the Author

I'm a Southern girl who firmly believes mornings should be outlawed. My perfect day would include lounging on a hammock with a good book, carbohydrates, and the people around me randomly breaking into choreographed song and dance routines. It would not include bacon, cleaning, or anything requiring patience.

Made in the USA
Lexington, KY
02 August 2018